## Are You Ready for a Change?

In a time of increasing shortages, waste of resources, loss of confidence in big government and public spending, what hope is there for the future?

*The Land of the Possible* is a fascinating projection of an alternative society infinitely more attractive than the present. Yet it is no visionary dream. Based on technology we already possess, and applying what we already know about social structures and group psychology, it offers a clear-headed proposal for a better world we could achieve by the end of this century.

*Future Shock* forecast the sweeping changes that lie ahead. *Walden Two* depicted a new kind of planned society.

Now visit *The Land of the Possible*, the future we might build by the choices we make now.

# LAND OF THE POSSIBLE

## A Report of the
## First Visit to Prire

by Mary Alice White, Ph.D.

A Warner Communications Company

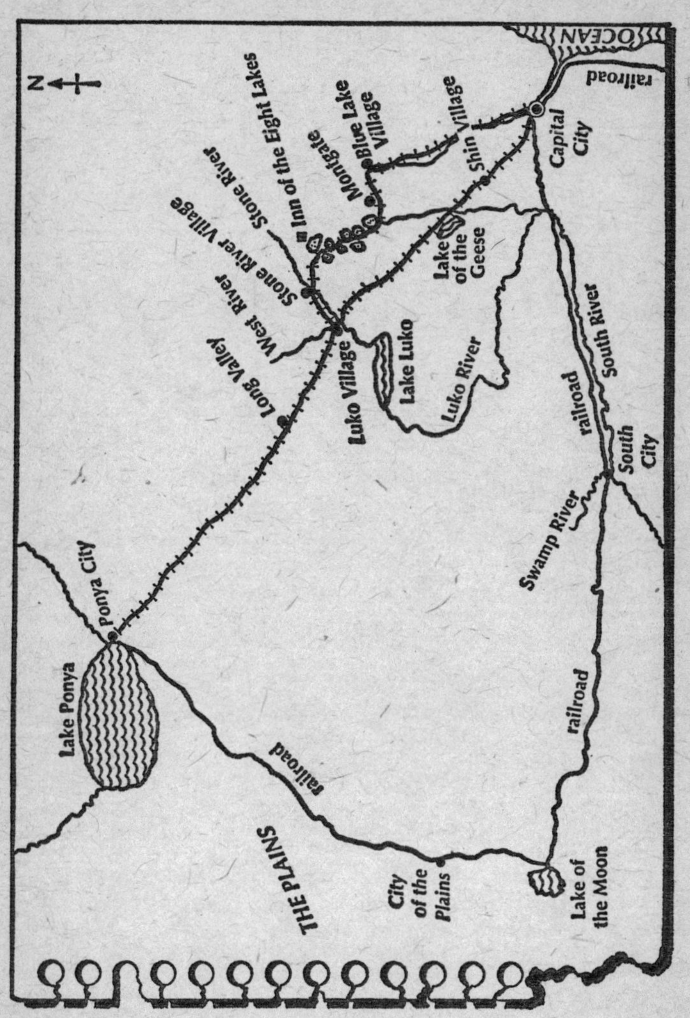

SCHEMATIC MAP OF PRIRE IN MY NOTEBOOK.
ITINERARY FOLLOWED IS SHOWN AS
SCALE IS APPROXIMATELY 7.8 MM = 100 U.S. MILES
N
OCEAN
railroad
Capital City
Shin Village
Blue Lake Village
Montage
Inn of the Eight Lakes
Stone River Village
Stone River
West River
Lake of the Geese
Luko Village
Lake Luko
Luko River
Long Valley
South River
railroad
Swamp River
South City
Ponya City
Lake Ponya
railroad
railroad
THE PLAINS
City of the Plains
Lake of the Moon

# Letter of Transmittal

Mr. Chairman and Honorable Members of the Joint Sub-Committee on National Resources:

It gives me great pleasure to transmit to you my report of the first visit to Prire. In it I attempt to portray exactly the conditions as I observed them there during this exploratory visit. I have set down what I observed, in order, as objectively as I could. In those areas where I had no expertise, I have tried to report what I saw as factually as I could, so that those readers more expert may be able to form an opinion from the information I gathered.

I wish to thank the National Resources Foundation for making it possible for me to spend this past year at the Resources Study Center, where I could prepare myself for this trip, and my university for granting me the necessary leave. I would like to acknowledge my indebtedness to Professors Gene Duval, Paula Matthew, and Harry Biele of the Resources Study Center, all of whom provided me with so much help in my studies of Prire; and to Douglas Lake Feer, Bellows Professor of Behavioral Conservation at Berkeley, who first suggested these studies of Prire to me.

I would like to take this opportunity to thank the members of the Sub-Committee for entrusting me with such an important mission. It is my hope that I have carried it out in a responsible way. I realize that much of what I report will be controversial, perhaps even not believed, but I hope that my past record of scholarship will give credence to these contents.

In the event the Sub-Committee should plan a second visit to Prire, I would be very pleased indeed if I could share in the planning and arrangements, and would be glad to contribute in any way I could.

Finally, I wish to acknowledge my deep gratitude to Dr. Maserli Bo, Chairman of the Overseers of the Future of Prire, who made my trip not only as worthwhile as possible, but who was the epitome of graciousness and hospitality, I would also like to thank all the various officials whom I met while in Prire, each of whom made it possible for me to return with so much information that will be useful to our own national planning.

Respectfully submitted,

*Charles Aldworth, Ph.D.*
DIRECTOR OF STUDIES FOR THE JOINT SUB-COMMITTEE
ON NATIONAL RESOURCES

# 1

## Sunday, June 17th

My first view of Prire was a surprise. As we came in over the Prire countryside, it looked so familiar and yet so different. I saw hedgerows, green rolling fields, good stands of oats and corn and wheat, many vegetable gardens and orchards, all of which I had seen before, in many countries. But there was something different. I kept studying the countryside below trying to identify what it was. Then it occurred to me that the difference lay not in what I could see, but in what was missing. From the air I could see no long highways filled with traffic. We passed over two medium-sized towns and I realized in retrospect that I had seen no smoke and no brown gray cover over those towns. I kept searching for evidence of a transportation system and it was a long time before I saw what appeared to be some form of railroad which connected the countryside below. From the air the track was a very thin ribbon, with some trains very short in the number of cars and some very long. I wondered if what I had heard about the Prire transportation system would prove to be true.

Everywhere I looked I saw an agriculture that was lush. Around each farm or group of farms, there were groves of trees and judging from the air, these must have been planted deliberately and cultivated. There were dots of little people in the fields, and again I had to remind myself of what was missing. I saw nothing that I could recognize as a farm tractor although I did see what appeared to be horses and oxen from the air. This was in early June and the first cutting of hay was taking place. I peered down to see how the hay was being handled but I could not make it out. I thought I saw horse-drawn mowers and hay wagons but I could not be sure. Some of the hay was stacked in the fields in a very unusual pattern, as though much of it was being stored out of doors rather than a barn.

As we began to circle in a lowering spiral, I could see that the capital was free of that brownish gray smog that I had become so accustomed to. As we flew lower, I was surprised to see how many people were about in the streets. I wondered if it were a special day or a celebration because the streets were full in all directions of people walking about. I could not pick up any signs of industry on the outskirts, but buildings appeared which may have housed some type of manufacturing. There was no sign from smokestacks that would tell me if this was a holiday or whether the plants were operating with clean exhaust. We passed over a body of water with people fishing from boats and I decided that this must be a national holiday. There were hundreds of these little boats all over the water, and people were picnicking in groups on the shore.

We touched down and after a long wait taxied up to the passenger terminal. What was most surprising to me about the airport was that I saw no other planes around and no activity whatsoever. We were the only plane on the field and there were no mobs of people anywhere to be seen, even inside the building area. (I didn't think it wise to ask questions from the outset, but I learned later that the airport was not used except for emergencies or to accomodate occasional visitors such as myself. Apparently airplanes are very rare, I presume because of their use of energy. I don't think I saw a single airplane overhead the entire time I was in Prire.)

I gathered my suitcase, my dictating machine, my typewriter and all of my notepads, and with as much excitement as I had ever felt in my life I went through the open door and down the stairs, with the help of the co-pilot. As I came to the bottom of the steps I saw a small group of people moving toward our plane. As the group came closer I recognized that the leader, tall and thin, must be Dr. Bo (I use the English version for the sake of simplicity.) He looked just like his pictures although he seemed much more vigorous as he walked toward me with a welcoming smile. He shook my hand cordially and asked if I had had a nice trip. I replied that it had been a very long one and I was quite tired but I had been very excited at flying over the Prire countryside and had been impressed with what seemed to be a booming agriculture.

"Thank you for noticing," he replied. "That is

one of the nicest compliments you could give us. We are delighted that a visitor such as yourself notices what we have done in this regard." He introduced me to the group that was with him. I must say they had gone out of their way to make me feel an honored guest. Outside of Dr. Bo, who I knew was chairman of the Overseers of the Future, there was a representative from Resources and Returns, from Community Service, and a Trustee for Human Resources. Dr. Bo introduced each of these in turn and identified them as representing the committees I had read about. Arrangements were made for the pilot and co-pilot to be cared for during my visit. Dr. Bo then asked if I would like to stay as a guest in his own home, at least for the first night, and I was glad to accept. I had not looked forward to spending time in some strange hotel or whatever kind of arrangement they maintained, and welcomed the opportunity to talk with Dr. Bo informally. Everybody helped me put my equipment into what Dr. Bo referred as the "transit." This was a small vehicle somewhat resembling an automobile but much simpler and powered by some energy source that I could not identify. I know only that it was not a combustion engine because it was almost noiseless.

We traveled perhaps fifteen minutes at quite a slow pace to Dr. Bo's home. As we passed through the streets of the capital I was busy looking at everything I could possibly see. I saw so many people walking in the streets and so very few transits that I asked Dr. Bo whether this was a holiday of some kind as I'd also seen people boating as we came in.

"No, this is a regular working day for us. You are surprised perhaps of the number of people who are not at work as you think of work. I'll be glad to explain that to you later. But they're all busy doing a different kind of work." I saw one- and two-story houses or apartment houses, I did not know which, set back with small green areas and trees along each of the streets we traveled. I saw very few density areas such as we are used to, few of what we would call apartment houses or office buildings. Every building seemed to have an area of green around it with shrubbery and trees. There was a sort of tram or streetcar that moved quietly down the center of the street and carried passengers. There were almost no transits in view; perhaps we passed five or ten. People were riding bicycles, some were pushing carts but mostly they were walking. It was a lovely day in June and many of the stores had their wares out on the street. I could not help noticing that the fruits and vegetables were very good looking and appeared quite fresh.

It is very hard to describe the difference in the feel of Capital City from anything that I had seen in our country or in Europe. The streets were absolutely alive with people walking, chatting, some sitting at what I would call an outdoor cafe, others busy on errands of some nature that I did not understand. But what one felt was that the city was alive in a way that was unhurried yet purposeful. Everywhere I looked there were people on the sidewalks or on the trams, going about some business. They looked to be happy, if one can make that kind of judgment. People were smiling and talking to each other in a friendly fashion and I was surprised at how many seemed to know each other. After all, the capital is a good-sized city and I saw none of the strangeness and rudeness often found in a city of this size. I made a note to ask Dr. Bo about that later. The other thing I noticed in this short ride was the cleanliness that I saw everywhere. The air was sparkling clear and had many good smells—I could smell peonies, and lilacs, and what I thought was honeysuckle and many flowers that I could not identify. Everywhere I looked flowers had been planted and I was reminded of England or Denmark. The streets looked as though they had just been swept and I could not see a paper or a can anywhere. I realized with surprise that I had not seen any dogs either. I don't think I saw more than ten dogs during my entire stay in Prire.

It seemed to me that the city had some kind of pattern. Every few blocks—I couldn't count how many—there would be an open square or garden area where children were playing, sometimes alone, sometimes in groups. Most of these squares or gardens were planted with flowers but I noticed a few that were given over to vegetable gardens or small orchards. At first, I thought, who would want to eat vegetables grown in the middle of a city? Then I realized, of course, that here the air was clean and there was no smog. Apparently the fruits and vegetables were growing well and seemed undisturbed by vandals.

By the time I reached Dr. Bo's house it was almost two o'clock by my time. I reset my watch at Dr. Bo's suggestion and found it was just noon Prire time. I was surprised that our times had come so close but I realized later that I had lost at least a day somewhere en route, so I gave up trying to compute the time differential. I felt remarkably well considering the long trip but I had taken the precaution of exercising regularly in the plane during the flight.

My notes on Dr. Bo's house are worth comment-

14

ing upon as he had one of the more charming houses that I was to visit during my stay. As Chairman of the Overseers of the Future, Dr. Bo was of course a most distinguished member of the community, if not the leading citizen of Capital City. Consequently one would expect him to have a special home, but it was not a palatial mansion, nothing like that. It was set on a somewhat larger lot than those I had seen and had a wall around it. He parked the "transsit" outside the wall and we went through the gate, carrying my luggage. The gate led into an inner courtyard which contained flowers and vegetables and I could see small nut trees and fruit trees on the side yard at my right. The house was made of a material I did not recognize but it looked like a kind of stone with a rather pinkish cast which was very pretty in the clear light. The house was set back within this courtyard and, as I was to learn later, there was another yard at the back, so that the house stood within a four-sided enclosure. As we started to enter the door Dr. Bo removed his shoes and put on house shoes. Some had been provided for me so of course I followed the custom. I was reminded of a similar custom in Japan which I have always thought was a sensible one. Yet everything looked so clean it did not seem necessary. He showed me to my room, which was upstairs on the left, a very light and airy corner room, quite simply furnished but charming. It was lined with bookcases filled with some of Dr. Bo's books. There was a chair by the window which looked most comfortable for reading, and a washstand basin which reminded me of a Colonial bedroom. Apparently this was not an antique, however, but was actually used. The bathroom next to the bedroom contained a toilet unlike any

I had seen before which operated without water. I did not know what the mechanism was, but it was absolutely quiet and without any odor whatever. I finally concluded that I was to take my bowl and put it under a faucet and fill it. The faucet was metered, I think, because it ran only until a certain amount of water was dispensed. After I washed up I saw a place where I was to dispose of the water. I guessed that this was some sort of filtering system and that the water was cleansed and returned for use for washing. I noticed there was another water outlet in the bathroom for drinking water because the faucet was so labeled. Everything was clean and neat but I would not say luxurious. There was what I thought to be a shower stall at one end of the bathroom. I was anxious to get downstairs to meet with Dr. Bo so I didn't take time to unpack except for a few clothes and to grab a notebook and my dictating machine.

I went quickly downstairs where he was waiting in what was the living room. This room also was simply furnished but I found it very pleasant. Again there were bookcases, from ceiling to floor, and comfortable chairs and low tables. There was a contrivance, which I learned later was a fireplace, set below the level of the floor, unlike any fireplace I had ever seen before. Dr. Bo explained later that it was a very efficient heater. Since this was a marvelous June day there was no need for a fire, but I was anxious for a cold snap to see how it would work.

From each of the windows one had a lovely view of flowers and vegetables or fruit trees or nut trees, and the effect was one of being in the country even though we were in the middle of the capital city. Against the walls of the outer garden were vines; some were flower vines but some appeared to be cucumber vines and I think others were some sort of fruit. I could not see any lawn and as I thought back on it I had not seen any lawn as we came through the streets and I made a note to ask Dr. Bo about that later.

As I sat down I had a sudden feeling of joy that—at last—I was here in Prire, after all those months of planning and meeting and trying to get this visit made possible. I must have uttered a sigh of relief or pleasure because Dr. Bo turned to look at me in a sort of quizzical way and said:

"It must be quite a surprise and change for you to be here in Prire. How do you find us?"

"Dr. Bo, I am overwhelmed by so many new things. I am also so excited to be here that I don't think I can answer any questions just yet. I must say that the streets look clean and the people look happy and healthy and everywhere I turn I see gardens and growing things and greenness which is a delight to me."

"You shall see much more of this in good time," Dr. Bo replied with a gentle smile. "We would not like to expose a visitor such as you to too much change at once because it is not good for you. We also want to take good care of your health while you are here. Why don't you join me for a light lunch and then you can have a little rest before we begin to talk and start our visits?" He then led me into a small dining room where a light lunch was laid out by what I assume was his housekeeper. I had read that Dr. Bo was a widower and assumed that he lived here in the house with only the housekeeper but I learned later that I was quite wrong about that.

I was eager to taste the food, to see if it would

be different. I found in front of me a bowl of something like yogurt only much thicker and with a somewhat different taste, perhaps closer to clabber. Around me were dishes of various fruits, some of which I recognized, and which I saw Dr. Bo slice into his bowl, so I did the same. I recognized dried apricots and fresh apples, of course, but there was something like a plum that I did not know which was absolutely delicious. I cut these up into my bowl of what I call clabber, watching Dr. Bo as he cut his up. There also was a kind of bread on the table which I was familiar with. It seemed to be homemade of whole wheat and had a nut-like flavor to it. There was a paste of some kind that he spread on his bread and I did also. It looked something like peanut butter but had a totally different taste, something between fresh fish and a lemony taste. I found it odd but likable. For dessert I had another one of those things that looked like a plum but did not taste like one. I kept trying to identify the flavor and decided that the closest thing I could come to was a lichee nut. We had milk to drink and a fruit punch that I found very refreshing.

Dr. Bo was most courteous throughout the luncheon, answering my questions about life in Prire. As we talked, I had a chance to look at him a bit more carefully. His face was distinguished—long and thin, I would say intelligent. He had piercing blue eyes that held your gaze in a commanding way. His hair was gray, cut loosely to his collar. He was wearing a blue shirt and pants that seemed to be chosen for their comfort rather than for any particular appearance. They did not speak of an expensive cloth although I don't know what it was. It looked to be cotton. He wore a pair of what I would have

18

called sneakers and socks. I was most impressed with the man's energy. As we talked he was enthusiastic and full of laughter, obviously delighted to answer questions about his country and its way of life. I kept reminding myself that he was, by my calculations, a good 82 and I could not reconcile his age with the alert, energetic man before me.

I was even more surprised, in view of this energy, when he said right after lunch that it was customary for people in Prire to take a nap. I did not mind because I could have slept a day at least but I was surprised that this was a habit. (Over the next few days I came to appreciate it more and more and decided it was an extremely civilized way to live.) Dr. Bo asked me if I thought I would have any trouble taking a nap, and I told him I did not think I would. He suggested, however, that if I did I would find a mat in my room if I cared to do exercises. I told him that I didn't think I would need any exercise and would be glad for the chance to rest.

When I woke up it must have been near 3 o'clock Prire time. Dr. Bo was waiting for me downstairs when I got there. He suggested that I might like to take an informal walk around parts of the capital to see something of urban life before we started on the official visit tomorrow. I told him I'd be delighted to do so.

We left the house, but instead of going in the "transit," which was nowhere to be seen (I learned later that these were used only rarely), we walked to a nearby station somewhat resembling the entrance to a subway. We went downstairs on a moving platform and I noticed they also had one coming up which made it convenient for elderly people. Everything about this subway was a pleasant contrast to those in our land. There must have been air shafts somewhere because the air was as good as it was above. The station was brightly lighted, with attractive murals on the walls, and extremely clean. The thing that surprised me the most was the lack of noise. Instead of having my ears shattered when a train pulled in or passed through, the trains were almost noiseless. Dr. Bo explained later that they had developed materials for a wheel that was almost noise-free.

We apparently were in an express station because the train we entered went by several stops and took us to what Dr. Bo explained was a central park of the capital in the downtown section, which I was anxious to see. The subway car itself is worth mentioning as an exceptionally pleasant mode of travel. The seats were comfortably padded and clean as could be; there were no defacing graffiti. Inside were attractive murals and photographs. It was when I was sitting in the car and we were moving almost noiselessly, at a very fast rate of speed that I realized that there was no advertising in the car and that I had seen none since I had arrived. This made me realize for the third of fourth time that it took an effort for me to identify what was missing.

When we reached our stop Dr. Bo led me off and we went up a moving ramp. As we did so I noticed some large trains of a different appearance had come into the station and were unloading onto large moving platforms. I asked Dr. Bo what these were and he explained that they were freight subway trains which moved material within the city. Large cargoes were moved on electric platforms that could be handled by one person. These were backed into freight subway cars that were than picked up by an express train which moved them around as needed. These freight cars I noticed, went up in a special freight elevator to the surface and then were driven to their destination. This explained the absence of trucks that I had noticed on our first drive —in fact the lack of almost all automobiles of any kind. I was most impressed by the speed of this system and the marvelous quiet. Dr. Bo and I could talk in a perfectly normal tone of voice as the subway train carried us from the station near his home to this downtown area.

When the moving ramp delivered us at street level, we were in the heart of the capital. I could see the capitol building off to my left, and right ahead of us was a large park. We did not go into the park but Dr. Bo explained that there were parks like this throughout the city and were used both for recreation and for the growing of flowers, trees and some small plots.

He brought me here to show me some of the various types of housing that were part of the capital. Off to the right was a building perhaps six stories high which, he explained, contained apartments for those who liked a denser pattern of urban living and did not want to be bothered with the house and small garden that I had seen in other areas. At street level there were shops everywhere I turned. I could not see any street floor part of a building as far as I looked that did not have some sort of store in it. As we walked along the street to our right which branched off from the park, we passed store after store with merchandise in the window or on the stands outside. I saw fruits of all kinds, and vegetables and occasionally fish of some kind. As we turned the corner we came to a large market set in a small park—perhaps a block square —and here there were for sale every sort of fruit and vegetable imaginable, as well as prepared food. As we passed along the stalls I marveled at the variety of well-grown food products including some that I would have judged to be out of season for this time in June. For example, I noticed cucumbers and tomatoes as well as eggplant and squash and asked if they were shipped from some other part of the country. He said no, that all food was locally grown, most of it in garden areas set aside around each of the cities. But they made a great deal of use of solar-heated greenhouse farms where it was possible to bring in crops a good deal earlier than we would normally. He said it was a policy to try to extend the growing season as much as possible so as to provide a variety of fresh fruit and vegetables year-round to residents of each city.

As we walked along the stalls I noticed many people with large carts who were apparently doing their week's shopping. I asked Dr. Bo how they would get these carts home if they lived at a distance. He pointed out that they had two choices. They could take one of the subway trains especially designed for people with carts—known as the mini-freight subway—which ran to all parts of the city, or there were trams that were especially designed to handle carts.

The quality of the products was impressive, and the market was exceptionally clean. But it was not until after the first few minutes that again I realized something was missing, and what was missing, of course, was the use of paper bags and plastic containers with which I was so familiar. Apparently everyone brought their own containers, for I noticed that from each cart people were bringing out containers into which they packed their produce.

Here in the market I had the same impression I had had earlier, that the people I saw seemed busy and were happy in appearance. I noticed also that they spoke to each other by name as though they knew each other. I remarked to Dr. Bo about this.

"You were very quick to pick that up," he said. "We've had visitors here who missed that completely. This is because of the way in which we've arranged the city. Each city is broken into a village so that it is possible for people within a village to know each other by sight. This is part of our whole principle of personal responsibility. We wanted very much to get away from the anonymity of the large cities of the past. The people you see here are part of a city and enjoy all the benefits of urban living, yet they are also part of the village and know the people in it, the people who run the shops, and the people who bring their produce here to market."

From the market we walked a few blocks to another park, perhaps three blocks square, where we saw a group of young people engaged in a series of what I assumed were fitness exercises. Around the park was a track; it was now about 5 o'clock in the afternoon and I saw people of all ages running around the track apparently on some sort of self-exercise regimen. The park itself was most attractive with areas around small pools where one could sit and be quiet.

The quietness of the city was totally comforting. There were people everywhere I looked, some of them in a hurry, others strolling in a leisurely way or sitting at the outdoor cafes, two or three of which could be found in every block. There was the hum of the city so that you knew that there were people and life going on about you, but there was none of the noise that I was accustomed to—no automobile noise, no screeching of brakes, no truck rumbling, nothing. I could not even hear the subway under the ground. The trams would come by every minute or so and discharge passengers but even the doors were quiet in operation. It seemed to me that one heard here all the pleasant noises of the city with none of the unpleasant ones.

Dr. Bo and I sat on a bench near one of the pools. I noticed that each area had been designed to be a niche of its own, landscaped in very much of a Japanese manner, to enhance the view and to make a different reflection in the pool. There were people sitting in these niches around the park wherever I looked and again I wondered where all the people came from. It seemed to me as though all the city were out in the streets or in the parks and yet I knew that some must be at work.

As we left the park we walked toward a different subway and I noticed the stores more carefully this time. There were still the fruit and vegetables stores that I had seen earlier, and the cafes which were filled, but I also noticed stores for furniture and for hardware and for clothing. I did not see these closely enough to make any judgment about the quality of the merchandise but the clothes looked adequate as far as I could tell. The people in the streets were dressed in a very simple fashion, nothing that I would call chic. The men wore trousers or shorts, occasionally some wore a long skirt of the kind that I had seen in pictures of the East Indies. The women wore both skirts and pants and loose blouses. Their shoes were of leather or a substance like it, and again were simply constructed flat shoes with some sort of bouncy looking sole. They seemed to be comfortable, judging from the way in which people walked. I noticed that they were all walking with free long strides, both the men and the women. They looked to be people who did a great deal of walking, with well developed leg muscles. The physical fitness of the people was impressive. I cannot recall seeing one person in a hundred who appeared to be overweight. Neither did they seem to be thin; rather, they looked to be well fed and in good health. I was impressed with the good color of their skin and their sparkle as they talked. The women wore their hair in a natural style, many of them wearing it long, either piled up on their head or held back with some sort of a band. I did not see any hair that looked to be colored nor did I see any evidence of hair styling.

It is very hard to convey in words the mood of the city as I sampled it that first day, walking around a small part of it with Dr. Bo. If I had to describe the feeling of the city in two words, I would say "purposive" and "enjoying." People seemed to have a purpose in what they were doing, whether it was shopping or going somewhere. Yet they also expressed a sense of enjoyment that was reflected in whatever they did, whether it was having a drink with a friend at a cafe table, or shopping in the market. I noticed that people had conversations with each other before a purchase was made and often lingered to talk further after the purchase was completed.

We returned home for an early supper after which I thanked Dr. Bo and excused myself, for I felt suddenly very tired, and I wanted to make notes in my journal before I forgot them. I lay on my bed and tried to review the images that I had seen earlier that day and asked myself what had I seen that I had forgotten to note down. As I went over the images, and again, I began to realize that the most striking thing was what was missing.

I had not seen or heard of the following:
> anyone who looked poor
> anyone who looked hungry
> a policeman
> anyone fighting with anyone else
> an advertising sign
> excessive noise
> traffic
> exhaust from cars
> trucks
> traffic jams
> airplanes overhead
> noise from buses
> teenagers in groups on the streets
> anyone who looked unemployed
> anyone standing on a corner with nothing to do
> children on the streets, except for pre-schoolers who were with their parents
> none of that hard-shell anonymous behavior so common in cities when transactions take place between strangers
> an excessive pace of movement
> fat people
> unhealthy looking people
> unpleasant looking people
> dogs
> cats

        garbage
        trash
        litter
        garbage cans
        political posters
        graffiti
        dirt in the street
        pollution
    I then made a list of what I had seen that I had
noted that day and the list looked like this:
        happy looking people
        pleasant interactions among people
        people who looked busy without being
            pressured
        people who had the time to enjoy a con-
            versation or talk with a friend
        healthy looking people
        many different little shops
        cafes both inside and outside
        people in the streets everywhere
        flowers
        fresh vegetables
        parks
        green areas where one could walk or play
            games
        trees
        buildings that did not obstruct a view of
            the sky
        pleasant and quiet transportation
        streets that apparently were safe, at least
            at that time of day
        a sense of country within the city
        a sense that people somehow knew each
            other and were not afraid of each other

a sense of intimacy in a city neighborhood

clean skies

pure air

—The contrast between the lists was impressive but I withheld judgment. I knew that in Prire no claim had been made that human nature had been changed. Knowing that we had a very busy day tomorrow I decided I would have to ask Dr. Bo about all the things I had seen and those I had not seen. I finished my notes, turned off the light, and must have fallen asleep right away.

# 2

# Monday, June 18th

I woke up the next morning feeling refreshed and anxious to start our trip. At breakfast Dr. Bo told me that today we would visit Blue Lake Village which was a rural village designed along cooperative lines. I had read about Blue Lake and it was one of those places I had been most anxious to see. I had heard it was something of a showplace but I still wanted to see it.

After breakfast we took a train for about two hours in a northwesterly direction from the capital. The train was very much like the subway that I had ridden the day before. It was extremely quiet with comfortable seats, and not too brightly lit. Although it was a warm June day the train was not air-conditioned, but there were fans in the ceiling which apparently worked off the air brought in by the train and turned at a very high rate of speed. I am not a good judge of speed but we were going faster than any train I had been on so I imagine it was 150 miles per hour or better. During the morning an older man came through the car selling fruit, bread, and fruit juice, all of which looked very attractive, but I was not hungry. I asked about meals on longer trips and Dr. Bo told me that there were cars that provided meals of varying cost.

We got to talking about Blue Lake Village as the train went through the countryside and I asked Dr. Bo if Blue Lake was not one of the showpieces. He said it was, but it was still one of things that I should see.

"It will give you a good basis for comparison," Dr. Bo said. "As you know, we are going to visit several communities, some of which have been successful, and some of which have not. Blue Lake is one of the more stable successful communities and I thought you would be interested in seeing that."

"Do you mean that some of the communities that were not successful are ended?" I asked.

"Yes" Dr. Bo replied. "We see no reason to keep on with experiments that do not work. We encourage experimentation in Prire because we feel that it takes different kinds of communities for different kinds of people to live in. We encourage our young people to develop new kinds of communities. One of the quickest ways for a society to become rigid and unresponsive particularly to its young people, is to deny them a chance to build their own experiments. Young people need that chance to try their hand at making a better world. So we encourage it and always have a certain portion of our land for new communities, and others are built upon those that died before them. Blue Lake was such a community many, many years ago and was the invention of some young people who were dissatisfied with the types of communities available to them."

"How do you mean that a community works?" I asked. "How does anybody decide, and who decides, when a community is no longer viable?"

"That's a good question and a very tough one," Dr. Bo replied. "Sometimes the communities die on their own because the people become dissatisfied and choose to join another village or community or city. There are certain basic criteria set up by the Committee on Resources and Returns and by the Overseers of the Future. The rules are very simple. No community can abuse the land or its resources or what lies under the land or over it. No community may abuse the wildlife or vegetation, and must have an approved conservation plan that is carried out. And then of course there is the rule for all communities, both cities and villages, that no one inhabitant or community may interfere with the rights or pleasures of another." Dr. Bo looked at me as he finished as though to see how I would react.

"That sounds very reasonable," I said, "but it seems to me it would be very difficult to carry out. What would be interference with another community, for example?"

"An example" Dr. Bo answered, "might be the cutting down of more wood than the conservation plan called for which in turn would affect the water table for another community, or the diversion of water so as to deprive another community, or any form of disposal of waste that interfered with the health or esthetic enjoyment of the next community."

"Would a community start some sort of action in

law against another community, or bring it up on charges before some sort of committee or commission." I asked.

"Yes," Dr. Bo answered, "one community can indeed start an action against another community in order to protect its own rights. In the examples such as I just gave they would bring up a case to the Regional Resources and Returns Committee and there would be an immediate hearing and a decision within a few days."

"Within a few days. You must have done something to improve the legal system if that's what happens," I joked. Dr. Bo smiled and said, "Yes, as you say, we have done something about a legal system. You will get a chance to see it."

Dr. Bo then called my attention to the land that we were passing through as he did not want me to miss anything. The impression I had had from the air was essentially correct. I saw a variety of what appeared to be small farms or homesteads varying in size from quite small to what Dr. Bo said were farms of 150–200 acres. Again I was struck by the fact that I saw very few tractors and no heavy farm machinery. I did see horses being used and mules and some oxen. The houses we passed were simple in structure but seemed comfortable and clean and well-kept on the outside. They were made of wood or stone. The out-buildings were numerous and seemed to be traditional farm out-buildings. I recognized chicken houses, stables, storage sheds, drying sheds—I was surprised by the number of these— and occasionally I saw a root cellar on the side of a hill, larger than I was used to. I was enchanted by the silhouettes of windmills all over the landscape as far as I could see. A few were of a design that I was familiar with, but there were many other designs that I had never seen before. They flashed brilliantly in the sun as they turned on their poles.

As I passed farm after farm, watching mostly those at a distance because our speed was too great to catch much of the foreground, I began to discern a pattern of how the land was used. I questioned Dr. Bo about it and he confirmed my impression. It seemed to me that vegetable and crop lands had been laid out but that each unit seemed to have proportionate land in wood and the whole thing gave one the impression of ecological planning rather than haphazard farming. There were ponds, sometimes two or three on each of the farms. There also were solar greenhouses which Dr. Bo identified for me and each farm had at least two of these facing south. The ponds appeared to be located below the poultry yards or pig pens. I guessed, and it proved correct, that this was part of the design to use the animal waste to fertilize the pond to increase the fish productivity in them. On some farms I could see irrigation channels, on others I did not, but Dr. Bo explained that some were using underground irrigation systems as an experiment.

I could not see the people very clearly because of the speed of the train. I certainly saw them at work in the fields and in the garden and caring for the animals. I was struck again with the air of purpose without rush. In fact many of the farmers would wave at the train as we went by and I saw people in our car waving back.

When we stopped at the next station I noticed that people got into our car, and other cars like it, who appeared to be passengers, but that there were cars farther down on the train that accepted people with carts and other heavy things to be moved. Dr. Bo explained that this is one way of handling heavy transport. It would be possible, for example, for a person with produce to sell to take it on a cart and go into a special car and ride to the next area or larger city to sell it. I noticed also what I would call freight trains which carried very heavy loads and were especially designed for that rather than passenger service. I noticed that they were using the same type of electrical wagon to move material that I had seen in Capital City although some of them here were much larger.

As we got closer to Blue Lake Village I noticed that there was one field where the hay was already being cut. The hay was being piled up in stacks by groups of people. I could not tell whether they were young or old at this distance but there were large numbers of people in the field helping to stack the hay. It seemed to me that they were stacking right in the field and tying some sort of cover over it rather than putting it in a barn. I asked Dr. Bo about this because it was obvious from the number of people employed that machinery was being used. He explained that this was a farm on the outskirts of Blue Lake and was run as part of an agricultural cooperative. This meant that the people of the area got together and helped each other hay and went from one farm to the other rather than investing in a lot of individual machinery. He said that there was nothing new about this, that in fact he had read that this had been a practice in our own country some time ago. I agreed that this was true but that the custom had gone out of favor. I said I had heard from some of my relatives great stories about harvest time and that each farm took great pride in the noontime dinner that they would prepare for the neighbors who came in to help with the haying, or later with the harvesting of the grains. Dr. Bo laughed when he heard this and said:

"Human nature, as I will tell you several times during our trip, hasn't changed very much. It is a matter of pride among people here at Blue Lake as it is in other cooperative agricultural villages to prepare as good a meal as possible when the neighbors come in to help with haying or with building a new barn or with any major venture. There is a feast, and each one tries to outdo the other. We must try to get to one of these if we possibly can because you will enjoy it."

As we approached Blue Lake Village I looked out of the window eagerly to get a feeling for the type of country we were in. I could see rolling hills perhaps four to five thousand feet high in the distance. Dr. Bo told me that was where our train would stop. We came up through a long valley with hills on both sides of us, passing a long and narrow lake which was not Blue Lake as I thought but was called Clear Lake. Dr. Bo said it was very deep and provided excellent fishing. The hills were covered with conifers and with beech, birch, oak and sugar maples. Most of the fields were not yet cut and were green with new hay. Everything looked tidy and well-cared for. As the train slowed down I looked intently at the outskirts of Blue Lake Village. I saw smaller homesteads the closer we got to what I presumed to be the center of town. I did not see discarded machinery, automobiles or trash, and of course there were no advertising billboards. There were two roads coming out of Blue Lake Village. I saw many wagons and carriages, but only two trucks and three transits of the kind Dr. Bo had used in Capital City. I had looked at the scene for some time before I realized that there were no telephone or utility wires and I had not seen any during the trip. The skyline was entirely free in all directions.

As the train pulled into Blue Lake Village we got our luggage together and stepped off the train. A committee was there to meet us, but instead of flowers or other honorary presents, we were offered cold fruit juice at an outdoor cafe which was part of the station. I thought it was unusual to have an outdoor cafe in the middle of a railroad station because I associate stations with noise and dirt and confusion. But here, of course, the trains moved silently and there was no dirt.

The committee which met us consisted of five people. My notes show their names and positions as follows:

Madame Young, Chairman of the Blue Lake Overseers;

Mr. Boratan, member of the Blue Lake Overseers;

Mr. Kulip, Chairman of the Blue Lake Resources and Returns Committee;

Mr. Malo, Chairman Community Service of Blue Lake;

and Dr. Posic, who was chairman of the Health Improvement Guardianship Committee of Blue Lake.

I realized that such an important committee had not turned out to greet me, but to welcome Dr. Bo who was one of the most prominent men in Prire society. It was clear that they were delighted to see him again and to have him visit Blue Lake even if he did bring with him a visitor as ignorant as I who was probably about to ask thousands of the same questions that they had had from other visitors. They could not have been more hospitable. They were in no rush to move me off to see everything on the schedule but instead allowed us time to enjoy our fruit juice as they inquired pleasantly about my trip and my impressions of Prire so far.

I was able to tell them with enthusiasm that I had enjoyed my visit to Capital City and was particularly impressed with the countryside as we came through it this morning. Dr. Bo told of our conversation about the cooperative haying tradition.

Mr. Kulip immediately suggested that we go to a farm where the haying was in progress to see how this was done. Afterwards, we could join them for lunch if we wished. I readily agreed and I could see Dr. Bo thought it would be fun to do, so off we went in a rather larger transit than I had seen before which could easily hold the seven of us and our luggage. Mr. Kulip was the driver. The road left Blue Lake Village almost immediately so I did not have much chance to see it but it looked rather like a New England village. There was a large square, almost large enough to be considered a small park, in the center of town with stores around it and roads leading out into the countryside. We took one of these and after perhaps twenty minutes arrived at a large farm where haying was in progress. I had not brought haying clothes with me but Mr. Malo of the Community Service quickly found me a cotton shirt and pants to wear and off we went into the field to join the haying.

When we arrived I found that the crew consisted of people of almost all ages. The youngest were about high school age, while the oldest was probably older than Dr. Bo, but he could still swing a mighty good hay fork. The hay was well dried and lying in windrows and our job was pitch it up into a hayrick. There was a young woman on top of the rick I was assigned to who was laying the hay out very carefully around a pole. When we had finished piling it to suit her, a large canopy was brought out and attacked to the pole which ran right up through the center of the rick. The canopy was then spread out, almost like a circular circus tent, and staked at the sides with ample room left between the rick and the canopy for ventilation. The whole job took about ten minutes and it struck me as a very clever arrangement. I saw that there were ricks like this going up all over the field. It was a particularly colorful sight because the canopies were all of different colors—red, orange, blue, green, yellow and purple—so from a distance it looked like an outdoor carnival.

As soon as the hay had all been piled into ricks we walked to the house for midday dinner. I noticed that all the members of our committee, including Madame Young and Dr. Posic, who was female, had immediately set to work to help with the haying and that Dr. Bo had also done his share. Everyone seemed good-natured and happy with the progress had made that morning, and each person in our crew came up to speak to me, hoping I would enjoy my visit to Prire and particularly my visit to Blue Lake Village.

I was impressed again with the great hospitality extended to me. Altogether there were perhaps forty of us. We sat down to eat at tables outside the kitchen of the house under a couple of beautiful old sugar maples. They had put planks together on saw horses, which was very familiar to me, covering this improvised table with colored cloths. I noticed one difference from the farm dinners I had known before. Usually the farm dinners were cooked and served by the women of the house while the men worked in the fields, but here there was a complete mixing of sexes. Both men and women worked in the fields and both men and women had helped with the preparation of the food. After we washed up we sat down at the table. Fortunately I had remembered that it was a custom on Prire to say grace so I saved myself the embarrassment of starting to eat by waiting for my neighbors. Everyone bowed their head and a grace was said which as I remember went something like this:

> Let us be thankful for the goodness of our land, the helpfulness of our neighbors, and the way of life we have chosen. Let us remember these now—this afternoon and this evening, and let each of us serve these well.

Up and down the plank table was a harvest dinner like none I had ever seen before. I had expected to find the cold hams and the salads and the cole slaw and the pies, all of which were present, but I had not expected to see the variety of baked dishes, delicious vegetable dishes and cheeses of all kinds. For refreshments we had a fruit punch of some kind which was very thirst-quenching. I think it had limes in it and perhaps some mint although it seemed early in the season for mint to me. For dessert there were the pies and a homemade ice cream that I found delicious.

When we had finished I noticed that each person took his or her dishes to the kitchen where they were being washed and stacked. I imitated my neighbors and found that one washed one's own dishes and stacked them to dry. I thought that this made a lot of sense because otherwise there would have been a enormous dishwashing for the forty people who were there.

I had expected we would return to the fields to do more haying, but instead everyone prepared to take a little siesta. I remembered then that that had happened yesterday. A nap was apparently part of the daily routine in Prire. I was personally very pleased, for a nap seemed the most desirable thing in the world at that point. Each person who had worked on the haying had brought with him a little sort of sleeping mat made of reeds which he stretched out on the lawn and promptly fell asleep. I was offered a couch inside the house and took it very gratefully and found myself asleep in no time.

About an hour later we were awakened and the crew went back to finish the hay. Dr. Bo and I and Madame Young and Mr. Boratan and Mr. Kulip and Mr. Malo and Dr. Posic then got in the transit to tour the Blue Lake community. Dr. Bo asked me to sit with Madame Young (I have used the word madame here, although that is not a literal translation. There are two forms of address for both males and females in Prire. For women it is close to Miss for the young women and Madame for the older women, with a cut-off point at about seventeen to eighteen. This does not refer to marital status but refers to the age when young people are considered to be adults. For boys the closest equivalent would be Master for those who were under seventeen or so, and Mister for the adult male in Prire.) Dr. Bo had asked Madame Young to sit with me as we

40

traveled as he said he wanted me to get a picture of what the Overseers of the Future did in a community such as Blue Lake. I found her a very lively companion. Mme. Young was somewhere in her forties, I would judge, quite small, very vivacious, with snapping brown eyes that seemed to photograph everything she looked at, the condition of the fields and what needed to be done.

Madame Young was Chairman of the Blue Lake Committee of the Overseers of the Future. As she explained to me, the Overseers of the Future was the paramount committee in each community, paralleling the National Overseers of the Future for the entire Prire society. It would be hard to draw a parallel to the power held by these Overseers but perhaps the closest thing would be something like our own Supreme Court except this was not part of the legal system, but of the political system. In order to understand the Overseers of the Future, one has to understand first that in Prire long-term planning takes precedence over short-term planning. I found this very hard to get used to in my short visit but it is essential to understanding how Prire works. The Overseers of the Future, who are the guardians of the long-term future of Prire, have the most political power of any group so that they control all interim and short-term decisions in terms of their effect on the future generations of Prire.

"In Blue Lake," Madame Young explained to me, "all plans to alter the land of the use of it, or the distribution of the population, must be approved by the Overseers of the Future before they can go into effect."

I thought that this sounded like a bureaucratic knothole. It certainly would have been in any other system but Madame Young told me that until I understood the entire system of public service, I could not understand how such decisions were reached rapidly and effectively.

Madame Young introduced me to the whole nature of public service in Prire which is very hard to describe. It is hard to know where to begin because it is so different from anything we have known and is based on a whole different set of assumptions. First of all, one has to understand that everybody has at least two jobs, only one of which is what we would call a "job," i.e., work in an occupation of some kind, but they also have a second "job" which is some form of community service. These take about equal time during the week although there is a lot of variation in it. The community service job is the training ground for public service. As Madame Young explained to me, records are kept on the performance of every person doing community service from the time they start, which is at about twelve years of age. One of the most important functions of the Overseers of the Future is to decide the eligibility of candidates to run for public office. This is done on the basis of their previous record, beginning as early as age twelve. If a person has done a good job in a particular service function at this early age, the name then goes into a pool of those who are eligible to be considered for the next office, and so on up. This system means that by the time one gets to a major office—for example, an Overseer of the Future of Blue Lake or member of the Resources and Returns Committee or the Health Improvement Guardianship—any of these chances to serve are limited to those candidates who have been deemed eligible on the basis of their previous record in lesser jobs. This judgment is made by the Overseers of the Future. I learned later that this judgment is subject to appeal but that this process is not used often.

Perhaps it would be useful here to mention the importance of records in Prire. Records are kept on all kinds of citizenship behavior with electronic equipment, though I gathered that a very fine and hard line was kept between the recording of public behavior and private behavior. Private behavior is not controlled by any of the committees of the society, but everyone is aware that his public behavior will be recorded.

One interesting sidelight of the record-keeping that amused me when I thought of its possible application to our society is that particular attention is paid to the record of predictions and promises made by people in public life. Not only is the record kept on promises broken or promises realized, but the ability to forecast accurately what is going to happen is considered a most important skill in Prire and a prime consideration in the selection of candidates for Overseer. Periodically people in public office are asked to make predictions about the future—the harvest for this year or the rainfall or economic resources over the next five years or whatever. Each official's predictions are later compared with actual events. (I imagined what would happen in our own society if we had such a procedure. I conjured up an image of people testifying before a Senate Committee and being asked at the outset, "Well, Mr. So-and-So of the National XYZ Institute, before you testify I would like to refer to your record on predictions and we find that your accuracy ratio on a scale of 0-1000 is .021. Therefore your testimony in this regard will be weighted with the factor of .021.") I thought it was an interesting idea because it does tend to make people more careful about the truthfulness of what they say about the future and also provides a way of estimating the worth of their future statements.

Madame Young admitted that not everyone found community service to his liking and that it was to be expected that some would like it and do well and that some would like it and not do well, and that some would not like it at all. Nevertheless, all are required to give a certain amount of time each week to the community and I gather there is quite a bit of latitude about the kinds of jobs one performs.

It was at about this time that we stopped at what I thought was a park but Madame Young explained that it was an important part of every community in Prire and was known as the Resources Inventory Park. I have never seen anything quite like it. Inside the park were grown examples of each of the flora and fauna that existed within Blue Lake, but in addition there were exhibits which were maintained on a daily basis of the resources of all kinds that lay within the Blue Lake community. I saw some children I would judge to be about ten under the leadership of a young woman of perhaps eighteen who were bringing in their field notes from a visit to one of the marshy areas; they reported that there were six pairs of red-winged blackbirds to be found on the South Marsh Pond, not the four that had been reported earlier. This information was translated immediately into a display which showed all the wildlife to be found in that particular area. In other displays one could see not only the wildlife but also mineral resources, water resources, analyses of the water in various parts of Blue Lake, soil composition, and the wood lot stands that existed with their mixture. In other places was a complete record of the crops being grown and of last year's productivity and the year before and the year before that. This concern about record keeping I would have thought rather stultifying, but that is not at all how it appeared to those involved in the Resources Inventory Park. The people took enormous satisfaction in the resources within Blue Lake and in seeing them increase. Everyone was delighted with the report on the red-winged blackbirds, much as I suppose an enthusiastic bird-watching group might be. The sense I got from watching the people coming to and fro and posting new information on these exhibits was one of community pride that the ecological bounty of Blue Lake was so high and apparently increasing.

One sidelight of this visit to the Resources Inventory Park was a chance to see how some of these community service jobs worked. I was pleased to see that many older people were actively involved in the work at Resources Inventory Park. Some apparently had been leading groups out to examine various parts of Blue Lake. I saw one frail looking older gentleman who, I was told, was the expert on tree resources. He had just come back from a walk up a nearby mountain with a group of people ranging in age from their eighties to the early teens. He was in charge of mapping the timber resources of that area. I recalled that I had not seen any older people sitting around on benches in Capital City and it occurred to me that perhaps one reason I had not was that they were all involved in some way in a community service job.

I learned later that the two jobs meant that people could experience various roles. For example, one person might hold a very responsible job in his given occupation but in his community service job he might hold a much less responsible post and in fact be the employee of someone whom he bossed at his occupational job. Having two occupations meant that people were seen in more than one dimension as far as their skills and usefulness to the community were concerned.

After we left the Resources Inventory Park I told Madame Young how impressed I was with it and what a splendid idea it seemed to me that everyone took so much pride in the resources of their community. I asked her if it was not true that some people would not enjoy this and in fact would resist having to give any time to the community. She told me that there had been such people in Blue Lake but they no longer lived there. I asked her what had happened to them, wondering if they were kept in some sort of concentration camp. She explained that people who did not take to that type of community were free to move to another that was more to their liking. As I visited other communities, she told me, I would see how much variety there was and how free people were to go to other communities. Blue Lake was a self-selecting community and housed the people who wanted to live that way, who enjoyed a cooperative type of community, but obviously it was not everybody's cup of tea. I was a little relieved to hear this because I knew that Blue Lake was seen as an ideal showplace but I could not imagine everyone would want to live in such a community.

After leaving the Resources Inventory Park we walked to the Community Service Building, where Mr. Malo was the host. This was situated in the park in the middle of the town which had reminded me of a New England town in its layout. Mr. Malo had wanted me to see the variety of community services that were being performed. Part of what I saw I had anticipated. I saw a building with rooms for all kinds of familiar activities such as hobby rooms, craft rooms, and rooms for games. There was an attached gym, but I did not see any health facilities, which I learned were in the Health Improvement Guardianship quarters. To my surprise the hobby and craft rooms were not filled with classes; in fact, there was no one in them at all. I asked where the people were. Mr. Malo explained that everybody was out on his community service job, and that these rooms were used only in late afternoons, evenings, and weekends. The community service jobs, he explained were serious jobs which occupied people as much as their occupational jobs did.

I had to talk with him for some time before I grasped the idea that Blue Lake Village was actually run by the people in it, who gave roughly half their time to running the community and the other half to what we would call "a job." The entire structure of the village depended upon the half-time efforts of the people in it. I, of course, was curious how people got paid and whether they lived on just half a salary. This was not explained to me until much later but I will insert a brief explanation here so that it becomes clear. In Blue Lake Village and in all other cooperative types of communities in Prire, an individual is paid for two jobs. One "job," as we understand the term, is where he works at his occupation, whether it is being a forester or a dentist or an artist or a statesman or a cook or a gardener or a craftsman or whatever. Half of his income comes from that occupational job. The other half of his income comes from his community service job to which he gives almost equal time. Some people alternate their days, and other alternate weeks. There is a wide variety of time allocation and there does not seem to be any one schedule. The money for community service comes from the tax resources of each village. It is paid back to its members on the basis of the work that they do, including the skill level at which they work and the manner in which they do the job. I began to understand why I had seen that purposive mood in Capital City. Probably I had seen people doing their community service jobs, maintaining the buildings, or the streets, or cleaning them or doing whatever job was necessary to keep Capital City functioning well.

In part of Dr. Malo's building, set back a distance behind a lovely courtyard, was a Child Care Center where I saw children, from infancy to about three, being cared for. I gathered that children three and over were in more formal schooling environments. I was impressed with what we would call the preschool facility. The building itself was well laid out, clean, and cheerful. The people working there (both women and men, by the way, of all ages) impressed one as interested and concerned and very much on the job. The infants were not being taught anything that I could detect. They were very healthy; all the children had good color and were active. The one- and two-year-olds had all sorts of activity materials available to them. I was reminded more of a Montessori preschool than anything else I could think of because it seemed to me that the activities were quite deliberate and well-planned. Everything a child did there was something to be learned from. It seemed to me that great stress was placed upon cooperation. Most of the materials required at least two children to work with them together and the toys were engineered in such a way that they would not work unless two children cooperated to make them work. I gathered this was very early education in the value of cooperation. Mr. Malo was anxious for me to see as many of the pre-school rooms as possible so I think I saw almost all of them in the building.

I noticed two things, or possibly three, that would be different from anything in our own schools. First of all, I noticed, a very high rate of approval being given to all the children. All of the workers seemed to be conscious of the importance of praising children for whatever they were doing that was right, or any attempt to do the appropriate thing. Second, it seemed to me that the teachers were acutely aware of how they used their approvals. I saw nothing that I would call a random use of the teachers' attention. They were very clear about what they wanted the children to learn and were applying their attention and approval to that end. The third thing I saw that was different was the use of some punishment. In what was otherwise a very serene and happy atmosphere I was quite surprised to see two or three instances where a child was punished physically. One child was slapped quite hard for refusing to share some building blocks. I noticed that the teacher came across the room immediately when he caught sight of what he must have viewed as noncooperation, reprimanded the child, and slapped him on the arm rather sharply.

As we came outside I asked Mr. Malo about this use of punishment. He did not seem the least embarrassed about it. He said that he had hoped I would see some examples of punishment which was why he had taken me to all the rooms. He said that their own experience and records indicated that although the carrot was effective about 90 percent of the time, the stick was needed about 10 percent of the time to get a child to adopt cooperative behaviors. He said that teachers in all of the schools abided by very strict conditions for using punishment. It was used only when the transgression was so severe as to require it to be terminated immediately. When a child behaved in such a way, the teachers had a standard procedure which was that the punishment be immediate, that it be as severe as was consistent with the child's welfare, and that the child be given a chance to behave differently and appropriately immediately. I recalled what I had just seen when the child had been reprimanded and slapped for not sharing the building blocks. The teacher immediately gave the child a chance to share the blocks with his playmate, and had in fact complimented him immediately on how well he was playing. Mr. Malo explained their philosophy of educating young children. He said the behavior of children was like a stream of water. If you did not want it to go a certain way, you had to dam it up, but then you had to give it another outlet so that it would run the course that you wanted it to go. He said that is what punishment did—it acted as a dam to stop the water from going one way, but that you had to provide the right course for the water to flow and this had to be done immediately.

My impression of the children in the community service preschool was that they were healthy and apparently happy and that they were certainly learning lessons in cooperation at an early age. Classes also contained the usual educational materials of letters and numbers and a few maps and so on, but there was much more in the way of plants and flowers than one would find in our own of preschool classrooms. I gathered that the care of nature's products is a very early matter of concern in raising children in Blue Lake. I was told later that the children had a garden in the little courtyard where they raised small flowers and that even the two-year-olds were taught how to tend and water them. I am not sure how much they understood of what they were doing but I thought it was a charming notion that they should be raising flowers at such an early age.

Mr. Malo then took me down to what was called the Responsive Center, a kind of chart room with all kinds of communications equipment, with maps of Blue Lake Village all over the walls with a series of grids on them. Mr. Malo explained that this was the nerve center for the maintenance of Blue Lake and that each of the grids represented a service where there could be a possible breakdown. At first I thought that he meant that this was where they just handled complaints about water or energy supply breakdown but I learned that he did indeed mean the entire community. Calls were coming in about all kinds of matters, such as a request by what I guessed was an older woman who was living alone and wanted to know if somebody could pick up her food from the store and bring it by, as she was not feeling very well that day. The Controller talked into a microphone, and shortly replied to the woman that a neighbor was going that way and would be glad to pick up the order for her. Another call came in requesting that one of the big transits be permitted to go out of its way to pick up a mother and child where the mother had difficulty walking because of a recent accident. The Controller got on the microphone again and a bus driver was asked to detour from the route to accomodate this particular person. I listened in on another call which was that of a frightened woman who said her child was choking. The Controller called the Health Improvement Guardianship to dispatch an emergency unit immediately. A nurse or possibly a physician came on then and told her what to do until the unit got there.

I did not have the time to see what all the other charts and grids were about but I gathered that almost any kind of request would be handled here and I assume some complaints as well. It seemed to me that the Responsive Center was a combination of police station, emergency station, hospital—almost anything of concern to the community would be referred here and the job of the people running it was indeed to be responsive, which is why I suppose it was called the Responsive Center. One advantage of such a center was that anybody who was alone or who was not entirely well had the resources of the community made available to them immediately through the phone or the use of what looked like a television set-up. I wondered if they did not have people who made a nuisance of themselves but I did not see any while I was there.

We had time for only one more visit before the end of the afternoon and that had to be a short one. Dr. Posic took me across the square to the building which was the Health Improvement Guardianship. I gathered this was something like our public health clinics but I was a bit wrong in that first impression. The Health Improvement Guardianship, at least in Blue Lake Village, comprised all of the health services, and all of the health care personnel were under the supervision of the Health Improvement Guardianship which focused its attention on health improvement directly.

I had expected to see a large waiting room such as we see in our own public health clinics, with their hard chairs and the eternally stoic patients who wait for their name to be called. Instead I was surprised to see that the first room on my left had a big sign over the door saying Nutritional Research. Dr. Posic explained that their Nutritional Research Department was very excited about a new source of protein which they thought they had developed from two new grains, one of which was a very ancient grain going back to Egypt and one of which was a new development. She asked me to try a wafer as we walked through the Nutrition Department and I found it fairly tasty, rather like something I had eaten at Dr. Bo's house the previous day. She explained that this was one of the new proteins that they had developed last year.

I could not resist asking Dr. Posic where the clinic was because I had not seen it yet. She asked what I meant by the word clinic. I explained that a clinic is where people went to get health care who could not afford to go to a private physician. She looked puzzled and said that they did not have anything called a "clinic" in Blue Lake, and in fact, she did not know of one in all of Prire.

"Everyone in Blue Lake has their own health team and can see them whenever they need to!" she replied. "Why would they have to come to a what you call a 'clinic' and wait to see them?"

I decided that I was only muddying the water with my question so I asked her to explain how the health teams worked. She explained that each health team consisted of between five and ten individual health practitioners with a variety of skills. It would include a physician practitioner, a nutrition practitioner, a fitness practitioner, and a psychology practitioner, and at the head of the team would be the Health Habits Counselor. As she explained it to me, every person in Prire had access to such a team throughout his life from the moment of birth. I gathered that one could change a team if one did not like the particular members.

I was curious about the Health Habits Counselor which was a new idea to me and also the fact that such a person would be chief of the team. Dr. Posic explained that the emphasis of the health team, as of the Health Improvement Guardianship, was on the conservation of health rather than the treatment of illness. The Health Habits Counselors were those who had the most direct contact with each person and knew all their habits, from what they ate to how they got exercise, to how they spent their time, how they slept, how they relaxed, their recreational habits and so on. The Health Habits Counselor was responsible for helping each person to build up those habits that were most congenial to his own health. She indicated a great deal of individuality was recognized in these habits and that there had been a lot of research into individual differences.

I remarked to Dr. Posic that I had been very impressed with the healthy appearance of the people I had seen in Capital City and in Blue Lake and that I had not seen any cases of what I would call overweight nor of severe underweight. Dr. Posic seemed very pleased with my observation about what her Health Improvement Guardianship staff had been able to accomplish. She explained that they had been able to achieve this over a long period of time through health education and through the development of health habits. Each person was given training in the establishment of health habits and in the use of self-reward to encourage life-long habits of health. She said another thing that had helped was the education of parents in developing the right health habits in their own children. There were no foods available except naturally grown foods and she explained that the use of sweets was very carefully handled and limited to honey, fruits, and the very restricted use of sugar cane. She felt that it was fairly easy to develop and maintain good health in an environment where there was so little that was bad to eat, and thought that Blue Lake was unusually lucky in being able to control what was available to eat. It would be a much harder job if there were all kinds of foods available that were unhealthy for people but of course the philosophy of Prire was that such things were not available.

I did not have enough time to speak with Dr. Posic about all of the aspects of their health care program but I gathered that the teams went to the people rather than the people coming to the teams. Each member of the team apparently was available for a visit but they made regular calls in people's homes. I also got the impression that the Health

Habits Counselor was a regular part of the school program and had a chance to teach youngsters how to form such habits early.

We had to cut this visit short so that we would be on time for dinner which was being held at Mr. Kulip's home, who was Chairman of the Blue Lake Resources and Returns Committee. (I was beginning to worry about my own health habits since I had had very little exercise and had eaten quite a large noon meal, but all of my Blue Lake hosts and hostesses told me not to worry about it as there was nothing in Prire food that would be bad for me. Interestingly, I did not gain weight on my trip.)

Mr. Kulip's home was on the edge of Blue Lake itself in a perfectly lovely setting although the house itself was simple, as were all the homes that I saw around Blue Lake. It was a small farm of about twenty acres but was very intensively cultivated. I saw no piece of ground that was not making some sort of return. I had the opportunity to walk in his vegetable garden for a few minutes before supper with Dr. Bo and I was impressed with the quality of what I saw there. Tomatoes, zucchini, squash— all were further advanced for June than I was used to seeing. I saw that corn was planted, winter squash, melons, sweet potatoes, cauliflower, broccoli, something that looked like collards, potatoes, beans, both bush and pole, and in one corner of his garden he had what he called a winter garden which was going to be planted in parsnips, turnips, celeries and a new kind of onion he described to me. He had a special bed of asparagus which was shooting up and another one of Jerusalem artichokes. He had a small orchard quite intensively planted with dwarf fruits—apple, pear, peach, cherry, crabapple, plum and apricot. He had a number of apricot trees and told me they were important in the diet in Blue Lake.

From what he described of their techniques of gardening, I gathered that they were ones which we are essentially familiar with but done much more intensively and with a lot more attention paid to storage. I gathered that Mr. Kulip's family could live throughout the year on what they produced because they had a very extensive storeroom in the cellar, which I visited after dinner. They also had a large root cellar and were still eating carrots and potatoes from the previous year's harvest. At the rear of his house was a sort of greenhouse, although unlike any I had seen before. It was solar heated, he explained. Many of his young vegetable plants had been started there and he now had some flowers that he was preparing to put out. It was semi-circular in appearance, attached to the wall of his house which faced south, and contained a series of vertical veins that could be adjusted to make the most of the sun's reflection, which was absorbed in the shield at the rear of the greenhouse. One part of the greenhouse was set aside for hydroponics and I saw some fascinating vegetable plants being grown in water. He explained that they were like a potato in their nutritious qualities but bore a fruit much like a tomato.

Before dinner Mr. Kulip insisted we all taste his wine, which he had made the previous summer from the berries on the farm which he called "summer berries." I thought it was quite good berry wine although a little too sweet, but everyone seemed to enjoy it. I asked if anyone might make his own wine in Blue Lake and was told that indeed one could; in fact, it was encouraged. I found the dinner meal better than anything I had had so far as it was made entirely from things grown on Mr. Kulip's farm and obviously he took great pride in that. Mme. Kulip had helped him cook the meal and both of them were admirable cooks. We had two different casseroles whose ingredients I could not identify except to say they tasted like fresh vegetables with some nuts in them, and one had some cheese topping. The salad was excellent and we had a *feta*-type of cheese for dessert with a plum that I had never tasted before, rather yellowish in color and a little tart. Mr. and Mme. Kulip did not want us to help clear up the dishes but I noticed that everybody helped just the same and I assume this was part of the cooperative spirit of Blue Lake, so I did my share. I must say it went very efficiently and soon we were on their porch overlooking Blue Lake which was a lovely sight.

There were boats out on the lake with people fishing and again I had that odd sensation of something missing until I realized that of course there were no motors and no water-skiers, and no speedboats. The boats were all either rowboats or canoes and it was a very quiet and pleasant sight. Mr. Kulip told me that the fishing there was very good, as of course care was taken to maintain the lake as a healthy environment for fish. The lake was fertilized regularly with manure from the various animals kept by the farms around it. This was done under the direction of a local Water Committee. Fish were a main part of the diet of the people in Blue Lake, so great care was taken to preserve the fish population and to make sure that nothing was wasted. He said he was sorry that I was not coming a little later, or had not come a little earlier, as I was in between the good fishing. I said this sounded like every fishing place I had ever been in my life where they always told you that you came just too late for the good fishing or that the good fishing had not started yet. He thought that was very funny but said it was true nevertheless that this time in June was a time when they fished very carefully so as not to disturb the nests of the breeding fish in the Lake.

I asked Mr. Kulip if he would tell me something about the work of the Resources and Returns Committee in Blue Lake as this was my first chance to talk with him, and he was delighted. He said that the main job his committee had was of guarding the resources of the Blue Lake Community but they were also responsible for seeing that a proper return was made from each of those resources. The resources included not only the land itself, which was the interest of a number of committees in Blue Lake, but also the resources in the earth, the use of timber, of water, of air power or wind, and so on. The function of the committee was to adopt a plan, which was modified on a yearly basis, that would provide Blue Lake an adequate supply of food, first of all, and ensure that all natural resources above, below, and in and on the land were used in a way that would conserve their availability for future generations. I asked him if all forms of energy came under his committee. He said that they did, and that furthermore they were constantly doing experiments to test various forms of energy that would be less depleting than those they now used. I commented on the presence of windmills and he said that these were very useful and efficient, that they used water power, electricity, some gas and coal, and some oil, but that each was considered as part of a master plan for the use of all energy resources.

I was curious about the word "Returns" in the committee's name and asked about that. He said that Returns here meant returns not only of the resources but that people were considered a resource as well, so that his committee helped to establish what returns were made for the work that was carried out. Apparently there was a very complex system of payment in Blue Lake (I think that this was true of the other communities I visited and I am not sure that I grasped the complexity of it). Payment was made in the money of Prire for the work that one did (remember that work is two kinds of jobs, the occupational job and the community service job) but other forms of payment were also used, such as vouchers, for return labor. Where one person contributed labor to the community for some sort of community project, he would get a voucher back for other people's labor to help him with his own projects. There also was a widespread use of points which could be converted to a number of things, such as larger land space if the need could be demonstrated and the points had been earned; toward the purchase of farm equipment; for improvement to one's house; for food delicacies; for clothes or jewelry; and so on. He explained that points could also be applied toward a special vacation or even to having one's house cleaned. I gathered that there were an enormous number of choices to which these points could be applied. It is a very curious system and I could not understand how people would work for a combination of income, vouchers and points. Probably one would have to live in Prire for some time to understand the variety of options that were open to any one person in return for his work.

Dr. Bo interjected that it would be hard for a person like myself, coming from the background I did, to understand that there were motivators as strong as money—in fact some even stronger—and that probably I would not believe that on such a short visit. I said that it seemed to me that the history of man showed a history of greed for money and power, and that I did not see how this was going to change. Dr. Bo said that he would not quite agree with the notion that the history of man was nothing more than a greed for power and money, but he would certainly agree that the desire for money and power were very strong sources of motivation in human beings, that this had not changed in any way in the planning of Prire but that they simply used these motivators for other ends. He explained that in Prire there was a definite intention to limit the range of money that could be earned by people in different occupations and that it was also part of the plan to make it impossible for any one person to amass a fortune. Under those circumstances it was essential that other forms of returns be utilized such as vouchers and points toward desirable services, or goods, or experiences. He stressed the word experience, saying that many people are motivated to be productive in return for some sort of desirable experience and that points made this quite possible.

An example he gave was of a man in his fifties who was a skilled repairman of agricultural machinery and who had always wanted to take painting lessons but had never had the opportunity. A member of the Committee on Resources and Returns pointed out to him that with the accumulation of extra points he could take lessons from the outstanding painter in Blue Lake Village, if he so wished it. This was an example of "Creative Return" in Mr. Kulip's terminology, in which they had matched the desire for an experience on the one hand, with the ability to acquire it through one's own productivity on the other hand. It had worked out very well apparently, and everyone was pleased. I was a little hesitant to accept the one-example argument, because people tend to repeat their favorite successful case but never the unsuccessful ones.

Dr. Bo apparently noticed my skepticism, because he made a point of asking me a few things about how things were run in our society.

"I understand that in your society the profit motive is considered to be the prime motivator of human beings, is that not so?"

I replied that that was indeed so and that it seemed to me our society had demonstrated the power of it.

"Quite so," Dr. Bo retorted rather sharply. "But don't you think that that might only prove that a society set up with only one form of return is going to see a lot of motivation for that one return?"

"Possibly so," I said, "but it seems to me that greed is an awfully basic human characteristic."

"No one is denying the motivating force of trying to acquire valuable possessions," Dr. Bo answered. "It is just that experiences sometimes can be as important or even more important than possessions.

"Tell me," he asked, "is it not true, as I have read, that there are many places in your society where people do hard work and dangerous work for no pay?"

"Not that I can think of," I answered. "Hard and dangerous work generally commands a premium pay."

"But," said Dr. Bo, "I believe I have read of something called a volunteer fire company. Don't they exist any more?"

"Oh, yes they exist." I had not thought of them.

Dr. Bo persisted. "Is it not true that people work for a volunteer fire department in your society, and in fact they pay dues, in order to go to fires and to help put them out?"

I answered that I thought this was true, and that I understood that these firemen were indeed volunteers.

Dr. Bo looked at me quizzically and said, "Now what would you call that motivation?"

"I don't think I would say, just off the top of my head," I answered, "but I suppose that volunteer firemen enjoy firefighting and the company of such people, and probably enjoy prestige in the town for doing such volunteer work."

"Quite so," replied Dr. Bo with a small smile. "Quite so. That's the sort of thing we have tried to build into the returns in Prire."

Mr. Kulip tried to explain to me that about half of an average person's income came from his "occupational income" and about half came from his "citizen income," which is the income he had earned for community service, in which he spends about half his time on a variety of schedules. Apparently this "citizen income" is also affected by the behavior of citizens in other aspects of their life. I gathered that citizens in Blue Lake, for example, would get points for the proper care of their land, for being helpful to their neighbors, for doing their part in collecting refuse, and so on, and also points would be taken away for uncooperative or nonconserving kinds of behavior and so on. I wondered how this was handled and whether there were local committees that handed out points both good and bad, and if so, if this did not create all kinds of resentment.

Mr. Kulip explained that there were indeed times when disputes had to be referred to the local Adjudication Committee, but that on the whole it worked fairly well because the behaviors were so clearly defined as to what would get you extra points and what would not.

Dr. Bo entered the conversation at this point and said that he thought probably I should understand more about the Law of Personal Effectiveness in order to understand how the checks and balances were made upon citizens living in Blue Lake and, in fact, in other Prire communities. I said I had read a little about this Law but would appreciate an explanation. Dr. Bo said that a basic part of the planning in Prire had been to deal with the problem of how to construct communities in such a way that people in them felt their own personal effectiveness, for people need to feel that what they do makes a difference. Their study of other societies had led them to the conclusion that cities and nations of a large size had lost this, for their people had developed a feeling of anonymity and of ineffectualness because they could never deal directly with a person who had the ability to change whatever was the problem in their life. It was partly a function of size but also a function of the Law of Personal Effectiveness that led the founders of Prire to the conclusion that the size of any of the communities of Prire would have to be limited, as an organizational unit, to not more than three thousand people and some might be much smaller than that.

I asked him how the capital city was managed because certainly that was well over three thousand, and in fact looked to be nearer to perhaps a half to three-quarters of a million. He said that the total city was that size but that each unit of the city or neighborhood was a unit of not more than three thousand. Within each unit there was a Responsive Center for dealing with any problem that came up in that community. These were not exactly independent communities, they were part of Capital City, but a great deal of autonomy was given them for the running of their affairs and that any member of a particular community could get an answer and action from his local administration on the same day that the complaint was made.

As Dr. Bo explained the Law of Personal Effectiveness to me, it had resulted in some very strong characteristics about both Prire and Blue Lake. Not only were the communities restricted in size so that people could know each other and have a sense of dealing with consistencies of human behavior over time (as well as its inconsistencies), but that the management of any phase of a community, such as Blue Lake for example, had to be responsive within twenty-four hours to a complaint or a question.

This emphasis on the responsiveness of any aspect of management was an interesting one to me as it seemed that it would increase the feeling of personal effectiveness if one could get a response back quickly from someone whom you knew on a name basis. I was curious, however, how this responsiveness was developed and maintained because I had seen it deteriorate in many situations in our own societies.

Dr. Bo said the answer again was a very simple one, that anyone in a managing capacity functioned under the same set of rewards as anybody else, namely, that their pay in Prire currency, or in points, or in vouchers, was dependent upon the responsiveness of their performance.

I asked how anybody could keep records of such things, and he said that too was simple, for each time there was a contact by a member of the community with someone in a managing capacity, a card was dropped in an appropriate location to indicate their satisfaction or dissatisfaction with the service from the person whose name appeared on it. These records were tallied, and the income for each management person was computed on a monthly basis from these satisfaction or dissatisfaction evaluations. I asked Dr. Bo that if this meant that they had gotten rid of the surly clerk phenomenon with which I was so familiar. He laughed and said he would not claim that they were that successful but hoped to achieve this over time because that kind of behavior simply does not pay off.

In the time I had left to talk with Mr. Kulip I inquired about how ownership of the natural resources was handled in Blue Lake. He indicated that in Blue Lake, as was true in all of Prire, none of the natural resources could belong to any one person. They all belonged to the Prire society and or to the community in which they were found, and the resources included all the water, the land, the woods, the fields, the flora and fauna, and everything that was in the earth, in the sea, and above it, including the air.

I asked if this meant that citizens did not own their land and he said that technically citizens did not own their land but that it was viewed as a kind of ownership because they had a lease for their life-time and for that of members of their immediate family, but not for their children. However, the children of the family had the first option on the lease of that land, provided they had demonstrated a record of being good guardians of these resources. I asked him if this meant that the land could stay in one family's hands over several generations. He said yes, indeed it could, in fact it usually happened that way where the family had a good record of being conserving people. I asked him if it was possible for one family to extend their leases so that they amassed quite a large farm of 500 or 2000 acres. He said no that was not possible, that there was a limit put on what any one family could own but that the range varied quite a bit. The smallest amount of land for a family would be approximately two acres but that would have to be a very fertile two acres to maintain the family, and that the largest holding would depend again on the quality of the land and the largest holding might perhaps be 200 acres. In the use of the land there were many limitations on what people could do without permission from either the Resources and Returns Committee or the Overseers of the Future or some other relevant group.

I did not like the sound of that because it seemed like red tape and bureaucracy before you could so much as divert a stream, and I said so. But Mr. Kulip explained that a citizen in Blue Lake was not dealing with some far away bureaucracy but with committees in his own town who were available to him immediately and from which he could get an immediate answer. He said if you wanted to move that stream on your property you would not have a lot of red tape and waiting because, first of all, there would be a plan already on file of the characteristics of that piece of land including its soil analysis, its topography, its water table and so on. I could make a request and give a reason for wanting to divert a brook or stream and I could have an answer within no more than one week. If I did not like the answer I could appeal it but I would have to demonstrate what I wanted to do was in the long-run interest of that piece of land and would not cause damage. I asked Mr. Kulip if permission was ever granted to change land for purely aesthetic reasons and he said that indeed that happened fairly often, and of course permission was given if nothing was done to alter the basic resources of that piece of property. He must have been a little bit irritated by my questions because he said to me rather sharply, "I don't know why we would not respond to a desire to improve aesthetic qualities. We consider aesthetics one of the resources of Blue Lake, as you can see for yourself."

I must say I had to agree with his point, sitting on his porch looking down on this perfectly lovely lake in a tranquil scene with productive farms all around the edge of the lake. It was as aesthetic a scene as I have ever looked at. I was not persuaded by what I had heard, however, that life would not be full of committees and requests and forms and all that, if one lived in Blue Lake Village. But I suppose they were right that one would have to live there for a while to know whether it was as bad as I feared or whether in fact the system was not somewhat more responsive than I imagined and that perhaps it worked as they claimed. I certainly could not judge in my short visit.

Since I was spending the night at Mr. Kulip's I decided not to pursue any more questions for fear I would upset him, and so for the balance of the evening I entertained them with some stories about life in our society which had them occasionally amused but more often shaking their heads and remarking that they certainly would not want to live in that kind of society and they wondered how anybody could stand it.

I was getting quite tired and so went to bed in a simple but charming room that looked over the lake. Dr. Bo stayed at Mme. Young's and Mr. Bortan, Mr. Malo and Dr. Posic went to their own homes for the night so I had said good-bye to them with many thanks for the generous hospitality they had shown me. Dr. Bo and I arranged to meet again in the morning.

# 3

## Tuesday, June 19th

The next morning Dr. Bo and I set off in a transit borrowed from Blue Lake Village to reach the Mountgate community, about an hour and a half away. Mountgate was not on the usual visitor's tour, although almost everyone visited Blue Lake which was an established cooperative village that had been successful over many generations.

According to what I had read, Mountgate community represented a type of community, fairly common in Prire, consisting of people not interested in a cooperative community but rather in freedom to live their own life-styles. Often these communities attracted artistic people, but sometimes people came just because they wished to live a life of independence and of nonparticipation. This particular community, Mountgate, was an artistic colony that had been going for five generations now and had attracted a succession of artists who found it a productive place to live.

I took the opportunity of being alone with Dr. Bo to ask him a number of questions about what I had seen so far. I was both puzzled and curious about the implications of some things I had heard at Blue Lake the day before, particularly about the means used to motivate people in Prire and about their governance. He was very patient in trying to explain this system to me, but I don't think I grasped it very thoroughly in the hour's talk. However, I will set down the outline of what he told me.

The basis for selection for citizens to become part of the governing system of Prire is their prior service in the community, of which complete records are kept. This had been indicated to me the day before at Blue Lake. Apparently the basis for being selected as a candidate for any office was one's recorded performance at a lower level job. The selection is done, I think, by the local Overseers of the Future. I asked Dr. Bo specifically whether it was not possible for scoundrels to get into public office as they had everywhere else in human history. He said it was possible, of course, but that it was very hard to confound the record of service, particularly in communities small enough so that officials were known by the people who selected them.

Dr. Bo described a special school for those who wanted to go on into public service. I was not clear exactly when one attended this school but I gather it was when one reached a certain level in public service, perhaps equivalent to city councilman in our society, or a member of the state legislature. I think the schooling is a requirement and not optional, and takes two years. The students are given a minimal subsistence while they attend, and do not hold office while they go to this school. As Dr. Bo described it, as of course he had attended the school himself as a younger man, the studies include service to Prire as well as budget analysis, legislative processes, evaluation of services, reading of performance records, techniques of interviewing, and demographic analysis of a community, etc. This school used behavioral situations to both train and evaluate its students. Dr. Bo described a major examination that he had taken many years ago and said that the same type of examination was still being used. The candidates are required to receive a dozen or more people from their community who have complaints. As they interview these residents, they are judged on the way they handle the interview and how they plan to deal with the complaint. Then their actual plan of follow-up is also evaluated so that a sample is taken of their ability to be responsive to the needs of the communities that they hope some day to represent.

Apparently considerable effort is made in this school to instill a moral ideology of service to Prire. Dr. Bo seemed reluctant to speak about this, but it was obviously an important part of the curriculum. The day before, in talking to the local trustees at Blue Lake, I had noticed that there was a very firm —almost fervent—commitment to service that seemed to go beyond a mere intellectual acceptance of the idea. It seemed to me to be closer to a strong belief or ideology. Dr. Bo said that I would see more of this later on as we visited other communities and I had the impression that he wanted to let me discover what this ideology was for myself.

After a young person, man or woman, had graduated from this school for service to Prire (not all graduated, I learned), they were eligible for a position in their own community. Another feature of this system was that each young person selected for office had assigned to him an older person, a man or woman who had a record of many years of service to Prire in a capacity as a trustee on one of the committees. The young man or woman then served an apprenticeship to this older person for some time before they went on into office on their own. I was reminded of the law clerk parallel in our own society. Apparently this was a deliberate attempt to provide a model for all kinds of behaviors and the apprentice practically lived with this older person who was available for counsel in all phases of his work and work contacts. Dr. Bo spoke with great fondness of his own mentor, the famous Madame Luko who was renowned in Prire as one of the great Overseers of the Future. He said that his two-year apprenticeship was the most important time of his life, and that he would never forget his indebtedness to her. Indeed, he had named his daughter after Madame Luko, and he hoped that I would have a chance to meet her while I was still in Prire.

I went back to the same question again and again with Dr. Bo, which was how did a society like Prire avoid exploitation? Had not Prire ever fallen into the hands of certain interests or leaders who came to power in one of the national committees? Dr. Bo replied that exploitation of the kind that I spoke of had been pretty well controlled for five or six generations now, but it had been a problem at the beginning. He attributed this freedom from exploitation to the fact that, first of all, it was impossible to build up a basis of wealth in Prire because the incentive system restricted the amount of currency that could be earned, although a wide selection of points and experiences were available for extra effort or productivity. Dr. Bo felt that the ban on hereditary private fortunes was another way to prevent exploitation, because it prevented the acquisition of power based on wealth. I wondered whether there were not groups of people with similar interests who would band together to bring influence to bear on the trustees or the Overseers or some other group. Dr. Bo said that such a possibility had always existed but so far the people of Prire had been successful in making the interest of the society as a whole the overriding one in the way they had organized its governance, in their education, and in the way in which people were rewarded in that soty.

"You must remember that we have been at this for a very long time," Dr. Bo said, "and have learned a lot from our own mistakes. But coming from the society that you do, it must be hard for you to understand how a system such as ours would operate."

"It is hard," I conceded, "it is very hard, indeed. What happens to all that energy that in our society goes into the making of money and acquisition of fortunes and of power? Do you pretend here that people have changed that much?"

"Not at all," Dr. Bo said quickly. "As you know, in Prire we do not pretend that we are changing human nature, only that we are getting it to work for more appropriate rewards. We are the same old animal we have always been. All we do in Prire is to try to make the desired behavior sufficiently attractive to our people."

"What about your industry? What about those who control the factories, and so on? Don't they try to improve their financial position and their power with your various Overseers and Trustees?" I asked.

"I think that you have a misunderstanding about how we operate our industry in Prire," Dr. Bo replied thoughtfully. "Our industry is limited to our national needs. As you probably know, we have no army so we have no arms industry to promote conflict. It was a long time ago, in fact, even before Madame Luko's time, that we finished our final evaluation on large versus small industries and decided to go the way of the small industrial unit and to limit industry only to what we needed now and in the future. We have no large industries, no centralized industrial facilities. Consequently, we have no large industrial empires."

"But don't you lose efficiency by having many small units rather than large centralized capacities?" I asked.

"Perhaps so, perhaps so," Dr. Bo nodded. "We have studied this quite carefully and we think we do lose something in the way of cost efficiency with smaller units but we are quite willing to pay the price in return for the social benefits that result from avoiding those large financial empires. You must realize also that the production of things is limited to our needs. We have no desire to increase consumption to match manufacturing surpluses."

"You make it sound as if Prire is almost free of lobbying and pressure groups. I can't believe that there is a society anywhere where there are not people trying to grab power or become part of the top power structure. It's been like that throughout history," I said a little bit heatedly. "Why should Prire be different?"

"I think we have a misunderstanding here," Dr. Bo remarked with deliberation. "People always have and always will have, I think, the desire for power in some form. If a society rewards people with money, then power will take that form. It is our view that the desire for power, as you describe it in your society, is the distraction of the desire to be well-thought of by others. In your society—I speak as only a student of course—with the hugeness that has grown up and the increasing distance between people, it seems to me that there are no longer the opportunities for respect at the more personal level. This has contributed to the desire for money and power as you describe it. Power here in Prire is the power that comes from being respected as a person who works for the long-term interests of Prire, whether this is at the local or the national level. The people who are held in most respect are those who serve the long-term needs of the country first."

"I find this very hard to believe," I said. "It sounds to me like you think that you have solved selfishness and I just can't accept that."

"Not at all," replied Dr. Bo quite quickly. "We have not done away with selfishness at all. It's just a question of redefining what is in one's own interests. If the environment is arranged in such a way that I'll gain more in the short run—as well as the long run—by being unselfish, then I'm being selfish in an unselfish way, am I not?"

"I don't think I follow you. What do you mean —being selfish in an unselfish way?"

"Let me give you an example. Let us say that someone steals chickens from his neighbor. In our system in Prire, Neighbor B whose chickens were stolen can go immediately to the Community Service, and either in person or through our visual system can bring his grievance before the local justices. Assuming that Neighbor B can prove his case against Neighbor A and that indeed the chickens were stolen, then Neighbor B can get his retribution from Neighbor A the following day, which is a matter of forty-eight hours from the time of the first incident."

"What do you mean by retribution?" I asked.

"In this particular instance the property protection code would indicate that Neighbor B is entitled to twice the value of his chickens from anything belonging to Neighbor A. The local justices would set the value and would have to approve what Neighbor B takes as retribution, but Neighbor B has the right to walk on Neighbor A's farm and select whatever he wishes that is of that value."

"It sounds to me like the retribution is swift and rather severe!" I exclaimed.

"Yes, that is correct. This is one way to make sure that stealing is not a rewarding way of life. The swiftness of it is very important, as is the double penalty. It really does not pay anyone to steal under such circumstances."

"Are you implying something about stealing, that sometimes stealing pays off?" I asked.

"Some stealing does pay off and where it does, it increases. I believe that in your society, from what I read, it pays a person to steal or to do what you call 'mug'. From what I read, the chances of being caught are very slim and there is no retribution to speak of."

"But if a mugger or a thief is caught in our society he faces the chance of going to jail for a long time."

"But that is not very effective, is it?" Dr. Bo asked. "This system of justice I read about in your country is entirely too slow to be effective and the chances of a person going to jail are much too small. If you won't take offense at my saying so, I think a problem in your country is that the justice is administered by lawyers rather than by those who have studied how to change behavior."

"But you have lawyers here in Prire, don't you?" I asked.

"Oh yes indeed, we do, but they are not permitted to run the system of justice. Our system of justice is based upon our knowledge of behavior and motivation, not upon some so-called accumulated wisdom of judges and lawyers. Unfortunately, legal systems are based upon legal precedents, not upon what works to change the behavior of people. And of course, like most systems, they have tended to serve the interests of those who run them, which are the lawyers and the judges," Dr. Bo commented.

I realized after this conversation that there was a lot I needed to learn about the justice and legal system of Prire which I hoped I would get to see in person. I could hardly believe what Dr. Bo was telling me and I was certainly not about to believe that such a system would be effective in cutting down crime.

During this conversation we had left Blue Lake Village and driven across a long fertile valley with a small river running through it. This was all farm country, very much like what I'd seen at Blue Lake, but as we approached Mountgate I noticed immediately how different it looked.

On the outskirts, there were a few farms but they were not particularly prosperous looking nor I should say, particularly well tended. I saw no intensive cultivation except a few gardens. A few places had a goat and some chickens but nothing gave the impression that this was a full-time farming community, for in fact it was not. Dr. Bo drove me around Mountgate for a while before we went to the center of the community and I could see that it was laid out very differently.

Mountgate consisted of a large number of dirt roads that rambled all over the hills with a farm here or a home there—I could hardly call them farms, more like a homestead I would say—but there was no great clumping of them together. Life here would be far more isolated than at Blue Lake, yet I suppose that if one had a way to get down the roads one could get into Mountgate village without too much difficulty. I asked about this and Dr. Bo explained that there was a large transit bus that went on regular rounds of these roads so that people could get into Mountgate village to shop and do whatever else they wished to do.

I took this opportunity to inquire about transportation because I had seen so few transits anywhere. He said that bus service was available in all of the farming communities and that occasionally an individual farm family might have a transit if it were needed, more likely a truck of some kind. But with a freight and passenger service available at the gate, it was not too often used. Many people preferred to use a horse and carriage for their pleasure driving. I asked about emergencies and how these were handled if someone were ill and he said there was an emergency health service in all of the communities, which was run by the Health Guardianship Committee. They operated an emergency ambulance and something like a helicopter.

We finally came into the village itself, which was laid out on the same principle as I had seen in Blue Lake and in Capital City. There was a park in the center of town and the shops were arranged around the park. An art show in progress in the park had attracted quite a crowd, people of all ages looking at the paintings. Dr. Bo asked me if I would like to see the exhibit and walk around and look at the shops. We strolled through the exhibit and I was impressed with the quality of what I saw although I don't view myself as being at all expert at such matters. Shops around the square were very interesting to me. This clearly was a village of people with artistic interests because the stores were full of artists' materials, records, books, musical instruments, weaving materials, potting materials—everything I could think of and a lot more I'd never seen before for all types of artistic work and handicrafts.

The people did not look much different from those at Blue Lake or in Capital City and they did not appear to be dressed any differently, perhaps a bit more casually if that's possible. I got the impression very quickly that their life was centered on their own artwork rather than in farming or in community service.

I asked Dr. Bo how such a community was managed if all the people were busy with their own artwork, for it would leave no one time for community service or the overseers' jobs, the trusteeships and things of that kind. Dr. Bo said there had been several attempts at solving that problem and

that at Mountgate the people had elected to receive
minimal services from Prire itself so as to cut down
the amount of time they had to spend on community
services. Apparently there is some sort of an agree-
ment between each community and the services in
Prire as a whole so that communities can elect to
accept a full range of services or a bare minimum,
in return for which they must contribute service to
the community and to Prire. This was a minimum
service community which accepted the necessary
services from Prire, including of course water and
utilities. The roads were maintained—to the extent
that they were maintained—by the members of
Mountgate. I must say they weren't in very good
shape but perhaps no one minded. They apparently
raised enough food to maintain themselves, but I
didn't see much evidence of cooperative farming;
it seemed as though each family more or less raised
its own food. Dr. Bo acknowledged that this was so
and said that it was a much less efficient system
than the one found at Blue Lake, but that after all
this was the choice of the people who lived there.

Apparently their main concern was not to spend
too much of their time in subsistence labor or in
community service, so that they could devote more
time to their own form of artwork. Dr. Bo explained
that anyone with artistic talent could elect to live
here or in a variety of other art-oriented communities in Prire, some of which maintained more community services and were more cooperatively organized. Mountgate, he said, represented the least
amount of organization of any of the art communities in this area and for that reason he thought I
would be interested in seeing it.

After we visited the booths we lunched at the

outdoor picnic table and I was interested to see that they charged currency for the lunch which Dr. Bo very graciously hosted. The sum of money I tried to translate, not too successfully, but I think it came to about between two and three dollars per person for the lunch, which was a fair amount of money in our terms but perhaps some of this went to help support one of the many art buildings around the square. The lunch, by the way, was quite pleasant if meager and had been contributed by various members of the community.

After lunch we visited one of the many halls that had been erected by the members of the community. I visited the music hall which was a small theater designed mainly for chamber music, holding perhaps 300 people at the most. It was extremely simple, made out of a native wood like pine. Dr. Bo said it had very good acoustic quality but I could not tell, of course. We passed by one of a series of art galleries but didn't have time to see the exhibits.

The feeling that I had just walking around Mountgate was that it was very much like the artistic summer colonies in our own society. The difference of course was that this was not a summer colony, but a full-time, year-round residence and I wondered how they met the problems of schooling and of community needs and so on.

Dr. Bo wanted me to visit with one or two of the families in Mountgate and introduced me to what I assumed was one of the overseers—if they had such things in this community. He in turn walked me down to one of the exhibits and introduced me to a young man and what I assumed to be his wife, both in their late twenties. They had with them a little four-year-old girl who was very interested in staring at me. I thought I looked pretty much like a Prire resident but as soon as I started to speak she detected my accent. Dr. Bo explained that I was a visitor from outside, at which they were interested and amazed that I would enjoy a chance to talk with them about their daily life in Mountgate.

I have no idea, of course, whether this couple was representative or was especially picked. Dr. Bo said that they were rather average for this community, but I have only his word for it. I chatted for perhaps 45 minutes and I will summarize what I learned. I never got their last name straight so I won't attempt that but the young man's name was Chee, his wife was named Ria, and their little girl was Misa.

Chee and Ria had met during their service. Each young person in Prire, I learned, spends two years in Prire service at about age eighteen or so. They had come from two very different communities quite far apart but were given permission to marry. I was very interested in the idea that they had to have permission to marry. Apparently young people can make an informal arrangement to live together without involving anyone else, but the marriage act is considered part of the future of Prire and requires permission. I think that one reason for this is that the act of marriage in Prire is intended to represent a stable life-long relationship which then becomes an important part of any community and also may have reproduction as its outcome. I was even more surprised to learn that Chee and Ria had had to obtain permission to have Misa. I asked many questions about this because I found it troubling that one had to get permission in order to have a child. Chee and Ria assured me that this is a very frequent procedure.

As Chee and Ria explained it to me, married couples who wish to have children must apply to the Human Resources Trustees for permission to have a child. I asked what happened if someone got pregnant by mistake, and they said an abortion was automatically required. I asked if people didn't try to have children on the sly who were not given permission to have children. They said that was practically impossible in Prire, and anyhow people would not do this. I didn't understand that at all. They explained that being given permission to become parents is a great honor and that they were extremely pleased that they were so chosen. Apparently potential parents go through a complete genetic work-up—naturally there are records available in Prire on that as well—and on the stability of the marriage and on their ability to become parents. All prospective parents who are given permission attend a "parenting school" for the period of the pregnancy and are required to continue attending parenting school on a regular basis until the child is eighteen. I was dumbfounded at this idea. Apparently the parenting school is particularly intensive during the first few years until the youngster starts formal schooling, which begins at age two, I believe.

I asked them if they did not resent having to go to parenting school and they said no, they did not, and they found it very helpful. They had available to them people who were experts on child health as well as members of their own family health team and they had educators and others who could help them with any sort of problem. They particularly found the Health Habit counselor a good source, they said, as she had helped them establish good health habits in Misa, who did indeed look as healthy as could be. She still was peering at me from behind her mother's long dress and was not about to come near such a funny stranger.

I asked if all the children I could see in Mountgate village were children of parents who had been approved for parenthood and they said yes, they all were. I asked what about couples who were not approved for parenting and how did they handle that? They said it was a disappointment to them but they got over it.

"Do couples sometimes divorce and marry another person in order to have children?" I asked, and the answer to that was yes, that does happen sometimes. But they said that at the time you are granted permission to marry, you are presented with the odds of your being approved to be parents so that you know whether or not the marriage is likely to lead to parenthood. I asked how parents were selected, and I was told it was a combination of a number of things. With complete family histories, the policy in Prire was to encourage those people to have children who had the best genetic endowment of health and intelligence and stability and imagination. People with bad family histories were not permitted to reproduce. (Dr. Bo explained to me later that day that this policy had almost completely eliminated a retarded population in two generations.)

This young couple was very earnest indeed, and they tried to explain to me that no one in Prire would want to have a child unless that child were going to be a credit to Prire. They looked endearingly at Misa and I could see how proud they were of her. They spoke of their hopes for her, that she would grow up and be a credit to whatever community she decided to live in. This raised an interesting question for me, which is the degree to which children returned as adults to the community in which they were raised. They explained that that happened part of the time, and part of the time young people moved off into communities of their choice, and very often that choice was very different from that of either parent. Sometimes children would elect to stay in the community if that suited them and they pointed out that there was one family in town that had chosen for four generations to stay in Mountgate.

I thought that Chee and Ria's account was a bit idealistic, particularly the notion that no one would want to have a child that would not be a credit to Prire. I asked Dr. Bo about this later as we were traveling to our next destination, and he agreed that this was a bit idealistic, that in fact there were some people in Prire who wanted to have children and who were not permitted to be parents. I asked him what was done about that and he said the abortions were enforced. I asked him if anything except a genetic history of illness or maladaptation was weighed in the permission to become parents. He said that there were other factors, such as the history of the particular couple and of their forebears as far as criminal activity and antisocial behavior was concerned. If there were a recurring history of antisocial behavior, permission to become parents was denied. He said it would be hard to prove, but it was his impression that this had contributed to the very low rate of crime in Prire although he would give credit as well to the swift way justice was administered. He said there was still a lot of controversy about the degree to which anti-social behavior was genetically based, but that in Prire they did not wish to increase the possibility of such a gene pool in their population.

My impression of this young couple was that they were dedicated and loyal to both Prire and Mountgate, and their counterparts could probably be found in any new society. I saw nothing particularly different about them except perhaps their willingness to limit their roles as parents to the criteria used in Prire.

I had the opportunity to speak to a number of artists who were displaying their works that day and not surprisingly they reported great enthusiasm for their way of life in Mountgate. They felt that they had gained a lot in terms of artistic freedom and time to work, and were quite willing to pay the consequences in lower services from Prire and from the community. However, they said, many artists did not like this rural type of artistic colony and preferred a more urban setting. Then asked if I had seen some of the artistic communities in Capital City. I said we had been much too rushed but I hoped to visit them before I left. There was a good deal of difference of opinion among them as to which type of community was best for artistic productivity. Some felt that the urban life had a lot to recommend it, with its concentration of talent and interaction among the various artists, whereas others felt that the quiet and peacefulness of the country contributed to their ability to be productive. The people I saw in Mountgate were certainly happy-looking and appeared enthusiastic about their type of community.

After I had visited as many of the booths as I could and talked with the artists displaying their work, Dr. Bo urged me to hurry up so that we would not be late for the ceremonies. I asked what these were but he refused to say anything more except that I would soon find out and see for myself. There were times when Dr. Bo's laissez-faire attitude toward me became almost annoying. However, he apparently felt that anything that he might say ahead of time might prejudice my views so I didn't push him on this. It was then about 3:45 and he urged us to join the crowd already hurrying toward the community hall.

The community hall was a very attractive rustic structure holding perhaps 500 people. It was made simply, like the other halls I had seen, and was used not only for public assemblies, but also for meetings and plays, for it had a stage. Today it was to be the scene for some sort of ceremony and the hall was decorated with many bowls of wild flowers on the stage and below it. We came in the back where wild flowers were arranged in attractive bouquets by the door. I asked Dr. Bo if it was not against Prire's values to pick wild flowers and he laughed at my question. He said it was permitted to pick wild flowers but only within certain limits, and he was quite sure that for today's ceremonies they would have been very circumspect. I wondered what he meant by that.

At 4:00 punctually a gentleman got up and addressed the group. I assume he was an overseer in Mountgate. The gist of his remarks was that he was opening the ceremony of the Commitment of the Young but that he had a few announcements to read before the ceremonies started. One notice was about some people who were planning to move out of the community to another one, indicating that their homes would be available. Another was about some newcomers who wanted to move to Mountgate. Dr. Bo whispered to me that this was a routine procedure so that anyone who might have objections to the new people coming in would have a chance to voice them to the Committee of Human Resources.

The chairman of the meeting then read a very unusual notice which went something like this: "Rone Tharsus wishes to have as his adoptive parents Carla and Olde Ven who have agreed to be his adoptive parents. Signed Rone Tharsus and Carla and Olde Ven." After reading the notice the chairman then said to the audience, "Anyone who has an approval to voice or an objection to utter should see the Committee on Human Resources within a two-week period or the adoption will go forward."

I whispered to Dr. Bo, "What kind of an adoption is this?" I had seen a young man about sixteen years of age and certainly he did not look like any orphan left at the door. Dr. Bo whispered back that it was not uncommon for young people in Prire to seek out adoptive parents. He said that many young people after the age of twelve found other adults, not necessarily a married couple, who were more congenial parents for them during adolescence, and very often there were adults who enjoyed playing that role. Under such circumstances, where it was agreeable to both the young boy or girl and to the adoptive parents, an adoption ceremony was held after the banns were posted. What I had just heard were the banns for this particular adoption. I asked him if the real parents of the young man or woman did not mind very much, and what happened to them. He said that sometimes they minded very much, but usually they realized that it was in the best interests of their child and were helped with this by the parenting school they attended, which sometimes helped to arrange such adoptions.

"It really works out quite well," Dr. Bo whispered to me quietly. "It often relieves the parents of stress at a time when they need relief and it gives the young person a chance to live with another family. Sometimes they appreciate their own families more, but in any event it gives them a chance to grow in a different environment at an important time in their life.

"If no one objects, what will happen?" I asked.

"There'll be an adoption ceremony in about a month," he said, "which will be attended by the youngster, his parents, the adoptive parents, and by members of the community. It is taken as a very solemn business. But I think we'd better be quiet now," Dr. Bo whispered to me.

The Committment of the Young ceremony was about to begin. Music began from a string orchestra at the back of the stage and young boys and girls filed up on the stage from both sides, dressed in clean white shirts and trousers and skirts. They all looked scrubbed to death with their hair tied back neatly, and on their faces that combination of fright and beaming pleasure that young people often show at such a public ceremony. They lined up at the back of the stage and sat down. I would judge that there were perhaps thirty of them. I could see that they were exchanging embarrassed looks with their families and friends who were all sitting down in the front rows. (I thought how universal this sort of thing was; it could have been a graduating class at an elementary school commencement.)

The ceremony opened with some songs, which I of course did not recognize but which seemed to have a spiritual quality to them, hymns almost. These were sung by everyone present, including Dr. Bo. Nobody needed a text, they all knew the songs from memory. Then the chairman introduced a woman whose name I did not catch but I gather was a leading artist of the town. She gave a typical commencement address, full of talk about the promise of the future and what young people have to look forward to and the importance of their loyalty to Prire and to its values and to Mountgate or whatever community they eventually decided to live in. It was quite inspirational and well done, I thought. She quoted some poetry, which of course was also unfamiliar to me, but by a well-known poet in Prire. Then the local chorus sang a chorale which Dr. Bo whispered to me was always sung at the ceremony of the Committment of the Young and was written by the well-known Prire composer Artimo. Even I had heard of his name. It was a gorgeous chorale and beautifully sung *a cappella*. Even though I could not follow the words, I was much moved by the beauty of the music and the voices. When the chorale ended everyone settled down in an expectant way. The chairman then moved to the front of the stage and read from a piece of paper as follows:

### The Commitment of the Young

I do solemnly commit myself to the way of life of Prire. I commit myself to put the welfare and future of Prire above my own immediate interests. I will work to make Prire a better society in my lifetime and that of future Prire generations. I hope to conduct myself in such a way that I may one day be chosen to serve Prire in whatever way my talents lie. I commit myself to that endeavor.

When he had finished reading this passage the boys and girls stood up and recited the same commitment out loud, and very solemnly. Then, much as in a commencement, each one walked up to the chairman as their name was called, and received a piece of paper which Dr. Bo whispered to me was a copy of the commitment which they had signed, and a badge of some sort. After the last young person had received his certificate and badge the chorus sang the closing song, a joyous-sounding one also by Artimo.

On the last two verses everyone joined in the singing including the children, and the ceremony came to a resounding end. The children filed out looking very excited and pleased, a few inevitably giggling as they walked down the aisle. Then everyone moved outside to a tent where there were ices and cookies and cakes and all kinds of things that the parents, I assume, had brought for the occasion. The spirit of the occasion was something like a combination of a Bar Mitzvah and a graduation ceremony, if I were to make a parallel to our society, but then it still would not contain the special quality of dedication to Prire society that I have tried to capture here.

As we were enjoying the refreshments, I asked Dr. Bo if all children made this commitment or were there some children who did not do it. He said that not all children made the commitment if they were not considered to be ready. The normal time for the Commitment of the Young, he said, was at twelve years but there were some children there today who were thirteen and one was fourteen. He described it as a very important point in a child's development, one toward which the child is pointed from about the age of eight. It respresents not only a commitment, but it marks the moving onto a stage of more responsibility and more freedom than before. I asked what these children would do now after making their commitment. He said that they began to have certain rights that younger children did not have. For example, children who wanted to could now seek out adoptive parents, which they could not do before they had made their commitment. But more important, they were eligible for serious responsibilities in the community, jobs, and the record of their performance was begun at this time. I was incredulous.

"Do you mean to say that in Prire the record of a person starts when they are twelve?" I asked.

"Oh yes," said Dr. Bo. "Yes indeed. We think twelve years is a good time to start people on their responsibilities and we find a lot of talent in young people which can be developed."

"But doesn't that mean that a lot of pranks and horseplay that young people do in their early years will be held against them later?"

"Not at all, we expect a certain amount of that but the amount is probably held down by the very fact that these young people take themselves quite seriously after age twelve. They know that what they do is being recorded for their future and they also are given a lot of responsibility and gain a great deal of respect from the community," Dr. Bo answered. "You'd be surprised to see how many adult jobs our young people can handle."

Dr. Bo then described the kinds of jobs performed by the children of Mountgate—staffing the various public halls, working in the library, supervision of the parks, maintenance of the ecological inventory (all the communities were required to keep this inventory), as well as helping in the maintenance of the roads, in which both boys and girls participated, and of the buildings themselves. Dr. Bo stressed again how much talent and ability was available in young people of this age and that it was a shame not to put it to use and give them both responsibilities and rewards at an early age. I was comparing this to our own children who were locked into junior and senior high schools during this period with such little chance to carry out responsible or mature tasks. I wondered how they handled the education of the young, but realized this would have to wait until I had a chance to visit some schools and see for myself. It seemed to me to be possible to work this out in a place like Mountgate, which was an essentially informal, rather rural community where people knew each other, but I found it hard to believe this could work in a larger or more organized community.

Dr. Bo must have sensed my skepticism because he added that I had to remember that every child in Prire was educated not only for his occupational life but also for his community life. This meant that every child had a specific skill such as carpentry or masonry or painting or road-building or well-digging or windmill-making or motor maintenance. He pointed out that even these twelve-year-olds that I had just seen had among them thirty or more skills and with very little supervision were quite capable of putting up a complete building or running a self-sustaining farm, if need be. They not only had direct instruction in their school, but also spent time as apprentices during their community service days with people skilled in their particular line of interest.

It seemed an interesting idea to me, although how workable I was not sure. I did agree that young people were kept much too dependent and immature in our society for too long a period of time, but I was not at all sure that they could be given the kinds of responsibilities that Dr. Bo talked about. I did recall that I had not seen any young people of this age hanging around corners of the capital city nor any evidence of crime of any kind. People left their possessions around anywhere, seemingly unconcerned about theft.

At this moment Dr. Bo thought we should be moving off as we had quite a distance to go that night in order to reach our destination for the following day. He explained that there was nothing en route that he thought would be of particular interest, so he had planned for us to stay at an inn that evening and get up early the next morning and drive on in the transit. I asked him why we were not taking a train for this part of our journey and he said we certainly could have taken the train but he thought taking the transit would give me more of a chance to see the countryside and talk to people. I thought that was extremely courteous of him because I realized that driving as much as he had at the age of 82 must certainly be fatiguing. He did not show any fatigue but his courtesy was such that I doubt I would have known anyhow. I wondered why he did not have a car and a chauffeur so that he didn't do the driving himself. But in all the days that I was in Prire I never saw an instance of anyone having a chauffeur.

We drove out of Mountgate and down out of the hills onto a plain for perhaps an hour and a half or so, past some marshes which reminded me of the terrain of northern Minnesota. We came over a small hill and down onto a road that led across a very large body of water which mingled with the marshes, being very shallow on our right but on the left developed into a large lake which had a river flowing through it. As we drove on, there seemed to be a series of interlocking lakes. The woods were all pines, hemlocks and spruces with very few houses or villages. I saw an occasional cabin and sometimes a somewhat larger house, but I would judge there was not a cabin per mile along the road we were taking. Dr. Bo explained that this was still another kind of community which we really did not have time to visit. Here people who wanted the most independent way of life and the least amount of interference might choose to live. He said there were several such communities available in Prire. These communities were considered to be minimum service communities, like Mountgate, but had very little in the way of organization or structure which Mountgate did. Here it was more or less a collection of individuals, each of whom wanted to go his own way, which he was permitted to do as long as there was no interference with the resources of the area, or with the rights of others. I wondered how such people existed since I saw no evidence of any work available it did not look like too prosperous a piece of land. Dr. Bo explained that they would fish and raise a little bit of food in their garden and do enough work from time to time to pay for whatever food or clothing they needed. He agreed that this was kind of a marginal life, but it suited certain people very well indeed.

"After all," he said with a sly smile, "not everybody likes cooperation."

I certainly agreed with that and was surprised to find communities such as this available in Prire. I asked him what kinds of people tended to live there, and he said a wide variety. They would be those one could find in any society who liked a marginal life and who valued their independence and freedom from routine more than they did services of any kind. Then there were those who simply liked a low level of contact with other human beings and found that very conducive to whatever they wanted to do. He said I might be surprised to know that some very prominent people had come from communities like these and in fact had returned to them later in their life. One of Prire's leading statesmen had retired to such a community and enjoyed being away from the telephone and visitors and so on. He said the philosophy of these communities was pretty much live-and-let-live and that on the whole it worked quite well.

Dr. Bo told me to keep watching the road as I would be seeing some very pretty views as we approached the inn where we were to stay. Our road followed first the border of one lake and then another, crossing a river each time, and I judged we must have gone over eight bridges at least. Dr. Bo asked me if I had been counting the bridges and I said that I had and had counted eight.

"Well, you are like everyone else, and that is

why it is called the Inn of the Eight Bridges," and he laughed.

At the eighth bridge we came around a corner, densely grown right to the edge of the road with hemlocks and spruce and pine and found a sign on our right, very simply done in wooden letters, reading "Inn of the Eight Bridges." We turned in a narrow, sandy road which wound down through a forest of huge towering trees. It was quite dark in there and it gave me almost an eerie feeling of how terrifying a primitive woods can be. At the end of a mile and a half we came out in a clearing and I looked across a small lake and saw the Inn of the Eight Bridges.

I have never seen a more beautiful setting in my life. The inn was across the water, set in a circle of azalea and rhododendron, and to our left was a waterfall, not very high but spilling over with a rush and tumble of lights in the late afternoon sun. Immediately ahead of us was a pier and a series of boats. Dr. Bo indicated we would park our car here and take a boat over to the inn. I thought this was very curious and wondered why the road had not been built over to the inn.

"That would interfere with the aesthetics," Dr. Bo said rather curtly.

With the help of two boatmen, we moved our gear into a boat and set off across the lake to the inn. The boat was like a very large freight canoe such as we have in our society but the bow and stern were raised higher. If anything, it looked like an Indian war canoe perhaps, except that it was deeper and wider and could carry a lot more baggage than we had brought. As they paddled us across the lake, I wished that I had brought a cam-

era with me but of course, I knew that that was
forbidden. I wished, also, that I had the talent of
an artist to capture it in my head for all time. The
lake was such a clear blue that I could look down
perhaps 12 to 15 feet and see bass, trout, perch
and blue gills. There were a few boats on the lake
fishing. The waterfall was to our left and as we
neared it I could see the river behind it, disappearing into the conifers. At the foot of the falls was a
great splashing and I saw some fisherman over there.
In the center of the lake and to our right was a
small island, apparently uninhabited, although it
had an open structure on it rather like a place for
picnicking which was quite large. Here a few boats
were drawn up and there were people moving about
on the shore.

We approached the inn and I could see that
the azaleas and rhododendrons were even more beautiful than I had glimpsed across the lake. There
must have been literally hundreds of them at the
edge of the woods and going back for a distance behind the inn. The azaleas were in full bloom on this
June evening and they made a stunning effect. The
inn itself was of simple architecture as everything
in Prire seemed to be so far. The first floor was
built of that same pink-like stone that I had seen in
the capital city, but the second floor was made of
wood. The contrast between the pink and the brown
was very pleasing in contrast to the blue lake. There
was a courtyard surrounding the inn much like the
one I had seen at Dr. Bo's house though much larger. Inside the courtyard as we walked in I could
see espaliered fruit trees all along the inside wall.
I glimpsed vegetable gardens in the back, but in
the front there was a cobbled area with tables set

out among the trees. In the center of the courtyard was a raised pool with a fountain which made a most tranquilizing sound. Small fruit trees were planted in tubs inside the courtyard and there were roses, peonies, marigolds, nasturtiums, pansies, petunias, geraniums, pinks and a host of other flowers that were new to me. To the right in the back of the courtyard I glimpsed a sort of greenhouse, and some bedding areas where no doubt these plants had been forced. We crossed the courtyard and entered the inn through a huge wooden door like the doors of a large hacienda in Mexico. Inside it was very cool, with a tile floor set in a symmetrical pattern. We were shown to our rooms on the second floor. I found that mine looked down on a second courtyard in back of the inn and the flower and vegetable gardens beyond. The room was small and modestly furnished, but quite comfortable, and the bed was good. There was a comfortable chair, a writing desk and an ample closet, and a bathroom very much like the one in Dr. Bo's house with a washstand and bowl. I was becoming an old hand at these arrangements and quickly found the drinking water outlet and enjoyed a refreshing glass of water. There was the usual exercise mat and a notice in the bathroom of the availability of a sauna. I unpacked what little I had and lay down on the bed for a few moments. I was so full of impressions that it was hard for me to record in my journal what had happened that day. I was glad I did because it was in this way that I was able to remember the Commitment of the Young that I had just heard a while ago. I decided to go through the exercise I had gone through at Dr. Bo's house on what was only the day before yesterday although I could not believe it—it seemed to me it must have been at least a year ago. The exercise was to note what was missing and what was present that was different from what I had experienced in our own society.

I had just noticed the lack of an ice bucket and the usual glasses on a tray when there was a knock on the door and a woman whom I took to be a member of the staff of the inn asked if there was anything I would like to have.

"No, thank you," I said, "I don't think so. We'll be having dinner shortly."

"Would you care to have a glass of the local wine? We think it's very good and our guests enjoy it."

"I would love some," I said, and went out on the balcony which adjoined Dr. Bo's room and asked him if he would join me in a glass of the local wine. He said he would be very pleased to, as he recalled it's being quite good.

Soon our wine arrived and we sat on the balcony looking down at the gardens and the other wing of the inn which was quite extensive. Beyond, we could see the lake, which was even more extensive than I had imagined. I asked Dr. Bo about the climate and what it was like here in the winter because it looked fairly cold to me judging from trees we had passed. He said it did get cold, although not bitterly so, but it was a favorite spot for ice fishing in the winter and that the inn was open year round. I asked how in the world people got to the inn during the winter over that ice, and he replied that it was quite an experience coming to the inn in the winter and taking a sled across the ice. I asked if they had ever lost anybody through the ice and he said no, they had not, as they are very careful. These arrangements sounded very impractical to me but I did admit that they had their aesthetic side.

We finished our wine and went down to dinner. It was such a lovely night we decided to eat out in the courtyard and were fortunate in getting a table near the fountain. It was one of the most peaceful scenes I have ever encountered, and for a moment the thought crossed my mind of how wonderful it might be to spend the rest of my life sitting at this table, by this fountain, near this pool. I was interrupted by Dr. Bo who explained that the inn was famous for its fish and in fact did not serve meat and he hoped I liked fish. I said I did very much and would take whatever he would recommend. He suggested a local fish whose name I did not recognize but which I found delicious. We were served a vegetable casserole again that I could not identify but which was a nice contrast to the fish for it was quite spicy. We had a salad fresh from the garden, and bowls of fruit for dessert served with very light cookies that were made with some kind of nut I think. They were unusually good. Dr. Bo must have realized I was enjoying the local wine, because he asked that another bottle be sent, of which I must say I drank more than he did.

Perhaps it was the wine or my fatigue, or perhaps it was all the new things I was seeing and doing, but I started talking to Dr. Bo in what may have been an over-enthusiastic manner about all that I had seen in Prire. I waxed eloquent in praise, as I recall, which must have seemed to him in some contrast with some of my earlier remarks. However, it was a beautiful night and I was all keyed up from my visit so that my exuberance, I think, was overlooked by him. We both decided to go to bed early as I knew he must be tired and certainly I was.

Before I went to bed I sat out on the balcony for perhaps half an hour listening to the sounds of the inn and smelling the odors that came up from the gardens. I wanted to soak up every sound and sensation into my mind so that I might remember it forever. I was afraid I would forget how beautiful it was. I thought to myself how nice it would be if only I could bring the family here. How Susan would enjoy the flowers and how Marjorie would love the fishing along with Jack. At that I became very homesick, thinking of my family and how far away they were and wishing they could share this with me. I decided that I had had a bit too much wine and I had better go to sleep which I did without writing any more in my journal.

# 4

# Wednesday, June 20th

The next morning Dr. Bo and I had a very early breakfast, this time at the edge of the courtyard facing the lake. It was a cool morning, perhaps 65°, and there was a slight westerly wind over the surface of the lake. Boats were out again which I had seen when I had awakened around six o'clock. We both chose to have a local fish for our breakfast which tasted very much like perch to me. This was served with homemade bread and fruit and milk. Right after breakfast we gathered our things together, and got into one of the canoe-like boats. We were paddled back to the other side of the lake where our transit was parked. I shall never forget the trip in the canoe back across the lake.

It was one of the most beautiful sights I have ever seen. It was a lovely June morning, with the sun sparkling on the waves made by our canoe. We passed some of the fishing boats I had seen earlier and found they were built very much like ours. The fishermen we passed were all making a good catch and several held up their strings of fish to show us as we went by. I turned to look back at the Inn of the Eight Bridges just before we reached the southern shore and tried to imprint it in my mind so that I might never forget it. Writing this, many days later, the image is still vivid in my mind.

As we got into the transit, Dr. Bo said we would be driving through a few villages on the way to the railroad which we would reach around noon. He had thought this drive would give me an opportunity to see the variety of communities available in Prire and he was pleased that I had enjoyed the inn as much as I had.

I had several questions about what I had seen yesterday at Mountgate. I pursued the question with him about the control over parenthood that I had found rather curious. I asked Dr. Bo if it did not happen that children who were born to approved parents were occasionally ill or deformed or retarded at birth. Dr. Bo agreed that this happened occasionally, that children were born who were physiologically inadequate and who would become mentally retarded or disabled. I asked him what was done about this. He explained that all children born in Prire were given an assessment as to their physiological health immediately at birth. If an infant's physiological state was fragile at the time of birth no measures were taken to increase its chances of survival. I was shocked to hear this, in comparison with our own practices.

"But isn't this some form of infanticide?" I exclaimed. Dr. Bo seemed put off by my question.

"This policy was given a great deal of thought before it was put into effect," Dr. Bo said. "We assume from the beginning that any decision has a price to be paid for it. We were well aware that if we made a decision to let certain infants die who were not physiologically sound, that we stood the chance of missing someone who could contribute a great deal to our society. So before we set up a policy we did some research on this. Of course, this was many, many years ago and I can only tell you the results from my own memory. Children were followed who had been unsound at birth. The original committee studied very carefully the costs of caring for them and of educating them. This was then contrasted with the outcome, to see how often a highly contributing member of society came from this group. I don't recall the exact figures, but it was something like one in two or three hundred from this group who made an outstanding contribution. The costs of education and care were compared to the contribution of that occasional member and as I recall it the ratio ran something like 5,000 or 10,000 to one in terms of the costs involved versus the contributions received from the occasional member."

"Do you mean to say that you figured out the life worth of an individual in so many dollars and cents?" I questioned.

"No, not exactly that way, and not in dollars and cents. We computed the cost of the time of people involved in caring for and educating these youngsters against the contributions to Prire society made by the occasional exceptional child from this group. Our research was based on time spent, on the theory that time could be spent in other ways which might benefit Prire more. The figure I quoted to you of the 5,000 to one or 10,000 to one is based on the usefulness of that time to the society as a whole."

"But that one person might be a Mozart or a Picasso or a Darwin," I protested.

"No, that did not really happen in our own research. But even so, there is a price to be paid for any decision. After we had looked at both sides of the question, we felt that we could not afford the social price of committing so much important time of our people in Prire to the education and care of a group of children who on the whole were not going to make an adequate contribution to the future of Prire. This is one of the functions of the Overseers of the Future—to look at the long-run benefits and deficits to Prire society for such a decision."

"It seems awfully callous to me," I said. "I don't see how physicians and nurses can stand by and see a child die."

"It's a matter of priorities," replied Dr. Bo. "In Prire we have had to set our priorities because we have only so many resources and we have to use them well. We looked at the long-term consequences of trying to save every infant, regardless of its capacity to survive, and found that we could not afford that kind of decision if we wanted Prire to be the sort of society we were trying to build. At least, that was the thinking of the people on the original committee, and as I said, that was many years ago. I think it was a wise decision. It certainly has proved to be a wise one in terms of our resources, for we do not have to commit the time, which is precious to us, to such care and education."

"But don't the parents object? Aren't they upset if a child is born to them in some way impaired and the child just dies?"

"I don't think you will find that today in Prire," Dr. Bo said. "The policy has been in effect so long that parents know, before they have a child, that the child must survive on its own, without special technical assistance, if it is to be a citizen in Prire."

"I don't know," I said, shaking my head. "It seems like an awfully cold kind of decision to make, and it must break the hearts of some parents."

"Not necessarily, because there can be other opportunities to have children, if that is so important," replied Dr. Bo.

My mind dwelled on this because it bothered me as a policy. It seemed heartless and I could not reconcile it with my own values. I was thinking about this, looking out at the countryside as we drove along. Across some fields behind a fence I saw a series of buildings that looked like some sort of a special institution. I could not see anyone moving about.

"What is that, Dr. Bo? Is that a prison or a school for the retarded or a mental hospital or what?" I pointed over to the right where I could see these clusters of buildings.

"That is a prison community," Dr. Bo answered me. "We may visit one of these in the next few days and you can go inside. We don't have schools for the retarded and we don't deal with our mentally ill in terms of hospitals."

"You don't have any schools for the retarded?" I asked.

"No, we do not, because of the policy I described earlier, which you thought rather cruel."

That gave me a moment's pause. I wondered if Dr. Bo was misleading me and they just did not call people retarded who were.

"What about your mental hospitals which you say you don't have? Surely you haven't wiped out all mental illness in Prire, have you?"

"No, we have not, although we take a somewhat different view than I understand you do. We don't put mentally ill people in hospitals. We have them in different kinds of communities if it is a chronic problem, but our first attempt is to get at the physiological basis of such an illness. We will try to work in a visit to one of these if we can find the time and if you are interested."

"I certainly am if we can manage it in the plan that you have made," I said gratefully. "Getting back to this parenthood thing—I know it must seem to you that I am full of questions, but this is so very different from some of our experiences that I really would like to ask you some more questions, if you don't mind."

"Go right ahead," said Dr. Bo, "We welcome your questions."

"What about divorces? Do you have any divorces in Prire?"

Oh, indeed we do. Not all marriages are perfect, as you probably would agree," he said smilingly. "Divorces are not necessary among our young people who are not married to each other. But when the marriage does take place, as you probably realize, it is a very serious matter in Prire. Not all such marriages are successful and parents may divorce each other and do so without prejudice."

"What about the children? What happens to them?"

"About the same things that happen to children anywhere, I suppose," replied Dr. Bo. "Sometimes the children will go with one parent or with the other. The only difference in Prire is they may elect to go with their adoptive parents if they have them and if they are old enough."

"You mean they would go with their adoptive parents rather than with either of their blood parents?" I asked.

"Oh yes, it happens rather frequently and it seems to work out quite well on the whole."

That gave me a lot to think about. I decided that I would have to put all of this conversation in the journal tonight. I thought I better spend more time looking at the countryside and save my questions until later.

We were now in a scarcely populated area, similar to the Eight Bridges section, driving along a two-lane dirt road. On our left was a river and an occasional house or cabin. The houses were getting to be more frequent and I asked Dr. Bo what village we were coming to. He said we were nearing Stone River Village, obviously named for the boulders in the river on our left.

"This is a small village, more on the cooperative side than you saw in Mountgate. It is essentially a farming village. It is not remarkable in any particular way but it was on our route to the railroad so I thought you might as well see it."

He slowed down the transit as we came into the village, which was laid out like the others, a central square with the town hall and other public buildings around the square. This was not as attractive

a village as either Blue Lake or Mountgate, although
the river which passed on the south side of the village was a pretty sight. There was a group of people gathered around the town hall and I noticed
that the Prire flag was at half mast over the entrance. I asked Dr. Bo if this was a national holiday
of some kind and he said no, that it was probably
a Passing Ceremony. I asked him what he meant by
a Passing Ceremony.

"That would be very, very hard to explain,"
Dr. Bo said with a deep sigh. "Perhaps the best
thing is for us to visit one if I can get permission."

He left the transit and walked over to the group
and talked to what I assume was one of the overseers because he came back very soon thereafter
and said he had received permission. He got in the
transit, shut the door and turned to me, speaking
very solemnly:

"You are going to see a very unusual ceremony.
I don't think any visitor has seen a Passing Ceremony. But I have asked permission for us to attend
because I think that you have so many questions
about what we do that can only be answered by
seeing how people experience them. I am sure you
would never take my word for it."

I was a little shaken by his words because I
did not know how he intended them. I felt as though
I was being put in my place for so many critical
questions. I felt badly about this because I did not
want to appear so critical of Prire.

"I hope you don't think I've been too critical,
Dr. Bo. It's just that so many of the things you tell
me are unusual to me and so contrary to my own
experience that I feel I have to ask some questions."

"No, that is perfectly all right, and we do not

112

object to questions," Dr. Bo said. "I feel, however, that any attempt to persuade you that our practices work would be hopeless. It is much better for you to experience these things yourself."

"I appreciate that, Dr. Bo, very much indeed, and I hope I can ask questions less critically."

"We do not want you to lose your sense of criticism," Dr. Bo said. "It is very valuable for us and for you."

"What is a Passing Ceremony?" I asked. "I would like to be prepared to understand what I am going to see."

"I think you had better see it and not let me try to explain it to you," Dr. Bo answered me. "We will be observers so we must be very quiet and not talk during the ceremony. I will answer any of your questions when we are back in the transit. Is that agreeable?"

"Yes, perfectly," I said, and followed him out of the transit.

The crowd in front of the town hall had gone inside except for the gentleman Dr. Bo had spoken to. He shook my hand and told me Dr. Bo and I would be welcome provided we sat at the back. He said that the members of the family had been asked if we could be present and had agreed.

We entered the hall, which was like the one I had seen at Mountgate, only smaller. It was a very simple room with a small stage in front and rows of benches across the hall. The group that we had seen was seated in the first few rows. Up on the little stage an elderly man and woman were seated side by side. The local overseer was on the stage at the right, leafing through a large book on the lectern. There were wild flowers on the stage as well as some yellow and red roses in small vases with ferns as a background. To our left was a musical instrument something like a piano. At a signal, a woman played what I thought was a rather solemn song. As it ended, the local overseer began to read from the book in front of him. What he read went something like this:

"The family and friends of Mr. and Mrs. Sadas of Stone River Village have gathered today to celebrate with them their Passing Ceremony. Having come to the decision that they wish to pass together at this time, in view of frail health and other considerations, Mr. and Mrs. Sadas have fulfilled the necessary time of the banns and have notified all of their children of their decision. This decision is in accordance with Prire policy on the Passing Ceremony and has been approved by the Stone River Self-Improvement Guardianship Committee, by the trustees of Human Resources, and by the Overseers of the Future, whom I represent here today." When he stopped, one woman down in the front row sobbed. Mr. Sadas, up on the stage, looked down and exclaimed, "Now Gladys, stop that! We've been all through this before. I'm not going to have you crying and carrying on on our Passing Day. Mother, tell her to stop!"

He turned to Mrs. Sadas who spoke sharply.

"Now Gladys, your father is right. This is no time for tears. We didn't ask you to come here for Passing Day to have you start to bellow like a stuck pig. Hush her up, son." The woman's sobs subsided.

The local overseer returned to reading more of the ceremony, which I cannot recall because I was busy watching Mr. and Mrs. Sadas. Mr. Sadas was a frail looking but very attractive older man, I would guess in his late sixties or early seventies. He seemed quite small in that chair up on the platform, but his eyes were alert. He had snow-white hair and a small white goatee, the skin on his face almost like parchment, with that translucent quality that one sometimes sees in older people who are not very well. Mrs. Sadas seemed a good deal younger than her husband, perhaps in her late fifties or early sixties. She had lovely white skin with a cap of snow-white hair which made her appear, in contrast, even younger. She was a bit plump and kept fidgeting with her dress, which was a long one. It was a color print of some flowers but it did not seem to fit her very well. Mr. Sadas was dressed in a business suit and I could see from the way it fit him that he had lost weight recently. Their chairs were placed side by side. They were holding hands as the overseer read on through the ceremony.

At this point I realized with a shock that what I was watching was a voluntary death. Apparently Mr. and Mrs. Sadas had reached a point at which they had decided to terminate their lives and had gone through whatever the Prire requirements were to do so, and now, today, was the actual day. Their family appeared to be gathered in the first few pews, as well as their friends. Among their friends I saw a number of people who were older than either Mr. or Mrs. Sadas.

At the end of the ceremony there was another song from the piano, this time a more lively one, and the group joined in singing the verses. Then each of the people on the benches filed up on the stage and walked across to Mr. and Mrs. Sadas to say good-bye to them. The tenor of this is hard to communicate but it was more like a good-bye at the end of a pleasant evening than a farewell in the face of death. I noticed that there were a few small children in the group, presumably the grandchildren, and one by one they came up and kissed their grandparents good-bye. After all had finished their good-byes, Mr. and Mrs. Sadas got up and moved toward a room off the left of the stage. I saw then how feeble he was and how she had to help him. A man and woman came out from that room to help them inside. The woman who had done the crying followed them in with her husband and five other people about her age. I assume they were the Sadas' own children and their husbands and wives. The door closed.

The overseer began to read again from the ceremony while everyone was seated and quiet in the hall. After what seemed like ages to me but was no more than ten minutes, the woman who had been sobbing and her husband and the other five adults came out of the room on the left. She was dabbing her eyes but the others were not. They returned to their seats and there was another song sung by all and the Overseer read some closing words from the book. Then the group filed out of the hall, talking quietly the way people do when they have seen something sad but satisfying. I overheard people discussing Mr. and Mrs. Sadas' life and what a happy marriage this had been and how fortunate they were in having the Passing Ceremony together.

As we walked out the door of the hall an older woman caught Dr. Bo by the sleeve and said, "Dr. Bo, isn't that you?"

"Mrs. Norg, how nice to see you. I didn't expect to see you here."

"I came over for the Sadas Passing Ceremony. Wasn't it beautiful?"

"Yes, very. He looked rather ill, and I'm glad they could arrange it together."

"Yes, it was one of their hopes always that they would have the Passing Ceremony together. Wasn't it nice that all of the children could be there?"

"Yes, it was. It was nice to see you, Mrs. Norg, but I must be off now with our visitor."

Mrs. Norg turned toward me and watching me closely, asked: "How did you like our Passing Ceremony?"

"I thought it was very unusual," I managed to say. "It did seem to be very pleasing to everyone."

I followed Dr. Bo back to the transit, with such mixed feelings that I did not know what I wanted to ask him first. We got into the transit and I said nothing. I thought about what I had just seen. I had to agree that the people involved seemed to be very accepting of this, particularly the participants, but it was beyond my understanding how people could go through such a ceremony. I decided not to approach this as critically as I had other things because I did not want to offend Dr. Bo.

"Well," Dr. Bo asked, "what did you think? Did you find us barbaric?"

"No, not barbaric," I replied. "It's such a new experience for me I don't know what I think."

"That's a very fair reply," said Dr. Bo. "I thought you would find it an unusual experience, but for us, it's not that strange. We go to Passing Ceremonies quite often."

"How do people feel about such things?" I

asked. "Isn't it awful to think of people selecting to die?"

"I think you'll have to answer those questions yourself," Dr. Bo replied. "You were there and you saw the people, you saw Mr. and Mrs. Sadas and their family."

Dr. Bo would not answer any more questions about the Passing Ceremony. He simply repeated that I was there and I had seen what the people felt. I suppose one could argue that it was better for them to be able to die together at a time they chose, than to have one left without the other or face a long and difficult illness. But the idea seemed so strange to me. I could not get over it. We drove along the Stone River in silence. I kept turning over in my mind what I had seen, trying to evaluate it.

It was perhaps a half hour before I realized we were approaching another town. Lost in my thoughts, I had not really seen the countryside at all. Dr. Bo broke the silence by saying we were approaching Luko Village, which was named in honor of Madame Luko, the historical personage that he had spoken so warmly about. He told me he had often come here with Madame Luko and had many fond memories of the village. He did not think we would have time to stop but he thought I would be interested in driving through it.

Luko Village was set in a broad valley where the Stone River met the West River, before it flowed into Lake Luko some miles below the village. Of all the communities I had seen so far, Luko Village had the best location from an agricultural point of view. The valley was lush, the fields green and stubby after their first cutting. There were several dairy farms in the distance and I thought I saw some pigs, which Dr. Bo confirmed later. Around the valley on the slopes were orchards. On the left I saw vineyards. Luko Village appeared to be an older town than some we had seen because the trees were quite old. Driving into town I noticed the old maples and chestnuts and guessed, correctly as it turned out, that Luko Village had been here over 300 years. Dr. Bo drove slowly through the streets so as to give me every opportunity to see as much as I could. Luko Village looked prosperous, a thriving agricultural town. It was certainly more prosperous than Mountgate and quite different in terrain from Blue Lake. The corn was already knee-high in the fields outside town, and all of the vegetable gardens we passed were full of growth.

We passed several groups of people clustered at the edge of the road and I inquired about what they were doing. Dr. Bo explained that they were getting their mail. I thought my question had been rather stupid because I realized when I looked at the next group that, of course, that was exactly what they were doing. They were like people I had seen everywhere at home coming to get their mail at the groups of mailboxes clustered at the side of the road. I did notice something unusual, however, in that all of them seemed to have the same color packet in their hand, a striped red and white envelope which everyone seemed to be getting. I asked Dr. Bo what the envelopes were.

"You are an observant person, I'll have to give you that," he chuckled. "This happens to be National Health Census Week and those are Health Census forms that go to every person in Prire today."

"What is your National Health Census?"

"It is a census of the health status of everyone in Prire. We collect this information once a year to get some picture of how the health of all of our citizens is faring and to pick up trends that might be useful. It also tells us about the degree to which our Health Improvement Guardianship is working in each of our regions and communities."

"What happens with those packages? Does each person just fill them out and return them? Don't you find people who don't return them?"

"I'm quite sure many people would not bother to fill them out and return them if we didn't make it worth their while," Dr. Bo answered with a smile. "You shouldn't be surprised that we make their return rewarding."

"What do you do?" I asked.

"Each person who returns the form completed correctly and on time receives a certificate in the mail for 20 Ploms."

"I calculated, not too quickly, that 20 Ploms would be about $5.00 in our currency.

"What do they do with this certificate? Do they turn it in with their tax and get a rebate?"

"They simply take it off their tax when they send the receipt in," Dr. Bo answered.

"How successful is your National Health Census with this method?" I asked.

"It is very successful. We get about 98 percent returns this way and of course it is possible for us to follow up the other 2 percent because each community does its own census and, therefore, knows who has returned it and who has not."

"What sorts of questions do you have on your Health Census?" I asked.

"Just about everything our Health Improvement

Guardianship Committee can think of," Dr. Bo answered.

"We pick up all kinds of information about levels of human energy, of well-being, mood, rest, exercise, a very long section on diet and dietary habits, and of course we have a long section on the care received from the local Health Improvement Guardianship. It is also a way of seeing how well they are serviced. Each person has a chance to comment on the good or bad aspects of the care they have received."

"What do you do with all these data?"

"They are looked at first at the local level because it is very important to our local community committee to have this kind of information. They keep one complete record of it. The other copy goes to the capital, to the National Health Improvement Guardianship Institute where the data are carefully analyzed. One thing that we do with these data that will interest you is that each Health Improvement Guardianship in each of the communities receives a rating based upon the returns of the people in that community. It is a weighted index from zero to ten, but it gives some estimate of how well the people of the community perceive their local Health Improvement Guardianship is performing."

"What do you do with these evaluations? Do you simply report them or what?" I asked.

"We report them, of course, to the local communities and to their local Health Improvement Guardianship Committees. But more than that, the Index for a local Health Improvement Guardianship Committee for this year will influence very much the amount of compensation the staff receives for the coming year."

"How does that work? That sounds very hard to manage, it seems to me."

"Well, let's take an example. Let us suppose that the Health Improvement Guardianship Committee here at Luko Village received a rating of 9 which is, of course, a very good rating. Let us suppose that at Stone River Village the local Health Improvement Guardianship got a rating of 2. Those ratings of 9 and 2 are figured into the basis for payment so that the total number of Ploms received by each member of that staff would vary by the rate of that Index."

"Do you think that has any effect on service?" I asked.

"I don't think my opinion would be worth much. I would rather let you see the figures on the indices for the past years. We find that when there has been a low rating, the rating tends to pick up the following year, meaning that people report that service has improved. It is one way of making a service responsive to the people it is supposed to serve. I do not think it's the perfect solution by any means, but I think it is better than not having such an evaluation. I always feel that service picks up in May when the Health Improvement Guardianship Committees know that the evaluations are coming out in June, but then of course, as you would say, that's only human," and Dr. Bo laughed with me over his joke.

"Does anything happen other than just a change in pay if a local committee gets a rating of a 2 or a 1?"

"Oh, yes indeed. I did not mean to leave the impression that it was just a matter of payment. No,

122

any low ratings like that are investigated by the local overseers first. Then they will request a visit from one of the regional or national groups to see where the problem is. Sometimes it is an administrator who is at fault or it may be one particular person on the team or one team that is penalizing everyone else. We try to get a team in for a site visit within a month after the evaluations. But that is not the most useful thing that we do with the evaluations."

"What do you mean, 'the most useful'?" I asked.

"I would rather you asked me about the high evaluations because I think that works better."

"What do you mean, 'works better'?"

"The local Health Improvement Guardianship Committees that get the highest ratings, the nines and the tens, are all publicized in our papers, both locally and nationally, and are open for visits. We arrange for local units with low ratings to visit those with the highest ratings to see how they work. It is considered quite an honor for the local Health Improvement Guardianship Committee to get a high rating and, of course, it increases the desirability of that community. You have to remember that there are always people who are looking to change communities in which to live and this kind of evaluation is one of the things that would attract new people to a community. There are evaluations of other aspects of a community as well. As you probably realize when we were in Blue Lake Village, this is one of the communities that has probably the highest rating—a 10 I think."

I thought these evaluations sounded rather sensible, something that we could use in our own society. They also seemed more workable than some other ideas I had heard expressed in Prire. But I was not clear on how people moved from one community to another.

"Can anybody move anywhere or is movement restricted, or how do you handle that?"

"I thought that we had discussed this yesterday or the day before, didn't we?" Dr. Bo replied. "The size of our communities varies from very small, such as the area we went through yesterday on the way to the Inn of the Eight Bridges, to the units in the capital city. The units don't go much above 3,000 although I think there are some that are a little bit larger."

"Why did you pick a figure like 3,000?" I asked.

"The rule of thumb that we use for the maximum size of any community is that it can be only as large as the Rule of Personal Identification permits. Do you know about that rule? Have you read about it?"

"I read a reference to it, but I didn't understand what it was," I answered.

"The Rule of Personal Identification is really quite simple. It says that no community shall be larger than that size which permits each individual in that town to be known by his name."

"But everyone is known by name, aren't they?" I asked.

"Everyone is known by name, but not everybody knows *you* by *your* name. In your society, for example, I understand that people have numbers and special signs in ink, and identification material and so on. Is that not true?"

"Yes, that is true. People in our society carry a number of different kinds of identification and also use numbers for a number of things."

"The Rule of Personal Identification would say that your society has units that are too large then, according to the views we have here in Prire. We believe that a person should live in a community where he is recognized by his or her name, in all of the contacts within that community. We are very strongly opposed to anonymity in any form."

"How does that rule work? Is it not quite a burden to have to memorize the names of 3,000 people?"

"No, it is not a burden if you've grown up with them and known their families and know who is related to whom and so on. It is fairly simple to learn the people in a community of that size over time. You have to remember that in our communities people come into contact with each other not only often, but in a variety of situations and roles. There is a lot of contact so that remembering a name becomes relatively easy."

"Why is this Rule so important?"

"We think the matter of Personal Identification is a crucial one for the quality of life in our society. It is very meaningful to us in Prire that none of us carries cards for anything. When we go to our libraries, we simply sign our name and do not have to present a card. When we order something the same thing is true. In our banking we simply use names to identify our accounts because of course we are known in the community where our banks serve us."

Suppose I'm dealing with someone from another community?"

"Any time you want to know something about a person, all you have to know is his name and village. For example, suppose I wanted to buy something from Mr. Boytan whom you met the other day in

Blue Lake, Let's say I lived in Capital City, which I do; it would then be very simple for me as a citizen in Prire to find out about Mr. Boytan and whether he is a person who could be counted on to represent what he had to sell honestly and whether he would be fair to deal with."

"Whom would you call to find that out?"

"In this particular example I would call the local Blue Lake Committee on Resources and Returns and indicate my query. As long as it did not invade Mr. Boytan's privacy I would be told about his economic behavior. You have to remember now we only use public behavior."

"But I would think that could be very unreliable depending upon who you had on these committees."

"You keep forgetting that we keep records on each of us from the age of twelve. As a matter of fact, there is nothing more reliable than a record of a person's behavior. We think that people who are reliable in the important behaviors should get rewards for this. If Mr. Boytan has been a responsible person, who has always paid his obligations on time, and is as dependable as the day is long, he should be rewarded in kind. What it means is that anyone from another community wishing to make a transaction with him would know right away that he was a man to be trusted on the basis of the local community's report."

"Well, I can see that would be convenient for Mr. Boytan, but what about the people who are not so reliable?"

"They do not have that trust extended to them. Again, you see, it is our philosophy here in Prire that people who behave responsibly and with consideration for others get rewarded for it. In some societies

126

the responsible people are penalized by the irresponsible people. We have never felt that was fair."

"I agree. It has always been one of my pet peeves that the responsible citizens in my country have to go through all kinds of inconveniences because a minority is irresponsible."

"Precisely. That is why we pay so much attention to the Rule of Personal Identification. We think it encourages responsibility and dependability, both of which are important to us. When people can behave anonymously they also behave irresponsibly. But if you know that your public behavior will be recorded from the time you're twelve on, and that how you behave will determine what privileges are available to you—you're inclined to make your record as good as you can. In other words, we try to see to it that responsible behavior pays off."

"Do you feel it really works?" I asked.

"Yes, we feel it works. We also think that the quality of interpersonal relations is greatly enhanced in a smaller community where people are known to each other. We have had visitors here tell us that in their societies there is much rudeness in the services of their own communities."

"I could tell you quite a few stories myself," I said. "It happens a lot."

"In our view, you see, this sets up a chain of ugly events between two people. The anonymous person is treated in an uncaring way by the stranger, in a community service, let us say, and then there comes retaliation somewhere along the line, perhaps with another contact during the day. We think this builds and builds into a very unpleasant set of events which destroys the nature of the human relationship."

"You seem to have made quite a study of this," I said.

Dr. Bo smiled. "Yes, this is one of the things I have specialized in. One of my special responsibilities as an overseer is the quality of life among people and it has been my hobby, you might say, to find ways to improve the contacts among people throughout the day."

"Do you really think it makes that much difference?" I asked.

"Yes, we do. As a matter of fact we have quite a bit of data on that. I am sure you have had experiences like those I have just described. In your society, don't you have places you have to go to get something from one of your community services?"

"Oh yes, unfortunately quite often. We have to go to our post offices, our automobile bureaus, to our town clerks, and to state agencies, and to federal agencies, and to our policemen, and to all kinds of what you call community agencies."

"Haven't you found that where the communities are small, the people are much more pleasant to deal with?" Dr. Bo asked curiously.

I thought about that for a moment. Scenes went flashing through my mind of hours spent waiting in line at the motor vehicle bureau, only to be told by a surly clerk to go to the next line, which was a block long, because I did not have a particular piece of paper. Or post office employees who were too busy talking to each other to come to the window. Or supermarket clerks who were more interested in discussing last night's adventures than they were in helping me to finish my purchases.

128

"Yes," I said with some emphasis. "Yes, such things happen to us, and too often."

"Are they not better in your smaller villages?" Dr. Bo asked.

"Probably so," I said, "Although you can get surly people anywhere, I suppose."

"Yes, you can, but with our continuous evaluation, we make sure that surly people either don't stay surly or they don't stay in those jobs." Dr. Bo said with some vigor.

By this time we were approaching West River Village where we would leave our transit and pick up the railroad for our next leg. Dr. Bo looked at his watch and said we didn't have very much time to catch our train. We would have to have our lunch in the station.

We drove into West River Village and found the station near the river. Dr. Bo parked the transit in a lot just behind the station, and we took our baggage into the station. I noticed he left the keys with the station master. We went into the restaurant, and having had many bad experiences in railroad stations, I was again surprised to find that it was extremely clean and attractive. We had fruit and a fish salad for lunch which I found excellent. I asked Dr. Bo about the transit and the keys. He explained that the transits were available for these kinds of responsibilities and that the particular transit we used could be picked up by the next person, who would get the keys from the station master. I asked him if transits were not stolen. Dr. Bo said that it rarely happened. I was curious about this and wanted to pursue it but Dr. Bo said we didn't have much time now but that I would get a chance later to ask a lot of questions about the legal system and how they handled such behaviors.

In a few minutes the train came in quietly and we boarded the first passenger car. This train was like the one we had taken from Capital City to Blue Lake Village and went very fast. Our trip would take about four hours, Dr. Bo said, and I settled down quickly for the Prire nap habit which I had become addicted to without a bit of trouble. As I went off to sleep I thought again about the Passing Ceremony and the quality of the relationship between Mr. and Mrs. Sadas. I wondered if this was one of the things that Dr. Bo meant about the quality of events. The Passing Ceremony gave them dignity, I thought, but who would believe me if I told them?

When I woke up I realized that I had had a longer nap than usual. Dr. Bo was watching the countryside from his seat across me next to the window. I apologized for taking such a long nap, but he said he thought it was good for me as I must be tired with all the new events. I asked him where we were and he said we were about 200 miles northwest of Luko Village and 400 miles from our destination which was Ponya City. This was one of the places I was most eager to visit for I had read about their schools and wanted to see them in operation.

We had left the river and were passing now through gently rolling countryside with open fields alternating with wooded areas in typical Prire pattern. The train made a stop at what looked to be a small town whose name was Long Valley. On the station platform I noticed a group of about ten boys I judged to be between twelve and fifteen who were talking excitedly to a young man about twenty-one. I pointed them out to Dr. Bo and asked him what a group like this would be doing at a railroad station in the afternoon. I added that this was the first group of young people I had seen who were apparently free to do as they pleased.

"They're not in school if that's what you mean," Dr. Bo explained, "but they're not free to do as they please. My guess is that this is a group of boys and their leader from one of our Educational Homes and they're waiting for another leader whom they are meeting at the station."

Dr. Bo proved to be quite right. In just a moment another young man of about twenty-one appeared from the back of our train carrying a knapsack and a large shopping bag. The young boys caught sight of him and ran forward to greet him and help him with his packages. As the train pulled out I could see all of them leaving the platform talking in a very excited way.

"What is an Educational Home?" I asked. "That is something I had not heard about."

"It is a home for young people who have shown some delinquent behavior," Dr. Bo said.

"How does such a home work?" I asked. "I didn't think you would have any delinquents in Prire."

"Yes, we have some delinquent young people, as does every society, although our rate is very low by comparison," Dr. Bo replied. "We have tried many different approaches over the years, but the one that seems to work best is the Educational Home. We found that putting a large number of delinquent boys together was about the worst thing to do because, of course, the only models available to them are the more successful delinquents. But it is foolish to put large numbers of young people together in any case, whether they're delinquent or not."

"But isn't it very expensive to keep young people in small groups? Surely there's a lot to be saved by housing them in a bigger institution."

"It depends on what you mean by savings," Dr. Bo answered. "You may save something on housing costs, or food costs, although I don't think that is necessarily true, but you certainly lose a lot in terms of effectiveness, and that is what we are after in our reeducation of such young people."

"Who goes to an Educational Home anyhow?" I asked.

"Any young person, although it tends to be boys rather than girls, who commit an act against the community which the community feels is severe enough, or has happened often enough, to warrant reeducation. Since we keep records on all public behavior from the age of twelve on up it is easy to tell when a young fellow is getting into trouble. He may be assigned to an Educational Home by the local community judge, but not until a number of people are heard."

"What do you mean by 'a number of people would be heard'?" I asked.

"We feel that it is a very serious decision and we want to make a good decision about a young person's future. So, not only would the people involved in the act against the community be heard, but also appearing would be all those who had worked with the young fellow in his community service job. The judge would hear from his boss and from his colleagues as well as from his neighbors and so on,

132

so that a pretty clear picture emerges of what kind of young man we are dealing with."

"How in the world do you get all of those people to go to court?" I asked. "That's a very real problem in terms of losing time for the people in our society."

"They don't go to court," Dr. Bo said. "I don't think I explained it properly to you. Although a judge hears from all of these people, the judges goes out to speak with them himself."

"You mean the judge would go to where the boy had worked, for example, and talk to his boss on his community service job and he would go to the school and to his neighborhood?"

"Yes," Dr. Bo replied, "he would do that. We think it is very important for the judge to speak with people directly in making such a decision. The same judge might not make all the visits. We would have three people involved if it were a serious matter, that is to say there would be three judges involved but each of them would have to do some of the talking to the people who know the youngster."

"Isn't this a very time-consuming procedure? I would think that it would take forever and you would never catch up with your work."

"No," Dr. Bo said, "it doesn't take all that long. As soon as an act of crime is committed that is serious enough to warrant such a hearing, the hearing is held within two days of the crime. Citizens of Prire are motivated to want to give information because for them this is someone in the community who will be returning to it. Everyone is motivated to make sure that that person returns with behavior that has been changed. A young man, let's call him John, will be sent away, but the community is not going to get rid of him. John is going to come back and the community is going to have to deal with him somehow."

"How do you decide on which Educational Home to send him to?"

"It depends on a number of things, but the major factor is how much change in behavior the judges feel is indicated. We keep records on all sorts of behaviors so that we have some idea of their likelihood of recurring. When we deal with a boy fourteen, who has, let us say, stolen three times articles of a certain value, and we know lots else about him and his background and his public behavior, we can make a fairly accurate prediction about the likelihood of that event recurring from our records. It is the likelihood of recurrence that determines more than anything else which Educational Home John would go to."

"Do you mean that a decision is made on the probability of recurrence rather than the seriousness of the deed?" I queried.

"Yes, that is correct," Dr. Bo answered, "as is true in the adult criminal code, as well. We take into the account not just the deed itself and how severe it was, but the probability that that behavior will recur. After all, the whole point of a legal system is to decrease the frequency of the criminal event, isn't it?", Dr. Bo asked.

"Yes, I agree with that, but doesn't the severity of the act tell you whether or not it is likely to recur? Isn't that the whole point of the common-law system that we use in our own society?"

"No, I don't think that is correct," Dr. Bo answered. "I think you will find that some severe acts of crime are very unlikely to recur, such as a

134

crime of passion as I think you call it in your society. Our records, which go back now for over 200 years, indicate that this kind of an act is very unlikely to recur. On the other hand, petty stealing is very likely to recur and lead to more serious acts. So we base our reeducation program largely around the probabilities of that behavior recurring, on the theory that it takes more reeducation to change a pattern that is likely to recur."

"What do you do in an Educational Home?" I asked.

"The home is staffed by our young people, all of whom do two years of national service as you know. We are very careful whom we pick because we want to pick the best possible models for young boys. The homes vary but, in general, we try to have about five boys to one educational counselor and we try not to have homes that are much larger than ten young people, including counselors. We have found it does not work to have large groups as I said earlier, because I think it takes away from the chance to model after the healthy older counselors."

"Well, how does this modeling take place? Don't the boys imitate each other, rather than the young man who is on his national service?"

"That is the tendency initially, of course, but we do all we can to make the counselor an influence in their lives by giving him control over all the rewards that are available. Like anyone else in Prire, these young people can earn money and points, and they can earn experiences. They have to grow their own food—or most of it—and they have community service jobs as well, and then they have jobs in their own home to do. If they are in school they have their school work, and if not in school they have an occupational job, so there are many opportunities for them to work for money or for points for experiences. The counselor is the one who has control over these."

"Where do you put your educational homes?" I asked. "Don't people object to having them in their community?"

"Well, you must remember that the young men in the educational home are right from the community. It is not as though one is receiving strangers, it is a question of regrouping people already in the community."

"Don't you ever get any young men who are what we would call hardened criminals, who don't react well to any attempt to change them?"

"Yes, it does happen occasionally, although it is quite rare."

"What do you do with them? Do you let them live in these Educational Homes right in the community?"

"No, we do not. If the act performed by a young person is an act that is punishable by death in the adult code, then they are put to death."

"You put them to death!" I exclaimed. "I'm very surprised to hear that in a place like Prire! Do you mean you would execute a boy of fifteen, for example?"

"It has happened," Dr. Bo said. "Let's say a boy of fifteen murders an older person in order to steal something from him. That crime would be punishable by death in the adult code, so it is punishable by death for the young person. You see, in Prire we look at the event in terms of its consequences to the victim. The victim was killed and it really makes no difference whether the person who did it was fifteen or fifty. The question is, what is the likelihood of that behavior being repeated? From our records we can tell, and therefore, the more serious the act and the more likely it is to be repeated, the more likely it is to have a death penalty attached to it."

"Do you think the death penalty has any effect as a deterrent?"

"It is only a deterrent, I think, when the punishment is extremely swift. That is one thing we do watch over very carefully—to see that criminal acts of this kind are handled through our court system within forty-eight hours. These don't happen very often though, let me assure you on that."

"It seems like an awfully drastic measure to me," I said. "I just can't imagine giving the death penalty to a young man like that."

"It all depends on your point of view," Dr. Bo said slowly. "You have to remember what our values are here in Prire. If that behavior is unlikely to be changed, then there really is no point in locking a person up for the rest of his life at the expense of our communities, is there?"

"Well no, I suppose not," I said, "But the death penalty is something that really sticks in my throat."

"You must not forget the importance of our records," Dr. Bo explained. "We do not impose the death penalty out of cruelty, but simply on the basis of pragmatism. We've found that our attempts to reeducate certain people were totally unsuccessful. We have figured out the cost in terms of time and personnel and expense to the community, and have decided that we could not afford to waste our resources that way. It is really as simple as that."

"Well, what about adults who commit crimes?

I assume that there are some that aren't put to death. What do you do with them? Do you have them in prisons, or what?"

"Our prison system, as you would call it, is based on the same principles that direct our educational homes. First of all, we do not put prisoners together in large groups because that only means that they will imitate each other. We put them in as small groups as possible. The prisons vary a good deal, from those intended for the worst offenders to the ones at the top which would have the most amount of freedom and privileges."

"Well, what happens to these people? I mean suppose you take an example like the John you mentioned before. Let's say John is thirty years old and has committed whatever crime it would be in Prire so that he would go to the worst of these prisons. What happens to him?"

"This John as you call him, if he had committed a crime short of the death penalty but very severe, would probably enter the prison that was at the end of the scale, which is to say, the most restricted. Being in the most restricted prison, he would not be accessible to his friends or family, so as to cut out all influences from the previous environment. This is the only prison in which we do this, but we do it for an initial period. Assuming his behavior is amenable he is able to earn money which is put in a savings account for family visits or his release, although he can buy things with it, up to a limit, while he is in prison. He can also earn points which can be exchanged for privileges, and he can earn experiences. These, of course, increase as you get to the most open prisons. Depending upon the circum-

138

stances, this John of yours might be there three months before he gets his first visit from his family, but he only does so if his behavior has merited it. If he continues to behave appropriately he can be moved out of that prison, and on to the next one, and so on up the line until he reaches the most open prison. But in all of our prisons the men do productive work. Not only do they raise their own food, but each prison has a particular thing that each makes which contributes to Prire society. Depending upon a man's previous skills he would be assigned to a prison where his skills would fit into the productivity of that particular prison."

"What kinds of things are made in prisons?" I asked.

"It varies depending upon the region and the community. As I said, they all grow their own foodstuffs so that they are self-sustaining. In some prisons that are located in good farmland areas they would also sell vegetables and grains to the nearby city. Some prisons raise pigs and cure their own ham and bacon. As a matter of fact, I think that we had one of our best hams at the farm in Blue Lake Village. Do you remember seeing it?"

"Yes, I do. I remember it looked very nice and I had a taste of it as well which was excellent."

"Well, that's a ham from our very famous prison which is located in the south and is really known for its pigs. In fact, it's called the Pig Prison. We consider them the best we have. We have prisons that make our telephones, some make fencing, some that are located near timber make furniture. It varies, but all prisons are self-supporting in terms of their own food and in terms of making a product."

"I assume that many of your prisoners learn skills while they're there and that they react well to the reeducation? Or do you find that it does not work with a large proportion?"

"It works for over 90 percent of our prisoners if by 'works' you mean their behavior changes while they're in prison. That is relatively easy to do. The real test is whether or not their behavior stays changed after they leave, and I would say we're about 70 percent successful there."

"What do you do about the 10 percent or so who do not change while they're in prison?"

"Well, this is probably going to upset you a bit, but if we find that the behavior does not change, that the prisoner does not respond to any of our attempts to reeducate his behavior, he has a second trial, so to speak, while he is in prison. We look at his whole record of behavior. If the record indicates that he is unlikely to change, then he receives the death penalty."

"You mean he could get the death penalty even if the original crime he committed did not call for one?" I was shocked.

"Yes. The death penalty is not given just for the original crime but for failure to change the behavior. Of course, we hope that the prisoners will move up through the various prisons and in fact, most do. But you always have to make provisions for the system that is not going to work with some people, and that is the way we have dealt with it. Again you must remember that we work from our records, not out of whim or out of emotion for or against the prisoner. And, secondly, you must remember that we make these decisions in terms of our resources:

140

We just don't feel we can spend our resources trying to reeducate someone when that effort fails, and when they are likely to return to society to commit more crimes against the citizens of Prire."

"In other words, you don't turn out any prisoners except successful ones, is that it?"

"That is correct," Dr. Bo answered.

"Do all of them return to their original communities?"

"No, not all, although most do because we've helped to maintain the ties there for them. As they've gotten into more privileged prisons they are living in the communities and have regular visits with their family, which we encourage."

"Do you have any problems with these visits?" I asked.

"I don't know what you mean but I suppose you mean the effects of these visits. Is that what you mean?"

"No, not really. What I wondered was whether these prisoners might produce children while they're still in prison and if that wouldn't be a problem."

"Oh no, that's not a problem," Dr. Bo smiled. "The prisoners are not permitted to have children."

"How do you manage that?" I asked with surprise.

"With a vasectomy," he answered. I swallowed hard.

"What about those prisoners who don't return to their communities, where do they go?"

"Some elect to stay at their prison. We have homes around the prisons, particularly those that are farming prisons, and sometimes prisoners come to like that life and want to stay there and have their family join them. Some become employees of the prison."

"Doesn't it give you some modeling problems?"

"Occasionally, but on the whole we think a very good model is a prisoner who has chosen to have a more productive and responsible life. Having ex-prisoners live on the prison farm or work in prison administration has worked well for us. The main point about our system, I think, as compared to what I've heard about yours, is that we make it possible for a prisoner not only to change his behavior but to have a payoff if he does it while he's still in prison. We feel there is absolutely nothing to be gained by keeping people locked up for a number of years if they are unable to demonstrate any real change in behavior, and if there are no rewards for the change while in prison. Prison life itself is absolutely maladaptive for outside life."

"I have to agree with you on that last point," I remarked. "Prison life doesn't prepare you for anything except to be in prison."

"Precisely, so we try to make prison life prepare people for a community life in a responsible manner."

By this time we were passing through rather flat country full of evergreens, with frequent glimpses of small lakes or ponds. We had passed through several villages since we left Long Valley, and I was interested to see how different they looked in their architecture. In one we went by I was quite sure I saw a very large solar heater, which Dr. Bo verified. The architecture was always very simple but varied quite a bit, using stone and timber. Some villages were laid out on a line along the railroad and others seemed to have much more density. Almost all of the villages seemed to be on or near a body of water. Dr. Bo explained that that was deliberate. Many of the ponds I saw were manmade rather than natural and provided the towns with local a water supply as well as fish.

He spent quite a bit of time explaining to me the use of the resources, which is a national code adopted by all the villages. I was familiar with this system, having read a good deal about it and I will not repeat it here, but it involves the utilization of all wastes, both solid and water; composting; the treatment of human wastes so that they can be used on the soil; the use of animal wastes. Everything used in the community is used, recycled, and used over again. This system had one result, at least, that I could see; there was no litter anywhere, no papers or cans or bottles lying around. I found that very agreeable.

We were getting nearer to Ponyo City now. The train came up a small grade and I could see Lake Ponyo over to our left. It looked immense. Ponyo City is the second or third largest city in Prire after Capital City and is situated in the northwest (see the map that I have drawn from memory). It is situated in a more northerly climate than Capital City. Everywhere I looked I could see the same landscape of evergreens and the occasional ponds or small lakes. I was surprised to see how empty the outskirts looked, considering the fact that the population of Ponyo City is around 300,000. Once again there were no smokestacks and smog on the outskirts. I remarked on this to Dr. Bo and he said he appreciated my noticing the difference. The aesthetic qualities of the cities in Prire were a matter of great concern to them. There were many people in Prire, he said, who had reservations about cities of this size at all. They had weighed the pros and cons of city life many times over the last few hundred years, and it was still a debate. But since there were people who preferred city life, they had maintained the cities and simply tried to work out some of the problems they posed. I asked him what these problems were and he told me that it was mainly a matter of size.

"It is size that is the enemy," he said. "Just by putting large groups of people together we find that the quality of life goes down. On the other hand, some improvements in terms of the cultural interaction of people are made possible by the city. We appreciate what this means to us culturally and in other ways, but bigness itself is something we try to avoid. We think the village units have been our best answer to this problem."

"Why are you so opposed to bigness?" I asked out of curiosity.

"I don't think any of us is opposed to bigness as a matter of opinion," Dr. Bo replied. "We are opposed the effects it has on the quality of life and on human events. We are opposed to anonymity because it breeds irresponsibility and antisocial behavior. That is why we have gone to great efforts to see that the Rule of Personal Identification is maintained in our cities."

The train pulled into Ponyo City station and we gathered our baggage and got off. Dr. Bo said that someone from the University would be meeting us. It turned out to be Mr. Pusiter, who was president of the local student association. Mr. Pusiter was a

144

short, affable young man with a sort of cynical sense
of humor whom I grew quite fond of in the few
hours we spent together. He had a University transit
and took us to the local Ponyo Gardens Hotel. This
was quite a comfortable hotel, a little bit more old-
fashioned than what I had seen in Capital City. But
the rooms were large and comfortable. We were due
at the house of the President of the University for
dinner so I had no time to stroll about the city. Dr.
Bo and I met with Mr. Pusiter a little later in the
lobby and drove over to President Chookbar's residence at the University. Dr. Bo had arranged this
dinner especially for me because he knew of my
interest in pursuing certain topics with the group
that was to be there.

The University is very pleasantly situated on a
slight hill overlooking the lake. The part that we
were in was only part of the campus but it was the
main campus. The major difference that struck me
between the Ponyo University campus and that of
campuses in our society was the lack of tall buildings. The campus was quite spread out and people
were either walking or bicycling from place to
place. Buildings were low, with large garden areas
around most of them. I could see a dairy farm off to
the back with the barns at the skyline. I assumed
that the University was self-supporting in its food
as with everything else I had seen in Prire, and this
proved correct. We drove up the hill to the President's house which was a modest residence but
with what must have been the best view in all of
Ponyo City of the lake and of the city below. It was
quite a lovely sight in the early evening.

We went inside and Dr. Bo shook hands with
President Chookbar who was an old friend of his,

I knew, and then introduced me to him. President Chookbar was an impressive man, very lively, vigorous, very interested in me and everything I had to say. He made me feel welcome and appeared to give me his total attention. The more I saw of him the more highly I regarded his intellect and his vitality. Waiting for us were Dr. Woll, a well-known economist in Prire; Dr. Lason, a renowned psychologist; Mr. Pusiter, and myself. President Chookbar invited us into his garden in the back as it was still too warm on the porch that overlooked the lake. I took great pleasure in walking in his flower and vegetable garden. He had an unusually attractive herb garden with many herbs that were familiar to me such as rosemary, woodruff, the various mints, germander, burnett, lovage, tarragon, and basil. There were other herbs there that I did not know which Dr. Chookbar identified for me and let me smell and rub between my fingers, all of which were delightfully new fragrances to me. He was obviously an excellent gardener and it was a pleasure to see the flowers and vegetables. I don't think I saw a better garden the entire time I was in Prire. It was clear that he did all his own work, or almost all of it, and apparently with a minimum of effort. I noticed he also had one of those solar greenhouses I had seen in some of the other communities.

We went in to dinner which was served by the students from the nutrition program at the University. I must say it was not too successful and was the only meal that I had in Prire that I did not think was first rate. We had some pork which was very much overcooked and dried out but the vegetables were fresh, if overdone. Dr. Chookbar served a local white wine which was very pleasant. What was of more interest to me was Dr. Chookbar's description of the local crafts represented on the table. He had a lovely silver set that he said was handmade about fifty years ago by a local craftsman just outside Ponyo City. It was as pretty silver as I have ever seen. The glassware came from the southwestern area, and was turned in goblet shapes, extremely simple but with a lovely line. I was quite taken with these and I'm sure if I had expressed much more admiration for them I would have been given a present of some, so I did not say anything further. The dishes also came from the Ponyo region and apparently were very well known. They were a clear white with a very high sheen to them but the reflections were warm rather than cold. I thought they were extremely attractive.

Dr. Bo described my background and the purpose of my visit to Prire to Dr. Woll and Dr. Lason and indicated to me that the dinner had been arranged to give me a chance to ask them questions about Prire.

"I think Dr. Aldworth has seen an awful lot in a very few days," explained Dr. Bo, "and has really not had the chance to assimilate much of what we have seen together. I thought this would give him a good chance to ask some questions of you experts."

"What can we explain for you?" asked Dr. Woll with interest. Dr. Woll was a rather small, vivacious and very intense woman of about forty. She reminded me a little bit of Madame Young at Blue Lake. She spoke very quickly and intensely so it was hard for me to follow her. I knew, however, that it was a remarkable opportunity for me to learn something about the economic system in Prire.

"We haven't had the chance to visit any of

your industry yet," I said to her, "but I'm not clear really about how your economic system of Resources and Returns really works."

"I'm sure that you would find this difficult. It is a very complicated system and one that is not easily grasped in such a short visit as yours. The basic principle is that each community owns the industry in it. We came to the decision many years ago that we would not have national companies or large industrial organizations because the very size of them produced so many problems that we had to cope with."

"What sorts of problems?" I asked.

"The bigness," she said, "led to all kinds of difficulties, cutting across community lines and developing a basic power that no one community could resist. It was this more than anything else that led us to the decision that no industry should be larger than what a community could own and manage itself."

"Doesn't that lead to a loss in efficiency?" I asked. "It seems to me that it must be an awful waste to have each community duplicate the same industries."

Dr. Woll smiled. "It depends upon what you mean by waste. If you mean could we produce some things for less effort, the answer is yes. If you mean that we duplicate some products in one community and then in another, the answer is yes, we do. But we do not consider that waste."

"But doesn't that cost more money? Aren't those goods more expensive produced this way?"

"Not really," she replied, "if you count into the expense all the related costs. We have done a very fine analysis of this going back for over 100 years, and we found that the large industrial unit was really not efficient at all when we counted in the costs of the resources used to build the plants themselves and to maintain them, the costs of transporting the finished products from one part of Prire to another, the cost of packaging, not to mention what those large units did to the quality of life which we, of course, put very high on the list of priorities. No, we think that when everything is taken into consideration, there's very little to be said for the so-called efficiency or savings of the large industrial unit."

"I find that hard to believe!" I exclaimed. "As you probably know, the efficiency of the cost savings of large industrial units has been well established in our society."

"Perhaps so," Dr. Woll said, smiling, "but I think you will find in the long run that one of our sayings will become true in your society. Here in Prire we say, 'Big only saves money, but small saves our planet.' You see, it's all a question of the frame of reference. We look at savings in terms of what it does to people and to the long-range resources of our planet and what it does to our society. The savings that matter are the savings in the long run, not the immediate savings. If you will permit me to say so, Dr. Aldworth, I think the economists in your country have been very short-sighted, at least those that I have read. They have been so specialized and so narrow in their interests that they have totally forgotten, or so it seems to me, what the economy does to its people and to the long-range resources."

"I should be glad to take that opinion back to my colleagues!" I joked. "Explain to me a little bit more about how the communities own their industries, would you?"

"It's much the same principle that I'm sure Dr. Bo has explained to you in other aspects of Prire life. In an economic design, we operate on the Principle of Local Responsibility. We have come to the conclusion based on our own experience and records that when an economic operation is owned by the people of the community, and is responsible to the people in that community, then the decisions tend to be in the interest of the community and not of the local industry. This is a very important point for us because we have insisted that the welfare of the communities come first over the economic success of the industry."

"But do your local industries make money? Are they economically healthy?"

"Making money isn't exactly the way we would see that," Dr. Woll replied. "We think they're economically healthy in the sense that they provide the services and products that are needed to the people who need them. All of our industry has to break even, but we are not profit motivated, as you must have guessed by now. Our local tractor plant, for example, just outside of Ponyo City, must make ends meet or it will make problems for that community. But we do not ask that those tractors be sold at exhorbitant prices in order to make a profit for the factory. Making ends meet, by the way, also means providing enough money for research to improve the product and to purchase materials for the next year. We definitely involve planning in our economy."

"What in the world is the motivation then for people to work in your industries? Why do people work hard at their job if there is no increase in their pay or in the profits?"

"I think Dr. Bo must have explained part of this to you. The rewards for an occupational job in Prire are highly varied and include not only money, but vouchers and points to be traded for a wide variety of things or experiences or privileges. Besides that, each person owns a share of the business so that they're run on what you would call a cooperative basis. The extent to which that particular industrial organization has a good year is reflected in the returns to the workers who own shares in it."

"You mean it's like a cooperative in the way it works?" I asked.

"Something like a cooperative, but there are two bases for return. One is the performance of the company, which is returned to the shareholders on a cooperative basis, but also individual performance rewarded with one of our three forms of reward. This means someone can be a hard worker in a company that does not do particularly well, and still be rewarded for the job he has turned in. The opposite is also true, the person who is lazy and does very little will not enjoy the same rewards that others get."

"Tell me, Dr. Lason," I said turning to her, "how do you explain this kind of motivation?"

Dr. Lason was a very tall woman in her early fifties with slightly graying hair. She had a very erect carriage. Her expression alternated between one of sweet kindness, and one of commanding authority. She had been very quiet during this interchange between Dr. Woll and me and I had noticed her listening with interest to my questions. Dr. Lason was probably the best-known psychologist in Prire and it was a great pleasure for me to be able to talk with her.

"How do I explain it?" said Dr. Lason very

slowly and with a smile. "You ask me only to explain human behavior, is that it?"

"Not exactly, I didn't mean to ask such a large question," I said hastily, "but tell me how you explain motivation to work on an occupational job with these rewards?"

"Well, I think the same way we would in any other society. Don't people in your society work for money and for bonuses and vacations and time off and titles or whatever else you have in your industries?" Dr. Lason asked.

"Yes, of course they do," I answered. "But I think everyone would agree that the main motivation is for the increase in income. In our society money is by far the most important motivator."

"I guess we would think that was a naive explanation," said Dr. Lason. "Or maybe we would say you have the cart and horse reversed. In a society such as I understand yours to be, where money is almost the only reward left, it is true that people will work very hard for money. Money becomes the medium to buy other things to improve their quality of life. Is it not true that in your society money can buy privacy, a piece of land, a view of trees, time at the seashore, can provide the illusion of meaningfulness in one's life?"

"Well, I don't know," I said, "I think some people feel that way, but there are a lot of people who feel that money is important for its own sake. Some people just like to earn money to have it, and to amass a fortune."

"Yes," Dr. Lason agreed, "I think that's true, that there are people in these societies who are greedy and want to have wealth. That is true here too. But I think it is naive to think that money is a prime motivator when a society is organized so that money is the only way by which one can buy these other experiences. If you build them into the life of your society, you provide a much richer array of rewarding experiences. This diminishes the importance of money. For example, here in Ponyo City, we think it is very important that everyone who lives here should have an attractive view. We have a wonderful lake and many of our houses face the lake, but we also have hills and views in all directions. One does not have to be wealthy to have an attractive view. Although I must say," she said turning to President Chookbar, "some of us have somewhat better views than others. I do think you have the finest view in all of Ponyo City."

"I agree," said President Chookbar laughingly. "This is one of the great privileges of being President of the University."

"I'm afraid I would have an awfully hard time convincing my colleagues of your idea of motivation, Dr. Lason. I don't mean any offense, you understand. I just think they would find it hard to believe that there could be other things as important as money in motivating people."

"Tell me, Dr. Aldworth, are your colleagues at your universities primarily motivated by money?"

"Well, no, they are not or they wouldn't be in academic life," I answered grudgingly.

"Then what motivates them, if I may ask?"

"Well, I suppose it's a variety of things. They think money is important but it is not that big an item in the average professor's life. I think that there are different motivators for different people. Some enjoy the good regard of their colleagues in the sense that they are thought to be scholarly or well-versed in their particular specialty; some enjoy teaching and being effective as a teacher with students; some enjoy being an authority; some like consulting with others; some like giving speeches; some like writing papers; some like the freedom of the academic life, I suppose; and I suppose there are some who like the status, or what there is of it."

"Well, that's really my point, Dr. Aldworth. I think you're quite right that there are varieties of things that motivate people. I'm sure that the teachers and professors in your society are not primarily motivated by money or they wouldn't have chosen that profession. The only difference between your thinking and ours is that in Prire we think that's true of all groups of people. We don't think human being are simple-minded at all. That is one reason we have used the Principle of Multiple Varied Rewards in designing so much of our society. This simply says that people are complex human beings, who prefer a variety of rewards, who prefer different rewards at different times in their lives, and who are highly individualized in the types of rewards that are meaningful to them. This means that no simplistic reward system is going to work very well. If money were the only reward we had in Prire, we would have some very unsatisfied people. So what we try to do is offer a wide array of different rewards that can be exchanged for different kinds of goods or experiences. Once you get the correct range of rewards, you can motivate almost anyone."

"You speak about rewards as though these things could be planned. Do you really go about it this way?"

"Yes, we do," Dr. Lason replied. "It was when we analyzed how these rewards were working that we hit upon many of the principles that we use today. For example, I don't think we would ever have gotten rid of our army and our heavy commitment to defense if we hadn't had the brains to sit down and analyze the rewards."

"How was that done?" I asked with great interest.

"I can't tell you how because this was done over a hundred years ago. But I know that what was involved was a careful analysis of the rewards of war-making. Some of these are quite obvious, of course, such as the money to be made off armaments, the status and power that accrues to those that win, not to mention the material gains, the excitement of it, the chance to change roles, to be brave, to win glory, the chance to fulfill patriotic needs, the giving of oneself to a higher end—all of these things operate. It is nonsense, of course, to speak of war as though it is not rewarding. War has been very rewarding in human history, or it would not have repeated itself so often. But was not until our forefathers a hundred years ago set out the analysis that we began to see the patterns of it. I think that this is one of our real breakthroughs."

"You mean when you found out that war was rewarding?"

"When we analyzed the rewards that war brought versus a nonwar situation. Not only war, I should say, but preparation for war, the maintenance of vigilance, of defense forces and of armaments—all of these were very reinforcing to important segments in any society. Isn't that true in your society?"

"I don't know," I said slowly, "I have to think about that. I have never thought about war as being rewarding before. I've always thought of it as a terrible waste and a dreadful experience. But I would have to agree with you that it has repeated itself throughout human history and therefore there must be something rewarding in it, or it would not recur. But what do you do about it? Suppose you do analyze those rewards? Then what happens?"

"What you do about it depends on the type of society you have," Dr. Lason replied. "I can only tell you what we have done in Prire. This of course happened a long time ago, but the major change came, I think, when we were able to understand the budget and appropriations process better than we had. It became clear to us that budget was policy and therefore control over that budget had to come back to the community level. As long as they were at a centralized level, budgets were going to be made by people who would in turn be rewarded by the outcomes. We wanted to change that by putting budgets in the hands of those who provide the funds and who in turn should receive the rewards from the services provided by those funds."

"And did you manage that?" I asked.

"As I say, this was some time ago and I don't view myself as an historian. But we feel that the key to our success was the drive to return the budget approval and appropriations process to the community level. The slogan at that time was 'No appropriation without participation'. It became quite a popular movement as more and more of our citizens felt they had a right to know where their tax money was going and what they were getting for it."

"Perhaps another thing that contributed to the success of this movement was our realization almost 200 years ago, I guess, that we in Prire society could not have everything—that there was just so much we could get in the way of service or outcomes out of our tax money. We recognized that tax money itself must have a ceiling to it, so we compared what we wanted to have happen and considered alternatives. This is a very different frame of mind than the growth frame of reference where the society assumes that there is no limit to anything, and that there can always be more and more appropriations, and more and more taxes, and more and more services, and more and more government undertakings. This change in our outlook was probably the most basic change because it is at the foundation of the philosophy of Prire, as you must have realized by now."

"Yes, I have caught on to that," I responded. "It's clear to me that the weighing of options is the core of the Prire society."

"That's quite correct, and I'm pleased that you see that. It is the weighing of these options that brought us to the budgetry process, because it seemed to us that the citizens who paid the taxes should have the chance to weigh the options themselves. This was the beginning of the Question and Answer Day and the Budget Day. I suppose you're familiar with these?"

"Not really, Dr. Lason, although I had read a little about them before I came," I answered. "Would you mind explaining them to me?"

"Not at all. They are both part of moving the appropriations process back into the hands of the citizens. As you know we are organized on a community basis and the communities in turn are organized into regional councils. We have six regional councils. Here in Ponyo City we are part of the Northwest Council. Capital City is part of the Southeast regional council. Question and Answer

Day occurs at the regional council level initially, when the questions are asked about the proposed budget and the alternatives. On all of our budgets we have alternative ways of making appropriations. On any particular subject we may have two, three, four, or even five different options about the size of an appropriation and the general outcome expected from it. For example, in Health Services we might have five different proposals up for the budget about how much is to be spent in the health area and the package of services that the average citizen could expect to receive from each of those appropriations. Each appropriation shows the amount of tax each citizen would have to pay to get these services. Once these alternatives are hashed out at the regional council they come back to the community for Question and Answer Day when each of the various proposals can be queried by citizens in the Question and Answer meeting. The representatives from the community and from the regional council are present to answer questions and to undergo a fair amount of heat, as a matter of fact, as often happens. Then there is the budget vote within the week, but not the same day as the Question and Answer Day."

"Why not the same day?" I asked. "Why don't you have your questioning and voting happen together?"

"That is a deliberate plan of ours to separate what can be a heated discussion, as I mentioned earlier, and the voting. We think it's best for people to have a few days to reflect on what they've heard and read before they actually vote. People need to collect themselves and not vote when their emotions are stirred up."

"I see. That makes some sense, I suppose, but

don't you lose a lot of your voters that way? How many people actually turn out to vote?"

"We get a very high percentage of people voting, but of course, this is part of our philosophy. We think voting is important so we make voting a rewarding experience for our citizens."

"What do you mean? Isn't voting itself enough of a reward?"

"Apparently not, if one looks at the voting figures of most societies outside of Prire. Each person receives a coupon against their tax which they can redeem so that participating in voting has an immediate payoff in terms of lessening their tax burden."

"You mean they get paid to vote?"

"I wouldn't call it exactly pay but it certainly is a coupon which reduces their tax. We have several of these options where people can reduce their tax through appropriate public service and by appropriate citizenship behavior. We find it works and we think it is a very good investment."

"How in the world do you ever get a budget together for all of Prire if you go through all this regional and local community process? It must take months and be a terrible hassle."

"Not at all," answered Dr. Lason. "It isn't an easy task because the budget is a very difficult matter as you are always weighing alternatives. But it is not as difficult as you might think. Using the health example I cited earlier, a percentage of the communities may vote for Option A, some for Option B, some for C and so on."

"What in the world do you do with all the different percentage votes?" I asked. "It seems to me you would never get a final budget!"

"No, it's not that difficult. Those communities that vote to tax themselves for a set of services under Option A in health, for example, receive such services. Other communities may vote for less participation. Some might vote for option E, let us say, which requires no services and no taxation. In other words, communities vote for what they want and they get what they vote for."

"It seems to me this is a terribly individualized system of budgeting. How in the world do you ever get any kind of national effort off the ground? How do you finance a large research program if you cannot get the communities to vote for it as a whole?" I asked.

"If it is an importance national effort, then it should be presented that way to the regional councils and the communities. It would be part of the responsibilities of the Overseers of the Future at the national level and the Resources and Returns Committee and all our other national committees to present this as an important national effort to the regional councils and to come up with a budget proposal that reflects the importance of this. The regional councils in turn, if they are persuaded, will form a budget option that stresses the national importance and would give it their own priority. Under these circumstances it is very likely to pass in most communities."

"But I don't see how you would ever get a defense budget, for example, or any kind of crisis or emergency funding. It seems like such an unresponsive system."

"I think you'll find it a more responsive system than most," Dr. Lason responded. "We budget for a two-year period at a time but with contingencies built into it. As for defense, I think you are aware that we gave that up quite a long time ago and have no army. But a comparable concern, to answer your question, might be the need, for example, to build up water reserves throughout all of Prire. That would be a national concern, not a regional one. We had a very bad three-year drought back in the nineties and at that time a national Water Resources Budget was passed almost unanimously by the communities in response to the very process I have outlined. It was clear to us and to the regional councils, and it was clear at the community level that we needed a national plan for water resources to meet the recurring problems of droughts. So a plan was drawn up, budgeted and it was passed and put into effect within six months. That is not too unresponsive, if I have read the history of your society correctly," Dr. Lason responded with a bit of a twinkle in her eyes.

"Well, I have to agree that in my society the budgeting process does take a long time and is really so complex almost nobody can follow it. But we can pass appropriations very quickly if there is an emergency of some kind as you probably know from reading about us," I answered, perhaps a little defensively.

"In Prire we can act in an emergency also," Dr. Lason said quickly. "We don't have many of them but we do have them occasionally. We have a system so that our national committees that feel there is a national emergency can convene the regional councils on 24-hour notice. But we don't have to use this very often, in fact it has been very rare in our history."

"I still am troubled about this whole question of

changing the rewards for wars," I said reflectively. "Some of what you said makes sense to me but I find it very hard to believe that you have found ways to avoid the warring impulse."

"The warring impulse?" Dr. Lason asked. "Are you implying that we have changed human nature?"

"Well, I'm wondering whether you have or have tried. It seems to me wars are part of 10,000 years of human history and I just can't believe that you have changed people's motivations or hereditary genes—or whatever—so that they don't make war anymore."

"We have not made war in Prire for 200 years," replied Dr. Lason, "if that's what you mean—but I don't think that's what you mean. We don't pretend that we have changed man's nature, as I'm sure Dr. Bo has told you. What we do claim is that we have managed man's make-up to some extent so that it is less destructive. We think man has inherited a predisposition to hunt and to compete and to fight for what is his, all of which have been very adaptive mechanisms in the past. Hunting is no longer an adaptive piece of behavior and we got rid of that over 200 years ago. On the other hand, farming is an adaptive behavior that goes back almost as far as hunting, and we have encouraged that."

"What do you do to replace the hunting instinct, if I may call it an instinct?" I asked.

"Yes, instinct is acceptable, or any other term that you like," she answered. "We have tried to use that same programming that lies within our genes for some other end. In the case of the combative program that you're referring to we have diverted this into sports and into endurance contests, into self-sufficiency competitions and into all sorts of out-of-doors skills which we feel tap the same type of genetic program. Our young people as well as the old take great pride in their skills in living with nature, in which they are quite expert."

The rest of the group, of course, had been listening to my conversation with Dr. Lason and had been watching my reaction to the things that she said.

I turned to Dr. Bo and said, "I have been informed, Dr. Bo, but I have not been persuaded! I am very impressed with the reasoning that Dr. Lason has explained, but it seems to me it would take a thousand years to change the behavior of the people in my own society to what Dr. Lason has been describing."

Dr. Bo looked around the group to see if anyone wished to answer. Seeing they did not, he turned to me and said in a very kindly way, "Dr. Aldworth, I think I could speak for all of us when I say the steps that Dr. Lason has described here are really not difficult. They are not hard after a society has come to the realization that it can not have everything, and that it has to make choices. The turning point in Prire, I am sure, was when our forefathers realized some 200 years ago that they could not spend 15 percent of their budget on defense, for example, on an army and related warlike behaviors, and at the same time have the quality of life they wanted. Societies must choose what they want, then they have to decide what they can afford. In Prire, we made our first job that of deciding the kind and quality of life we wanted; that then decided how we would spend our resources. It is really fairly simple once you reach the point of knowing you have to choose."

Dr. Chookbar then engaged the other members at the table in a description of the current arts exhibit at the University which he wanted us to see after dinner. I took this opportunity to turn to Mr. Pusiter to ask him a bit about student life at the University.

I will summarize our conversation here as I recall it. Apparently the Prire educational system is quite different from ours. (Both Dr. Chookbar and Dr. Bo verified the points that follow so Mr. Pusiter was not my only informant.) In Prire education is available to anyone who can meet the entrance requirements at the various stages of education. What is quite different from our system is that one can go to school at any time in one's life, at any age.

Education is compulsory from age six to twelve. At age twelve a young person can choose, with the cooperation of his parents, whether to stay in school or go to work. By work I mean an occupational job because everyone starts their community service work at age twelve. This would mean that a youngster who chooses not to go on in school would start working full-time at his occupational job and at his community service job just like an adult. This sounded like exploitation of child labor to me when I first heard about it, but I think that would be an unfair criticism. Children are not exploited in Prire, but are put to work at sensible jobs that they can handle. I was told that most of the children who choose to go to work at age twelve continue with their citizenship training at their own school and generally also take one or two vocationally related courses, so that their contact with school is continued on a regular basis, even though they do not attend school full time.

Those who choose to stay in school do so, going on to higher school, or to college, or graduate training, but of course spending two years in national service at about age twenty-one. Very few people go to school without interruption. The more typical pattern is to go through a period of training until completion, then work at an occupational job for a while, and then return for further training, and then go back to the occupational job. At the University, for example, people are enrolled at all levels from ages eighteen to eighty. One of the striking things about Prire is that there is no segregation by age in any part of the society. I found it very strange at first, but I came away with the feeling that it had much to recommend it. On the Student Council at Ponyo University, for example, Mr. Pusiter told me that one of the members of the student council was a man in his seventies, and another a lady in her upper sixties. I am sure this tends to give a much more stable and knowledgeable character to those student councils, rather than the turnover characteristics that we see in our own universities.

I asked Mr. Pusiter how he came to be at Ponyo City. He was a young man in his late twenties. He said he had done national service, and in the course of it had visited many parts of Prire, and had been attracted to the Ponyo City area. He had not yet been ready to go on to the university at that time so had selected his occupation which was that of a mathematics teacher. He had taught at his school in the southeast region for three years and then had decided to go on to the university for more training and had come to Ponyo University. I asked him how university life was for students, expecting to receive the usual complaints that I was familiar with. But I

165

sensed that student life was very different from what I knew of it in my own society. I think this was due partly to the fact that the students had all had some work experience, and were of different ages, so that one had a cross-section of society among the students in the university. It certainly was a long cry from the prolonged youth and dependency period that is forced upon the young people in our own society. Mr. Pusiter explained to me that students, when they finished their training, could elect to go to different communities. During national service young people were exposed to many communities and in the course of their occupations they might well be in different communities also.

I asked him how life varied in the communities in terms of being very rigid and moralistic to being freer and more open kinds of societies. He explained that communities varied tremendously in this regard and that people who chose a freer, more open life would seek out that kind of community to live in. He said this was true of universities as well and that they varied in their approach to learning. Ponyo University was known to be a very good university but also one that had a serious approach to learning and which had tested out its own teaching techniques. The university at the City of the Plains was quite different, he told me. There they belived in learning through experience and the use of apprenticeships. Those who preferred that type of learning went there.

Mr. Pusiter had come to Ponyo University to engage in a project to reorganize mathematics teaching. They were doing a two-year census of the use of mathematical skills in Prire, which is a very large undertaking. Based on their findings of what the people actually used in the way of mathematics in their occupational jobs and their community service jobs they were going to reorganize the curriculum. He told me this was done every couple of decades, so that the curriculum made sense in terms of its application. In discussing mathematics, teaching with him I was quite taken with one example he gave me. When the children in Prire are studying multiplication and division, it is the practice to bring in local carpenters and masons and farmers and accountants to give brief demonstrations in the classes of how they use these skills in their particular occupations.

I asked Mr. Pusiter about this option of children leaving school at age twelve about which I had many reservations. He told me a story about his own brother who was just not the type of youngster that liked school at all and had not done well at it. He had been slow at reading although he had done all right in mathematics. At the age of twelve his brother was absolutely determined to leave school and go to work although his parents were opposed to it. Both of Mr. Pusiter's parents had been teachers and I assume were very much in favor of education. His brother went to work as a baker's apprentice and apparently liked it very much and became quite good at it. He, of course, maintained his citizenship training which was required, and in addition took a course on grinding grains at school. Today, Mr. Pusiter told me, his brother has moved down into a community in the southwest region near the Lake of the Moon where he runs his own mill and grinds grain for the community, as well as having a bakery which he runs with his brother-in-law.

Mr. Pusiter asked me if that kind of life would be possible in our own society. I had to say that it was not, as we required our young people to attend school at least to the age of sixteen. He asked me if that did not cause a lot of problems when young people could be out and doing at a much earlier age. I said I thought it did cause a lot of problems which we had not yet solved. Mr. Pusiter said that he felt that the best thing that ever happened to his brother was to leave school and go to work at age twelve where he felt useful and was regarded well by the other people in the bakery. He said it was the turning point in his brother's life.

When we had finished dinner, Dr. Chookbar asked me if I had not had enough of Prire for one evening and I said I had not, that I was enjoying myself enormously and was learning much from everyone. He asked if I would be interested in walking across to the art exhibit that they had been talking about. I said I was not too tired and would be delighted. We walked out onto the porch as it was now dusk and looked out over Lake Ponyo. It was a striking scene. The University sat up on the hill behind Ponyo City, covering a very large area overlooking the lake which extended well beyond our view. As we walked across the campus I noticed that the students ranged in age from the early twenties up to the sixties and seventies. I had to collect myself from the slight shock I felt at seeing couples in their sixties walking around holding hands. I was reminded of our saying that it is too bad that youth is wasted on the young.

We passed through a tiled arcade and heard music coming from the end of it. As we approached we heard a quartet playing Mozart. My hosts saw I was interested and waited until it was finished. Dr. Chookbar asked me what I thought of the music and I said I thought it was very nice indeed, that I was very impressed with the quartet. He said that there were many such musical organizations around the university and that such concerts were very common. I thought that was a delightful idea.

We went into the art exhibition hall. The exhibit that they had been talking about was of the best that had been produced in the region for the year. It took my breath away, I must admit. We did not have the time to visit everything, but I went through rooms of crafts ranging from silverwork, to ceramics, to weaving, to leather-working, jewelry-making—I can't remember all the rooms—but I saw workmanship of a quality I have not seen before. These were not amateur craftsmen enjoying their hobbies. Clearly these were serious artisans.

We then went into the halls where paintings were exhibited. Although I consider myself a very poor judge of art, I was impressed with the high level of craftsmanship. Dr. Chookbar pointed out some of their famous artists to me and I was really dazzled by the quality of their work. I could see he was very pleased by my reaction. My hosts must have seen that I was drooping a bit because they called an end to our walk and we strolled back toward Dr. Chookbar's house. On the way we passed a small outdoor theater. I could hear the sounds of an opera. Dr. Chookbar said that this was a rehearsal of a student-written opera that would be performed later in the week. We paused to listen for a while, then walked back to Dr. Chookbar's house. He offered me a glass of the wine I found delicious and then Dr. Bo suggested we go back as he knew we were very tired. I was grateful for the suggestion because I really was near my limits. Mr. Pusiter drove us back to the hotel. This was one night when I did not feel I had any more questions to ask Dr. Bo. I went straight up to bed, and was barely able to write my journal notes before I fell asleep. What images marched through my mind before I went to sleep! This one day seems to have been a week of experiences for me. . . . Stone Rive Village, and Luko Village, and on through Long Valley to Ponyo City. What a strange and yet wonderful place Prire seemed to be. . . .

# 5

# Thursday, June 21st

When Dr. Bo awakened me the next morning, I felt as though I could have slept another day. But soon I was alert and looking forward to the day's outing as I knew we would be visiting schools in Ponyo City. Dr. Bo and I had a very pleasant breakfast in the hotel and were fortunate in getting a table near the window where we could look out over Ponyo Lake. I was impressed with the views at every place we visited and asked if this was a deliberate part of the planning. He told me that in planning places of work or of relaxation the aesthetics of a view were considered as important as the function that the particular facility served. The results certainly made a very agreeable experience for this visitor.

Shortly after breakfast, Madame Roos, who was

to be my guide for the day, arrived. Dr. Bo explained that he had other business in Ponyo City that day and that Madame Roos, who was from the local education committee, would be delighted to show me as much as possible. Dr. Bo said he had told Madame Roos of my interests and that they had planned a full day, as I was eager to see all that I could. Madame Roos suggested that we start with a drive to the Inlet Lower School which was just north of Ponyo City.

As we drove she told me about the Inlet Lower School. Like all the lower schools in Prire, it served children aged six through twelve years. (As I had mentioned earlier, at twelve children choose to go on to school full-time, or to work and study part-time, so that the higher schools are for both those who study full-time and for those who are taking part-time courses. In the lower school all children attend full-time and I gather that this is compulsory.) I asked her several questions about Inlet Lower School as we drove along the east border of Lake Ponyo, trying to assess how typical this school was. I could not get any data from her about what kind of population it served. According to Madame Roos there was roughly the same variation in the population as there was in other lower schools. Of course, I had to remind myself that the differences in income in Prire were so small that probably one did not get the great range in socioeconomic status that one does in our own society.

The Inlet Lower School was set up on a small plateau overlooking Ponyo Lake. The school itself was a modest looking L-shaped building of two stories holding, I would guess, 250–300 children. What was different were the large grounds around the school and the inevitable garden. I noticed a big shed to one side which housed gardening equipment. In our society this space would more likely have been for a field house and a football field. There were no children outside, but of course it was still early in the morning.

We visited several classrooms in which Madame Roos introduced me to the teacher and to the children. The children were unusually courteous, standing up to say "Good morning, Dr. Aldworth. We hope you enjoy your visit to Inlet Lower School." Their behavior was more like that of children in East Africa than that of any I had recalled seeing in our own society. It made me wonder how rigidly these children were being educated. The classrooms, like the building, were simple in structure, made of wood. Some seemed fairly conventional, with desks lined up facing the front where the teacher and blackboard were located. Other rooms had more materials, such as a library corner or a science corner. All the rooms, however, had an abundance of growing plants. Based on my brief observations, there was a heavy emphasis on the basic skills of reading, writing, and arithmetic. Madame Roos, in answering my question about this, added that speaking was the fourth major skill that children were taught in the early grades, speaking and listening to others who are speaking. She said that in Prire the ability to speak well is considered as important as the ability to write or to read. I picked up one of the readers in a class of seven-year-olds, comparable to our second grade. The reader consisted of many short stories, some of them fairy tales. Many of the stories ended with a moral, such as that laziness did not get anybody anywhere, but that hard work did. One story spoke about the value of honesty. Another was about respecting other people's property. There was a highly moralistic tone to these stories I thought. There were lots of other small reading books in these rooms, some not more than four or five pages in length. Each child had a chart of what he had read and the teacher assigned points for each step completed in the reading progress. I noticed the same sort of system for mathematics, writing, and speaking. The children seemed to take great pride in putting up points on their charts.

In one room for seven-year-olds I noticed two or three older children working with the younger children. Madame Roos explained this was their tutoring system, in which the older children in the school who were good students tutored the younger children who were having trouble in some phase of the learning. The particular tutoring lesson was designed by the teacher but the older child supervised and helped with the learning. I asked if this tutoring did not interfere with the progress of the older student. Madame Roos explained that time given for tutoring gave the older children points that they could use for their own independent study, or for special work with the teacher in an area of interest. She said that they had found that tutoring by the older children was a very successful technique because it gave the younger child a good model of what learning would lead to.

We had not been there more than an hour visiting classrooms when a musical theme came over the loudspeakers. About half the children in each classroom left for various destinations. Madame Roos could see that I was interested in what was happening and suggested that we go outside to watch the

174

work teams. As we watched the teams assemble she explained how they worked. Each team had as its captain one of the twelve-year-olds so that the team was composed of children of different ages from six to twelve. This made about seven children per team. Each team, she explained, had a particular job for the day and these jobs would rotate. Teams might work in the garden, or on the maintenance of the building, or they might repair equipment, or tend the flowers around the buildings, or help prepare the noon lunch, or they might be canning or freezing food for the next year. Each school, Madame Roos explained, was as independent as possible in growing its own food and in its own maintenance.

I asked how twelve-year-old children could possibly have the skills to help maintain a building. Madame Roos said that these skills were taught very early under the supervision of a local school mechanic who might have several buildings under his supervision. He would also have with him an apprentice who would be one of the young people who had decided not to go on to school after twelve. He and the teenage apprentice would take turns instructing the twelve-year-old leaders in the basics of the necessary skills. (I made a mental note to ask Dr. Bo how all this worked out with the unions.)

We strolled around the vegetable garden and watched the teams at work. I was quite impressed with the work that was being done, considering the fact that these were children from six to twelve. The twelve-year-olds were obviously used to being leaders and managed it quite well. The garden itself was under the supervision of an adult who I assumed was a teacher in the school, but a great deal of the responsibility fell upon the twelve-year-olds to see that the peas were picked properly and that the vines were not ripped out. Another team was putting some hay over some new seeds that had just been planted. The care that they took with the seeds and with the hay and where they walked was impressive for children of this age. Another team was spreading compost around some of the squash and shoots of corn. In what I called the machinery shed a team without any adult direction was sharpening hoes on a grinding wheel pedaled by a twelve-year-old. I noticed that they had a jig for the hoes so that the children could not get the angle wrong for grinding. Another team was marking out straight rows for more planting.

We walked around to the back of the school and found two more teams digging out young plants from the solar greenhouse to put in the flower bed. The flower beds were really lovely, and I so much enjoyed seeing them there. I've always been unhappy that our schools did not have more flowers around them. Madame Roos said that the children would all be trained in each phase of school and garden maintenance. They would work in the greenhouse, the garden, the maintenance of equipment, painting the school, and repairing its equipment.

We walked in the back door of the school and turned left into the kitchen where there were at least four teams at work under the supervision of a cook and her assistant. I checked immediately for the cleanliness of the kitchen because I am quite particular about that sort of thing. I was pleased to see that things were immaculate. I had visions of little children preparing the lunch that I was likely to eat and the prospect had filled me with dismay. But the children's hands were well scrubbed and everything was done quite carefully. The children were chopping up vegetables for the soup and helping to take bread out of the pans where they had cooled. The bread aroma was extremely tempting. The head cook, as I presumed her to be, explained that two of the teams had made the bread first thing that morning on getting to school early and it was just now ready to be taken out. Madame Roos asked me if I would not be interested in seeing what was going on in the classrooms while this activity was going on and I said I would indeed. I had already decided to question her about the loss of time from studies that would happen as the result of all these work teams.

We went back to the classrooms and found, of course, that half the children were still there and were receiving lots of individual attention from their teachers and from the tutors. There were tutors in every room I visited, some ten years old, some eleven, some twelve years old. It is always hard to judge a school when you're on a visit because you assume everyone is putting their best foot forward. But I have to report the tone of the school was one of seriousness, although not soberness. The children who acted as tutors were very serious about their work, they insisted that the children pay attention and were successful as far as I could see. The work teams, at least on the day I visited, were far more attentive to the task than I would have predicted. I did not think that twelve-year-olds could carry off this kind of responsibility as well as they did. The six-year-olds looked up to those twelve-year-old captains as though they were the principal of the school!

I asked Madame Roos how they had come to develop the work teams and tutoring systems. She said that they had found children so easily imitate other children that it is important to use this imitation in the right way. They had also found that children could accept responsibility at a much earlier age than people had thought in the past. They found that twelve-year-olds could be very effective team leaders if they are given the proper training and enough supervision and support. She said, "We find that our twelve-year-olds in Prire society are ready to become young citizens and we treat them that way. At age twelve they are starting on serious responsibilities and we find them an important source of leadership for our young people."

I thought of our own twelve-year-olds, many of them in sixth grade, and many of them without any sort of responsibility at school. I wondered how well they would be at leadership and decided they would probably be fine, if given the right kind of training and rewards for it. Madame Roos answered my questions about the curriculum and use of time. She said that they thought time was critical in education and tried to use every minute in a constructive way. The time spent at these jobs, she felt, was not a waste at all as the children were learning essential skills for life in Prire—independence, resourcefulness, growing one's own food and maintaining one's own environment. The school had its own woodlot farther out from the school and in back of the lake, where children worked to bring in the wood supply which was supplemented with oil heat. I saw no graffiti anywhere, nor did I in all of Prire. The bathroom that I visited was free of the usual written sayings. It was also neat and clean, much to my pleasant surprise. The library was run by a twelve-year-old at the time I visited it, but I understand there was a teacher who acted as a supervisor as well.

I inquired about physical education and Madame Roos told me that physical fitness was a very definite part of the instruction. Had we arrived earlier that morning we would have seen the children engaged in their physical fitness exercises, which they did again later that afternoon. I asked about sports and was told that sports were also stressed but that these took place after the regular school day.

At this point we were joined by Mr. Doob who was principal of Inlet Lower School and who apologized for not having been with us earlier but had been tied up in a planning meeting about the curriculum. I told him that it sounded very familiar to me and wondered what kind of curriculum problems existed in Prire, compared to our own society. He said they were debating the success of their curriculum in conservation. They were pleased to see that materials were being used better and that there was much less waste, but they were not as successful as they would have liked to be in the use of electricity.

I chatted with him about the curriculum for about 15 or 20 minutes and learned that it stressed not only the four basic skills—reading, writing, arithmetic and speaking,—but also included conservation of the resources of the school and of the environment, cooperative behavior, knowledge of another language and culture, and exercise in planned behavior. We did not have time to go into any kind of detail, but it was clear to me that the architecture of the curriculum closely reflected the values of Prire. Mr. Doob explained that they used a reward system for the desired behaviors and that children received a variety of rewards for the points they earned, including special experiences, merit badges, free time, special books and extra privileges.

The atmosphere of the school is very hard to convey. It was a little different than any school I have seen although it combined some characteristics of a work camp and a fairly business-like school atmosphere. I don't wish to give the impression that everyone went around grimly at his task, because that was not so. The children were pleasant and smiling and seemed to enjoy what they were doing. There was some kidding around, as one would expect, but not nearly as much as I have seen in our own schools.

Mr. Doob asked me if I would like to chat with a few teachers and I said indeed I would. He suggested we talk to the curriculum committee which was just finishing up in his office so we went in there and I was introduced to five or six of the teachers who varied in age from twenty to perhaps sixty. I told them that I was somewhat familiar with the schools in our own society and had talked with many teachers there. I wondered how teachers in Prire felt about their jobs.

Each responded that he or she liked the job although they felt it was a tough and demanding one. They said (and I was not surprised to hear this as I have heard it everywhere in our own society) that teaching a class full of children for five or six hours a day is one of the most difficult and draining jobs in the world. I agreed with them heartily and said I thought it was extremely demanding work. I asked them how they managed the stress of this. They told me they thought the work teams and the tutoring helped a great deal because they were able to deal with that half of the class that was not out working, each in turn, and it gave them a chance to give individual attention.

They found the tutors on the whole very helpful. Occasionally a tutor would not attend to his business and had to be corrected, but on the whole they felt that the children took this responsibility beyond their classroom. One might be responsible for a phase of maintenance, one for a part of the garden, one for some part of the preserving of food and so on, so that each teacher had two different sets of responsibilities. I asked them how they liked having the two jobs in the school. All but one said they liked it because it gave them the chance to see children in a different setting and to work with them differently.

I did not have a chance to visit the art and music rooms but I heard the music room as I went by and it sounded like the music rooms back home. I did notice that the loudspeaker system carried classical music, which surprised and enchanted me. The display outside the principal's office consisted of a series of designs for a garden plot ten feet by twenty. I gathered from those who won high commendation from the principal that it was an attempt to see how one could use the land for the most productivity.

Madame Roos' particular interest was in language learning and she made a point of having me listen to children learning in the language laboratory. All of them were expected to learn one other contemporary language fluently during the years in the lower school. I was not familiar with the languages they were learning so I cannot comment on their skill except to say that I saw two ten-year-olds carrying on a conversation about something with apparent fluency. She explained to me that the children in this group would be visiting in the country of their language study this summer and would return later to spend a whole school year there. This was part of the cirriculum, she explained, that attempted to teach responsible planetary behaviors and that one way to do this was to have children learn at an early age something about another society so that they would develop empathy for others who lived outside Prire.

As we walked along Inlet Lower School, the walls of the corridors as well as the walls of the classrooms were covered with sayings of an inspirational nature. Some had been done by the children in their art class, I assume. Some of those that I recall were "Reward those behaviors in others that you want to increase"; "Respect the right of others to do it their way"; "Was I considerate of my fellow human beings today?"; "Did I do my share today?"; "Is this bit of the planet better off today because I was here?" There were many more in a similar vein.

It was getting close to noon so Madame Roos suggested that we move along to our next stop which was to be the Bay Higher School. We drove south of Ponyo City to a little bay from which the school got its name. The higher schools in Prire accept children over twelve years old and up to eighteen or so. At eighteen the young men and women go into the national service or on to the university, but all must do their two years of national service sometime between the ages of eighteen and twenty-four.

The Bay Higher School, like most of the buildings I had seen in Prire, is built simply out of native wood and some stone. It was two stories high and, with 900 housed students, is one of the largest higher schools in Prire. When we arrived it was just about lunchtime so Madame Roos suggested we have our lunch at the school. Having been exposed to high-school cafeterias, I was not too anxious for this experience, but I was pleasantly surprised.

Apparently the same system I had seen at the lower school worked here at the higher school. There were teams of young people between the ages of thirteen and eighteen with seventeen- or eighteen-year-old leaders. Each team sat at its own table so that there were no more than six or eight at each small round table. Instead of the usual bedlam one finds in our cafeterias, it was relatively quiet and I could hear classical music over the loudspeakers. I was delighted to miss some of the signs of our usual cafeterias—no vending machines, no snack foods, no soft drinks.

Madame Roos and I took our trays and went to the serving line where we were offered a bowl of homemade soup that looked very good, some homemade bread which I took, peaches that had been canned from the previous year, and a piece of cheese. We took our trays to a vacant table over at one side of the cafeteria. I noticed as we went to our table that teachers were sitting at one table and next to them would be a student table and so on. I was very pleasantly surprised by the meal. It was very tasty and nutritious. The vegetable soup was particularly good. To my mind there is nothing in the world that can beat a good homemade bread.

I noticed that student teams were working in

the cafeteria, helping with the serving of food and cleaning up. I was particularly interested in what was done with waste. Each student brought his tray to a unit near where we were sitting and any leftover soup was put in one large can, any leftover bread in another, and the same with the dessert. Madame Roos told me that all the leftovers were used one way or another. Some were used to feed the chickens that the school maintained, some were turned into compost for the garden and some went to the pigs, but nothing was wasted. There were no paper napkins. Each child had his own napkin, tray, dishes and implements. After eating, he took his tray to the washing room where the team leader supervised the washing of the dishes which the youngster then put back in his locker.

When we had finished lunch, Madame Roos suggested that we look at some of the shops. We walked out through the back door of the cafeteria and I began to understand the layout of the higher school. Behind the cafeteria were a number of buildings such as would be needed to sustain a farm of a couple of hundred acres. (The acreage at the higher school itself I judged to be not more than ten acres.) The sheds out back contained the shops, such as a carpentry and a masonry shop, a paint shop, an electricity shop, a pipe shop and so on. I asked Madame Roos if we could step inside the masonry shop as I saw a class was going on. The teacher of the class, Mr. Arch, welcomed both of us and introduced us to the class, which stood and welcomed us to the school. I found this surprising but nevertheless it made me feel very welcome. Mr. Arch, a wiry fellow of about forty with blue eyes and sandy hair, was giving a lesson on the building of fireplaces. I knew from my own experience how tricky fireplaces could be so I was interested in following his lesson. He seemed to know exactly what he was doing as he explained the importance of the throat and the angle of the fireplace. The youngsters were working with stone but were not using cement in this lesson. He was simply showing them how to lay it out and to get the right pitch, and they would actually build the fireplace the next day. Mr. Arch explained to us that the school was building a summer kitchen for the canning from their garden and this class would build the fireplace. The class consisted of four teams of students and I was impressed again with the level of attention and decorum that was maintained by their leaders.

As we walked out of the class and on to the school grounds I could see that the carpentry class was busy setting up the summer kitchen. Madame Roos explained that they tried to make the training in the school as close to real life as possible. I asked her where they got their teachers. She said that Mr. Arch, for example, was a mason who gave two days a week to teaching the masonry class as his community service. Other people of Ponyo City who were in the trades would take on the teaching, and they selected those who were the better teachers. I asked her how good the preparation was, whether or not a youngster, for example, could go from a masonry class at Bay Higher School into the masonry trade. She said that was exactly the purpose of those classes. Not only did every student learn the academic skills to go as far as he wished but he or she was also required to learn a practical skill such as those that we had seen. I noticed that there were girls and boys mixed equally in the masonry and carpentry classes I saw. There were also classes in cooking, clothesmaking, certain kinds of office work, gardening, farming, and animal care, Madame Roos told me. The students could elect to pursue any one of these skills with more intensity. When they finished their training in the higher school, they were prepared to go out as apprentices to an existing carpenter or mason or chef or in whatever skill they chose. I asked what happened to those who decided to leave school at age twelve. She replied they would be attending these classes at the higher school and they also came for their citizenship classes. I asked then, "All children in Prire really go on attending school, isn't that right?"

"In the sense that they continue to take classes in their occupation, that is correct," Madame Roos replied, "but those who elect to go to work are not required to go on with their academic studies at this time. They can pick them up any time later if they wish, of course, and most do go on with some form of academic learning throughout their life."

"How do you manage the time schedule if they go to school and also work?" I asked.

"We'll, it's not very different from the schedules of everybody else in Prire," she answered with a smile, "We all split our time between our occupational job and our community service job. Those young people who want to go to work at age twelve go to school two days a week and work at their occupational job the other three days. We decided long ago that there was nothing holy about five days on the occupational job."

We came back through the school and I saw that on the right side were some athletic fields and beyond them some barns where I assumed the livestock

186

was kept. Classes were in session inside the school and we stopped at the door of several of them where the academic subjects were being taught. I saw classes in mathematics, literature, history, science, and they looked essentially like our classes. I would say that the level of attention was a good deal higher than in our high school classes but I saw no major differences in the equipment or methods of teaching. In the area which I would have called the library but they called a learning center, I saw the usual arrangement of books plus a number of learning devices which were not familiar to me but which were self-instructional and I gather were aimed at either increasing skill or helping a youngster who had a problem in that skill. Off to one side were individual cubicles for independent studying. Here too I was surprised to see how much responsibility the seventeen- and eighteen-year-olds had. There was a teacher or a librarian in charge but the seventeen- and eighteen-year-olds handled the materials and acted as advisors to the younger children who were coming in to use the center. We passed by two doors that were closed and I was told that these were the citizenship classes and that an important examination was being held now. She explained that in Prire citizenship behavior was no more taken for granted than was parental behavior or any other kind of behavior. Every student was expected to learn about Prire, how it was run, its history, and how its problems were being met. Annual examinations were held in citizenship for all of the young people in Prire up through age eighteen. I asked Madame Roos of what importance were the citizenship examinations. She told me they were quite important. It was only one kind of information about each young person, she said, and their behavioral record was more important. Nevertheless, their knowledge about Prire was a necessary part of their citizenship training. I asked her what happened if one flunked the test. She said that the students were required to repeat the course until they were able to pass that particular examination. I asked her if students got As and Bs and Cs, and if so were there different kinds of rewards? She said they didn't use that kind of a grading system, but that students who did exceptionally well were given commendations in citizenship which gave them priority in their choices for their national service.

Walking around the school I noted that I saw no graffiti and that the buildings seemed in excellent repair. I commented on this to Madame Roos most favorably and said that I was impressed with the care that seemed to be taken of the school property. She asked me if this was a problem in my country, and I said that it was a very serious problem in some places. She said that they had not had that problem since she could remember. What they had done was to make care of the school property an important behavior which was rewarded with points and privileges. Since the children themselves took care of the school plant, she added, she thought they were less likely to deface it. She also thought that the team leaders had a great influence on the conservation of school property.

"Our young people in Prire really are wonderful," Madame Roos remarked. "We give them a lot of responsibility as I'm sure you've seen, but they respond so well to it. I think it is good for young people to be given leadership, don't you?"

"Yes, I do," I answered. "I am impressed with

what I have seen. I think we make a mistake in my society to keep our young people so dependent for so very long. I remember reading somewhere that Nelson was captain of his own ship at seventeen and I've often thought of that when I have visited our own high schools."

"Yes, we think that young people can do so many things when it is asked of them," Madame Roos responded, "but, of course, we feel that way about old people too. You probably have noticed that older people are an important part of our life in Prire and we feel that they make an important contribution to our communities."

"Yes, I have noticed," I answered, "and it seems to me to be a good way to use the skills and experiences of older people."

"We think so," Madame Roos said. "We feel our older people are one of our great national assets."

She asked me what else I would like to see at the school. She didn't want to hurry me but we had to watch our schedule. I asked if I could talk with a few students if time permitted. She said I certainly could and we headed for the principal's office. Madame Ross introduced me to the principal, a Madame Jin, who was a most attractive woman in her late forties, quite thin, with short, curly hair and a very friendly manner.

"Of course you can," she replied to my question, "I'd be delighted to have you talk with some of our students. Who would you like to talk to?"

"I think I'd like to talk to some of your older students, some of your team leaders," I answered. "Would that be possible?"

"Of course that would be possible," she answered. "Why don't I just find out who's free right now and you can talk to them and use my office here."

She turned to the microphone near her desk and over the public address system asked if there were any team leaders free right now who could leave their team. She said that they had an important visitor to Prire who wanted the opportunity to talk wih some of the people at Bay Higher School. She reminded them to be sure that whatever team they were working with had enough to do for the next thirty minutes and to turn their team over to their assistant.

"We think this is a good practice for our leaders," she said. "We will often pull them in for a conference, a few at a time, and have their assistants take over so that we know that they are training their assistants in responsibility."

Within five minutes there were about twelve young people in her office. After they all had gathered, Madame Jin described my background and my visit to Prire, in which they seemed very interested, and explained that I wanted the opportunity to talk with some young people and that she was pleased that she could arrange it. Then she and Madame Roos left the room, which I thought was very considerate of them. I was immediately bombarded by questions from the young men and women wanting to know what I thought of Prire. I told them that I was very impressed with what I had seen, but that it was so different from my own society that I had not had a chance to digest what I had experienced. I tried to explain to them how hard it was to come such a long distance and have so many new experiences. They seemed to understand this, but I thought that they were particularly happy that I liked what I had seen in Prire.

"I am interested in the teams you have in schools which is a new idea to me," I said. "Do they really work? Do you like being team leaders?"

There was a chorus of answers, all affirmative.

"We like the teams," one boy answered, "because it gives us a chance to move up. I remember when I started out as a thirteen-year-old on a team and I thought I would never get to be leader, but you do. I think it's good training for citizenship."

"I think it teaches you responsibility," answered a girl in the corner of the room. "I notice how we all have changed since we went through being an assistant, and then finally a team leader. The little kids, they look up to you and they expect a lot of responsibility and good judgment from you. It puts you on your toes."

"Sometimes it's a pain," said the girl next to her. "I don't much like the business of having lunch with my team. Some of those little kids want to fool around too much. But they're good kids and they listen to you."

"What about the skill training? Do you think you really are learning how to do carpentry, or masonry, or farming, or whatever—or is it just pretend-leaning?" I asked.

"Oh, it's learning all right," said the boy on my left. "We learn a lot, and its very useful too. I help at home doing things I couldn't do before."

"Mr. Arch says I'm just a natural mason," said a girl sitting on the floor in front of me. "My mother says I inherited it from her father!"

"We really learn a lot," said a boy in the back.

"I've learned a lot about gardening. In fact, I've taught my father a few things."

They all agreed on the usefulness of what they learned and on the practicality of it. I gathered in talking with them that some of the teachers were better than others, but of course I expected that. I asked for a typical schedule and found out that they were not very typical at all. I gather that they all took the academic subjects if they were in school full-time, including advanced language and the study of another culture. They had all spent a year in another culture sometime during their higher school years. I asked them if there ever was a student who wanted to stay in the other culture and not come back to Prire. They said that it happened rarely, but that such a decision was fine. I then asked them what they would be doing next year since this was their last year in the higher school. About a third were going on to the university in the fall, another third were going straight to work. I asked them if they would finish their education here or whether they planned to do more studying later. Nearly all said they planned to go on to school after national service or a few years later. This confirmed what I had been told about education being a life-long program in Prire and not just a program for the early years of adulthood.

Then it was their turn, and my heavens, the questions they asked me! They asked me how students in our school liked their school, what they did after higher school, what they studied, how they dressed, what they did for their national service, and I had a hard job on my hands to explain to them how such things operated in our own society. They thought it too bad we did not have team leaders in our schools. They said they thought it must be very demeaning to be a young person in our society without any responsibilities. They could not understand why we did not have a national service. They were strongly of the opinion that young people should give two years to their country. They all thought it was a great experience to be on your own and away from your family at that time. They also said they looked forward to their national service because they had heard great stories about it from their older friends. They said that you did work hard, of course, but you met different people from all over Prire and you got to see a lot of the country and to broaden your horizons.

I saw by my watch that time was running short so I thanked them for their kindness and their time and they in turn thanked me for the opportunity of meeting with them.

Madame Roos and Madame Jin asked me how I enjoyed the meeting and I told them very much indeed, that it was one of the high points of my visit. They both seemed pleased with my response. Madame Roos then took me by the arm and said we simply had to leave or we would be way behind. We had quite a drive to reach a national service camp by 5:30 which was up one of the streams feeding Lake Ponyo. We thanked Madame Jin for her hospitality and off we went, with Madame Roos driving what I thought was a little too fast by Prire standards, but she was determined to keep to our schedule.

We left the road that ran around Lake Ponyo and turned right up a sandy road through some pines. We must have driven a mile and a half or two along this road with a stream on our right until we came to a clearing which led into some fields. To our left was a series of buildings, to the right was what I took to be a recreation area that ended at the stream. Madame Roos explained that this was a national service camp and that this particular one was there to improve the ecological resources of its assigned region. There was no one in sight outside, which bothered Madame Roos, but she decided that they were probably getting ready for supper as she knew they were expecting us.

We walked through the door of the main building, and then into a back room, which was quite a large hall. The buildings here were even simpler than those I had seen in other villages. They were faced with board and batten siding, roughly finished inside, but sturdy and as far as I could see well-built and certainly cleanly kept.

As we walked into the main hall we found out where everybody was. Young men and women were busy decorating the hall with colorful banners, others were putting flowers in vases around the tables, and more were involved in some activity on the stage at the end of the hall. Madame Roos located the two adults and introduced me to them. They turned out to be Mr. and Madame Chub, who were the directors of the camp. They were in their late thirties or early forties. Mr. Chub was a short, stocky fellow, very muscular looking, with a barrel chest, and his wife was the exact opposite, small, thin and frail-looking.

Madame Roos asked about the activities. Mr. and Madame Chub explained that the young people had planned on having a party that night and were going to put on some skits. He said they had not planned this for my arrival, in case I thought that, but had been planned some two weeks ago. It began as a birthday party for members who happened to have a birthday that day, but they decided to turn it into a general party because they had just finished a project on the brook. I asked about the project and was told that I'd have a chance to see it before dinner. Mr. and Madame Chub checked with several of the older people there—by older I mean perhaps twenty-two or twenty-three as the age range was only eighteen to twenty-four in these camps. They left some instructions about matters and then took me and Madame Roos on a walk down through the recreation area to the brook and then northward up the stream where there was a small footpath.

Mr. Chub explained that the project they had been working on was the restoration of the stream to make it more capable of producing fish and holding them in the waters. This was primarily a trout stream. He invited me to test the water and it was quite cold. The campers had built a series of holding dams along the upper reaches of the brook which were quite ingeniously constructed. They had made maximum use of trees in the area and of rocks in the stream so that it had a very natural look. They had formed a number of pools, both small and large, for quite some distance. We only walked perhaps a mile, but he said the project continued on for another three miles.

I asked Mr. and Madame Chub how the work was organized. They explained that there were work teams. I immediately asked if these were like the teams I had seen in the schools that day. They said that they were like them in many ways but that in the service camps, each person belonged to two different teams. One was a work team and one was a house team. The work team was for working on whatever project was at hand, and the house team was for meeting community responsibilities. The campers were organized so that they lived in a cabin with their house team. The idea was to give people at this age a chance to be exposed to at least two different peer leaders. The leaders were all in their twenties and were in their second year of national service. Madame Chub explained that one of the major responsibilities of the directors of a camp like this is to take great care in the organizing of the house and work teams to make sure that young people are getting good models in their leaders. I asked if friction ever occurred and they said it did, as one would expect. I asked what they did about it, and she answered that they generally tried to move people around on the teams, and occasionally they would have to remove a leader because he or she just did not seem to have the capacity for leadership, or was providing a poor model. Sometimes there would be a transfer to a different camp; but that on the whole the system seemed to work quite well. On our walk back to the camp I asked Mr. and Madame Chub how it happened that they were directors of the camp. They explained that they were doing this during their sabbatical. I was surprised at this answer and asked more about it which I will summarize here.

After national service (which takes two years when the young people of Prire are between the ages of eighteen and twenty-four), there is the opportunity for a sabbatical for all adults of Prire. The opportunity for a sabbatical occurs every seven years as it does in the academic tradition. Citizens of Prire can apply for sabbaticals at earlier or later times, according to what Mr. and Madame Chub told me, because this sabbatical of theirs was occuring in the fifth year since their last one. The adults in Prire may take a sabbatical which consists of nothing more than dropping their occupational job for a year and living off their community service income if they wish. This generally leads to a change in occupation, according to Madame Chub, but Mr. Chub did not agree with her. Some people elect to go into full-time community service during their sabbatical which is what Mr. and Madame Chub had elected to do. They had served as leaders in a national service camp during their last sabbatical and had been asked to return in their fifth year to take on this camp because of a change in personnel. I asked them if they did not find that it was upsetting to have to leave their homes and their jobs to come to be directors of a camp such as this.

"No, we love it," said Madame Chub. "We loved our work in the national service camps last time we did it, and we were very pleased to be asked back."

"It gives us a chance to do what we like to do anyhow," added Mr. Chub. "We love this type of life and we like working with young people."

I asked them what their regular jobs were and where they came from. They said they came from an area to the south of Ponyo City. Mr. Chub was an engineer in his occupation and a clock maker in his community service work. He maintained the clocks in his community. Madame Chub was a musician—a violinist—who played with the chamber orchestra in her community and also taught music at the higher school. Her community service job was as director of the drying and preserving of foods in her community. In my brief talks with her I found she had a fantastic knowledge of herbs and wild plants and I wished I had more time to spend with her. She walked me past the kitchen garden and I saw that she had planted a wide variety of herbs. The kitchen garden was very large. She explained that they raised all of their own food, with the exception of certain grains which they got in Ponyo City. But they ate their fresh food, and canned, dried and preserved all unused food. They also raised chickens and three pigs.

We walked back into the hall where we found a great deal of progress had taken place. The decorations were all up and a curtain was drawn across the stage. There was a buffet supper with the campers waiting for us to begin. Mr. Chub made a short introduction as to my background and the purpose of my visit to Prire about which he seemed very knowledgeable. I said how glad I was to be there, that I had visited two schools that day and felt that there was much to be learned from the Prire educational system. I also said that this was my first visit to a national service camp and that I would be very interested to see how it worked. I added that my own children, who were close to their age, would ask me all kinds of questions about their camp so that I hoped that I would go home well-informed. They laughed at that and I could see they were interested in hearing about what children in our own society did.

We then had our buffet supper which was very carefully arranged on the table. There was onion soup, baked beans of some kind that were very tasty, fresh salad, homemade bread, and what appeared to be a stewed corn dish. There was the usual fruit for dessert. It was very plain food, but quite good

and very wholesome. We sat at one of the four tables with perhaps eight or ten of the campers, and
I don't know when I have seen bigger appetites.
They all looked tan and healthy and quite strong. It
was about half boys and half girls—or I should say,
half young men and half young women. Their
conversation was very lively and cheerful. They
talked about having finished the last dam on the
brook. I would have called it a creek because it was
bigger than a brook, I thought. I asked them if any
of them had been fishing after all this work and
they thought that was very funny, because Mr. Chub
had promised one camper who was at our table, a
very avid fisherman I gathered, that he could go out
and fish the next morning as a treat for having completed the dam. He said he was sorry I was not going
to be there for breakfast because he had planned to
bring back one or two trout just for me to taste so
that I could compare them to the trout in my own
country. I was sorry that I couldn't be there because I would have enjoyed that very much.

During the dinner I asked many questions of
the young people at our table. I don't know if they
were especially selected to sit with us but they were
one quarter of the campers so I suppose it wasn't a
bad sample. I asked them many questions about
camp life and again to save time I will summarize
what I heard.

They all were enthusiastic about living in a
national service camp. For many of them this was
the second year of the two-year service and this
was the second camp they had been in. Some had
been in a city camp working in the parks; some had
been on a farm camp; some had been in the southwest in the plains area working on reforestation;

two had worked in Ponyo City itself on a new school being built. Other kinds of service that they told me about included hospital work, prison work, working in schools especially at the higher school level, work with elderly handicapped people, all types of conservation and ecological work, repairing of roads and bridges, repair and building of recreational facilities, and serving in recreational facilities in the preschool nurseries. I gathered that there was a very wide choice of service, and that a young person would serve in at least two different places during the two years. I learned also that there was a definite attempt to move a young person around Prire, away from his or her own community to one or two different areas during service so that he or she would have a better understanding of the different regions of Prire. I also assumed that the intent was to develop more national allegiance to Prire. This particular group came from almost all of the different regions—six—in Prire. They appeared to have become very good friends.

I asked them about the things that went wrong in these camps, thinking back on my own experiences in them. They said that sometimes there was trouble among the members, usually because one member was not doing his or her share. I asked them how they handled it. They said that it was usually handled in a very effective way. The team leader reported on the productivity of each person each day. The person who shirked his work was so reported and as a consequence got fewer points for the day. I asked them what difference the points made, and that made them all laugh. They said that points determined how much you ate, how much time off you got, how much salary was put aside for you, how much spending money you got—in fact, they determined everything while you were in national service. I asked what would happen if somebody just refused to do his share, and they felt that was also pretty funny. They said he would get very hungry! I gathered that they did not think that was a serious problem.

They said that the problems that came up were usually a matter of personality, in which case they would try to make reassignments to teams and sometimes this solved it. Occasionally a young man or woman just did not work out, perhaps because this was the sort of person who simply did not thrive in a close-living community of forty people. I felt that was an interesting idea, because it certainly occurred to me that not everybody would like this. They said that in that case that there were other national service opportunities for those people who liked to live a more secluded life and did not care for a cooperative community. They said this is just like Prire itself, where there were communities where one can practically be a hermit. In this case a person would be moved into a national service job which might be better suited to his level of tolerance for others.

I then brought up the question of what happened with young men and women in the age range of eighteen to twenty-four who were living together and what were some of the outcomes of this group living. They said that there was no group living. Young men and women were not permitted to live together during national service. I asked whether this was a moral stand or the reason for it, as I knew that in Prire nonmarried couples were permitted. They said that living together as a nonmarried couple was permitted after the national service, but not during it. During national service individuals had to be free to be moved around according to needs. It was also the view in Prire that until people had completed the national service, they were really not in a position to establish a mature and stable relationship.

I asked if this meant that, in effect, people could not get married in Prire before they had completed their national service, and they said that that was quite correct. Young people who wanted to get married would elect national service as soon as they could do it, which would be at eighteen, but in any case they could not marry before they were twenty. They also were not permitted to serve in the same camp together during the national service. I thought that was pretty rough on young people and asked them for their reaction, but they seemed to be very accepting of it. They said that marriage in Prire was a serious matter and most people did not marry anyhow until they were in their upper twenties. It was their opinion that it also saved a lot of marriages that would not have worked out. One young girl spoke up and said she was engaged to a young man who was also in national service and that she didn't think it hurt them to wait. She thought they would be sure of their feelings for each other if they had spent the two years not working together. I asked if she ever saw him and she said she did on her holidays and that that was permitted, in fact encouraged, so that they would have the same holiday time together.

Madame Chub remarked that she thought the system in Prire had many advantages because it meant that young people were experienced with other young people before making any final decisions in their lives. She thought it was a good thing for young people from one region to meet young people from another. Moving around during their national service would help them to mix with perhaps several hundred young people during the course of their service. I questioned her figures because it seemed to me that if a camp were like this one, with only forty people in it, and a young person served in two camps, they would only meet eighty people. Madame Chub explained young people coming into national service attended a training institute for the particular job they were going into, and these institutes were run for all the young people in that particular occupation. For example, if a young person were coming into this particular camp, they would have attended a national training institute for ecological work. This would be held at one place in Prire and would take perhaps six weeks and be attended by hundreds of young people. This training institute would be repeated before their second year service, in all likelihood, so that there was a great amount of mixing during the period of service.

I asked Mr. and Madame Chub how directors were found for all these various national service camps. They said that camp directors came from a variety of sources. Some people made it their occupation to be workers in the national service. Others came on their sabbaticals as the Chubs had. Still others would work about half-time in such a camp as part of their community service job. As an example of the latter, there was a biologist from Ponyo City whose community service job was to come to the camp and to consult with them about ways in which the stream could be improved for fish life. I began to see that through the community service jobs, many different skills could be utilized in patterns that were different from ours.

At the end of the supper I followed what I now knew was a Prire custom and we all washed our own dishes. We then moved the tables and chairs around so as to form an audience for the stage. The campers then put on their show which was as funny as any that I have seen. It was a typical take-off of camp life in which they imitated Mr. and Madame Chub, the biologist, and even the fish. There was one very funny scene about how they were trying to build a dam for fish so that the fish would have more fry. The campers playing the fish sang a song whose theme was "But I don't want to be a mother fish." Madame Chub played the piano, and there were two campers who played guitars so they had quite a good musical group. It was all a lot of good fun. Of course, I could not follow the inside jokes, but it broke up the campers and Mr. and Madame Chub a number of times. After the show was over they prepared to have a dance.

At this point Madame Roos suggested we better be getting back as she knew that I had to meet Dr. Bo by 10:00 that night at the railroad station. Dr. Bo had agreed to pick up my luggage and meet me at the train. We thanked Mr. and Madame Chub and the campers for a delightful evening. Madame Roos then drove me back to Ponyo City to the railroad station where I found Dr. Bo waiting for me.

I thanked Madame Roos for spending the day taking me around, and told Dr. Bo that she had been a most gracious and helpful host. She seemed to appreciate that as I knew she thought highly of Dr. Bo. Dr. Bo had my baggage with him and we went to the train where we headed to our sleeping compartment. It was quite a comfortable compartment with upper and lower beds, a small toilet of the type I described before, and a washstand. As we walked through the station Dr. Bo suggested we pick up a basket of fruit which we had done.

After we had settled down and were munching on our plums, he asked me if I had had a good day. I said I'd had a wonderful day and had enjoyed, in particular, talking to the young people at the higher school and at the camp. I said I did not know if they had been specially picked but certainly I was impressed with the general sense of well-being in them, and their very healthy attitudes, as well as their joy in living. Dr. Bo said he very much appreciated that observation, that it was felt in Prire that the degree to which their young people felt optimistic and useful and had something to look forward to was a very important sign about how healthy Prire society was. I said I agreed with that myself.

"Your young people seem remarkably healthy to me, I must say, Dr. Bo," I remarked. "I'm sure that there are problems among them, but they don't seem to be different from any I've ever heard before. What strikes me is their willingness to work in such things as a national service camp."

"You mean the work ethic, I suspect, don't you?" asked Dr. Bo.

"Yes, I guess I did mean that."

"We believe in the work ethic, you know," Dr. Bo replied. "We make no bones about it. Until a better principle comes along, we think people ought to work for what they receive, and that means everybody."

"How do you manage that?" I asked. "I gather you don't have any welfare or unemployment in Prire."

"No, we don't have any unemployment in Prire, and we certainly don't have any welfare. We have a few people who are handicapped due to an injury or an illness and they must be cared for, but no matter what the handicap, we find some way for those persons to be useful, to earn their keep so to speak. With some of our older people this is sometimes not possible, but as long as a person can do something useful, we will find a way for him to work in order to receive support."

"How do you manage the unemployment problem?" I asked. "It seems to me that either you must control jobs very strictly or limit your population."

"We have several ways of handling our employment," Dr. Bo answered. "You are quite right that one of them is population. We do control our population growth as you know, and we do projections to see what our population needs will be. But another control that we have over employment is the way in which we handle technological changes. Are you familiar with that?"

"No, I'm not," I answered. "I read a reference to it but I didn't understand it at the time."

"Well, we have a National Committee on Technology. We don't believe that inventions should stop or that people should stop having ideas about how to do things better, not by any means. But when there is a technological invention of some kind, it is always tested for a period of five years minimum. While it is being tested, not only is its effect looked at on the particular process—for example, a better communications system—but all the secondary effects are looked at also. One of these, of course, is employment. We would never let a technology change go through that would result in severe unemployment for some part of society. What just seems like a stupid judgment to us. There is no improvement in communications that would be worth the loss of jobs of many people."

"What sorts of effects do you look for?" I asked.

"We look for the effect on employment, but we also look for the effect on the quality of life and some long-term effects. For example, I have read that in your country that there was a change in the way that you harvested cotton, if I'm correct."

"Yes, that's true," I said.

"And as a result of that, many millions of your black people moved from your plains area into the cities. Is that correct also?"

"Not from the plains area," I replied with a smile, "but they did move from the southern agriculture area where cotton was grown, into the northern cities, because they were put out of work by the change in technology—yes, that part is correct."

"Well, to those of us here in Prire, it seems like a very funny state of affairs. We would have watched that experiment very carefully for a five-year period in a limited area. We would have seen that the coming of that technological improvement would result in the loss of employment to a particular segment of our society. We would have traced what happened to those people, and then we would have made some predictions about the larger effect, and would have decided not to change our cotton process, I'm quite sure."

"You mean you would have kept people picking cotton in the old-fashioned way?" I asked.

"Yes, of course we would," Dr. Bo answered. "Isn't that a lot better than having a huge unplanned migration in your society? Isn't it better than the result upon your cities and the quality of life for everybody involved? Do you think it is a good thing to disrupt people from one way of life to another without giving thought to it?"

"No, I don't, but I can't see holding back technological progress. It seems to me that you can't refuse to improve your processes just because it's going to mean that some people will have to move."

"It isn't just that some people are going to move to the city, Dr. Aldworth," replied Dr. Bo very slowly. "It means that people who have been essentially rural people are thrown out of work, not given training for more city-types of employment, families are disrupted, or so I read at least, they are unable to be self-employed and must go on what you call welfare. That's not just a simple effect at all. Compared with the harvesting of cotton, it seems to me that's a very large effect. Don't you agree?"

"I agree it's a large effect, but I'm a little appalled at the thought that in Prire you would forego technological progress for these reasons."

"I really have to question the term 'technological progress'," Dr. Bo said with what I thought was a bit of heat. "I don't know what you mean by progress if the lives of people go downhill as a result of some technological change. I would wager that the colored people that we were talking about—I believe you call them blacks, don't you?—I would wager that their lives have not been improved. I would guess that their lives were better when they were living a rural life. At least they had a way of keeping their families together if they had a piece of land."

"I don't know about that," I answered sharply. "I think many blacks would disagree that life down on the farm was better than life in the city. For many of them, coming to the cities was a chance to get a better education, and to move up in jobs, in the quality of their lives."

"Just because we monitor technological changes doesn't mean we would not think that education was important to the people in rural areas," Dr. Bo responded. "We are as concerned about the education of people who live off in the Stone River area, for example, as we are with that of the people in Capital City or Ponyo City or the people who live in the plains. We're also concerned about their employment and their ability to use their skills. They don't have to move to Capital City or Ponyo City to have those opportunities."

"I agree with that point, Dr. Bo, I agree with that very much," I answered, "but I don't see how you can turn the clock back. I don't see how you can keep people doing things in an old-fashioned way when there is an alternative that is easier or less expensive to use or does more work in a certain amount of time."

"Again, my dear Dr. Aldworth, it all depends on how you define progress," Dr. Bo replied. "We measure progress primarily by the quality of life that results, not in terms of how much gets produced. If producing more at less cost makes for an inferior quality of life, then we make a judgment against it. We stay 'old-fashioned' if you want to use that term. If progress means that people feel less happy with their lives, if they feel more harassed, less able to control their own lives, less productive, less independent, less resourceful, less useful—then we would say that that is not progress, but a deterioration in the lives of human beings."

"Very true," I agreed, "but it's very hard to measure quality of life. It is a lot easier to measure the cost of producing cotton, for example, or how many units of a product are produced. I can't imagine my being successful in persuading people in our society that something called the 'quality of life' was going to be impaired because of a technological change."

"Perhaps because you haven't taken the quality of life as seriously as you have your production costs?" asked Dr. Bo.

"I think we take it seriously, Dr. Bo," I answered. "I think the politicians in our society take it very seriously because it affects elections. But it's awfully hard to measure it in dollars and cents."

"Precisely," Dr. Bo remarked. "You can't measure it in currency. But don't you take other measurements of the quality of life in your society?"

"Like what?" I asked.

"Like our national census on the quality of life, for example. Don't you regularly take readings on how people in your society view their lives?"

"Not through a census. We have public opinion polls on all kinds of things."

"No," replied Dr. Bo, "I mean a national census every year or two which tries to feel the pulse of how the people in your society react to their lives."

"No, we don't have such a thing. Do you think that it is useful?" I asked.

"Absolutely," said Dr. Bo. "We take it very seriously and many of our decisions are based upon the reactions of the people in Prire to changes we have made. Of course, none of these changes take place, as I have told you, without an experiment of five or ten years ahead of time to determine what the effects might be. But we don't stop there. We pursue it, once a change is put in, to see what happens to people and how they react to things, so that we're always getting feedback on what we are doing to the quality of life. As I said, we take it very seriously."

"Well, it's an idea," I answered slowly. "Maybe it is something I could talk to them about. But I just don't see our Congress appropriating money for a national census on the quality of life."

As I got ready for bed I thought about such a census and the emphasis on the quality of life. I could not see how we could put that into effect in our society. I tried to imagine our government halting technological progress until experiments were made to see what effect they would have on the quality of life, and it seemed to me absolutely unworkable. I thought there was some merit to the idea, particularly in the fields that were dangerous to people's health. But it was hard to imagine that an industry would have to prove over a period of five or ten years that its changes would enhance the quality of life, rather than detract from it.

As I started to drift off to sleep I had images

of how attractive our rivers and lakes might be if technological changes had been monitored before they went into effect. . . . How sweet the air could be and how quiet the sky. . . .

# 6

# Friday, June 22nd

Our train pulled into Shin Village at 6:35, exactly on schedule. It was a glorious morning and I had been awake since 5:30 watching the early light stretch over the land. Dr. Bo and I got our baggage together and stepped off the train into the station where we were to have breakfast. The stop at Shin Village had been planned for me to see some of the industry of Prire. Shin Village was a community not more than an hour outside Capital City in a northwesterly direction and was on the direct rail line between the capital city and Ponyo City.

Outside the station were rows of blooming flower beds, which reminded me of England. Everywhere I looked in Prire I saw flowers and vegetables growing, which of course I enjoyed very much. Inside the station restaurant we sat down for breakfast. Dr. Bo told me that the area of Shin Village was particularly known for its cheeses. Northwest of Shin Village, Dr. Bo explained, was the Lake of the Geese which we had passed in the early morning. We ordered scrambled eggs that were delightfully fresh, fruit, homemade bread, toasted, and instead of jelly I tried some of the local Shin cheese that he had recommended. It was a blue cheese with a creamy texture, rather mild in flavor. Served on the coarse whole-wheat bread, it made a delicious if unconventional treat for breakfast. Dr. Bo had his usual herb tea but I took regular tea that morning. I was beginning to feel a bit tired from all our travels.

Dr. Bo had arranged for the loan of a transit from the stationmaster. We checked our bags with him and drove off. It was then about 8 o'clock and people were walking toward the factories. What surprised me was that the groups were so small. Dr. Bo stopped the transit opposite one plant, which he explained, was a steel fabricating plant. It was not large by our standards with only three or four hundred employees. Again I noticed that there was no black smoke coming out of the chimneys. He said that they had solved the pollution problem a long time ago. Here were made the basic units for their railroad cars and their trucks. We drove on up the same street, a distance of about three or four blocks, and he pointed out a pipe manufacturing plant where steel pipe was made. Again, this was a small factory rather than a large one. I asked Dr. Bo if he would drive me into the area where the workers lived. He said he'd be glad to. We turned a corner and he weaved back and forth for a few blocks until we came to what was now a familiar sight—the inevitable park or square. He said this was one of the communities from which workers came to work in the plants. These homes were simple, one- or two-family dwellings, but each had a yard and a garden. When we went around one block I had a chance to look into the backyards and saw that the gardens were being cultivated and that they were quite deep. I would say that their blocks were twice as deep as ours.

The people walking to work at the steel fabricating plant and the pipe manufacturing plant were dressed as I had seen people all over Prire—in very simple clothes. It was still cool in the morning and they had light jackets on. Both men and women were going to work. The plants themselves, from what I could see from the transit, had some attractive features. There were trees in the plant area, benches set out under a few trees, flowers around the windows, and what I thought were semi-dwarf apple trees in the back toward the railroad siding. The buildings themselves were clean, not sooty and grimy. I saw some trams arrive, discharging larger groups of employees for the plants. Others bicycled and still others walked. The age range of the workers interested me. I saw people as young as fourteen or fifteen going to work as well as people in their seventies, if not older. Dr. Bo explained that that was correct, that the work force was drawn from the whole range of ages from twelve on up.

Dr. Bo then turned right, skirting the downtown part of Shin Village, in an easterly direction. He stopped in front of a pottery plant and he suggested we make a visit inside. He said he had arranged for it to be available to us if I wished to go in, and I was delighted. Dr. Bo asked me if I knew anything about how Shin Village got its name. I said I did not. He said that Shin was the name of a very famous potter who lived about 125 years ago in this area. He had made the pottery of Shin famous all over Prire. This one factory still made pottery in his tradition, and was well-known throughout Prire. We left the transit near the front door and walked into a very unpretentious building, with skylights throughout its full length, which made all kinds of lovely sun and shadow patterns on the floor.

We heard noises toward the back so we walked through, turning right, and went into one of the drying rooms. This was a very plain room, perhaps 40 feet long, with a bare floor and sun pouring in through the skylight. Workers were moving back and forth arranging pottery on shelves for drying. Dr. Bo asked one worker about the process, and he explained that these had come out of the kiln some time ago, but would stay in the drying room for another day before being inspected and packed for shipment. We went back into the main room where we located the plant manager with whom Dr. Bo wanted me to speak. His name was Mr. Ononi, a short, dark, plump fellow with a very jolly smile. He toured us through the room where the pottery was shaped. I was surprised to see how much of this was done by hand. I had expected to see an extensive machine-operated plant. Instead I would say about 90 percent of the work was done by hand. We saw the glazing room where the designs were being painted on by hand with special brushes. In another room new designs were being created. Mr. Ononi was very proud to present his young son to us, who was an apprentice designer. He then took us into the finishing room which also contained their

216

displays. I gathered that people can come directly to the factory to buy pottery.

The display room was the high point of the visit for me. There I saw pottery of all kinds, from simple pottery—what I would call peasant pottery with bright colors—to elegant porcelains and sheer cups through which the light shone when you held them up the skylight. Some were as thin and fragile as could be, others much sturdier. I found the designs entrancing and immediately fell in love with a set of peasant dishes which had a goose design, with a very nice smooth finish to them. Dr. Bo saw that I liked them and he suggested that I might want to take a set back as a gift. I said I would like to very much, if I was permitted to make such a purchase, if I could afford it, and if we could have them delivered to the plane.

I told him I appreciated his kindness, but that I was here in Prire to learn about its ways and I had certainly learned one thing, which was that everyone had to earn what they got and I was not about to be an exception! Dr. Bo thought that was a very funny joke. I pulled out some Prire currency with which I was still not familiar. After a lot of help from Dr. Bo I managed to get the right amount for the dishes. They were not expensive, and I thought they would be lovely for breakfast or for when we had cook-outs. I knew Susan would love them. Mr. Ononi agreed to have them wrapped and delivered to the airport for me the following day. I thanked Mr. Ononi for the visit and told him how much we would enjoy his dishes.

As we went out the door, Dr. Bo said that he had arranged a special visit for me which was not on the official schedule but that he knew I would enjoy.

He drove three or four blocks and stopped in front of a one-family house. He explained that this was the home of one of the lowest paid workers in Shin Village. The husband of the family worked in the pottery plant we just visited and had given permission for us to visit his home at Dr. Bo's request. (I had wondered what Dr. Bo was doing in the back room while I was talking to Mr. Ononi.) Dr. Bo explained that he wanted me to see all sides of Prire and this was one side I really had not seen. It represented, he said, the least prosperous segment of Prire society. This worker was not skilled, but was one who simply moved the carts around in the pottery factory, what we would call an unskilled laborer. He and his wife lived in this small house. Ordinarily, Dr. Bo said, he might well live in a double-house, what we would call a two-family house, but in this instance, they lived in a one-family house. It was a small lot, perhaps a quarter acre—which was a small lot in Prire, however big it may seem to us.

Dr. Bo approached the door and talked to the woman there, I guess explaining that her husband had said it would be all right for Dr. Bo to come and bring a visitor. She agreed readily and we walked into the house. Her name was Madame Tors. It was a simple house, more like a cabin, and not particularly clean although it wasn't filthy. The breakfast dishes were still on the kitchen table and she offered us a cup of tea and a slice of bread. Dr. Bo said he would be very pleased to have some and I thought it wise to follow his example. She showed us the bedroom which was not large, nor particularly well-kept, but adequate, and the bathroom, which was like the baths I had seen in Prire except this one was not kept as well. We had our cup of tea and bread. I was surprised to find both of them excellent. I praised Madame Tors for her very good bread and tea. She was quite delighted. She said she wasn't much of a housekeeper, but she did like to cook, and Mr. Tors was very particular about what he took for his lunch.

She asked if we would like to see her garden and I said I would. We went out the back and almost the entire lot was planted in vegetables with flowers around the border. I was impressed with how much effort and labor had gone into the care of the plants and the flowers. It was clear that one or both of them spent a lot of time gardening. She said her specialty were the berry bushes at the back. Of course, they weren't ready yet this year, but she did have a jar of her best blueberry jam and she would like me to have it. She went down into the cellar, coming back with a jar of the jelly, which I thought was very nice on her part. I told her I would enjoy it very much, and that my wife would like it as well. I asked her if she had always lived in Shin Village. She and Mr. Tors had met during national service and had become engaged and had married as soon as their service was finished. She said he came from Shin Village and his folks had always worked in the pottery factory. Over on one side of the wall was a sideboard, with racks for plates, and she pointed out the attractive pottery plates standing there. Mr. Tors had gotten these at the plant because they had a slight imperfection and she was making a collection of them. She said they only used them for special occasions. Had she known we were coming she would have gotten them down for us to use. Dr. Bo indicated that our time was short, so I thanked her again for her hospitality and told her how much I would enjoy the blueberry jam and we left.

As soon as we had started off, Dr. Bo asked me what I thought of that visit. I said that I thought the house was a modest one, but if this was the poorest household that Prire had to offer, I did not think it was a bad situation at all. I pointed out that they had their own place to live, they had a garden with vegetables, an opportunity to put up food for the winter, and that they seemed comfortably off to me. Dr. Bo replied that this was typical of the level of unskilled workers living in a semi-urban environment.

"I am curious about one thing," I said. "I noticed that Madame Tors was not really much of a housekeeper but the outside of the place was kept up very nicely. I would have expected to see things left around like old toys—well, of course, they don't have any children—they don't own a transit—tires, no they wouldn't have that either—well, old hand tools for the garden, or old cans—"

"I think that you have gotten to the heart of it," replied Dr. Bo. "I am sure if we had that kind of thing available to be left around that it might be, by Madame Tors, or by others. Each family has its own containers for shopping. You are quite right, they do not own a transit, and they don't have children, so they have no toys."

"What about their not having any children," I said. "Is that their decision or is that a Prire decision?"

"I don't know in this particular case," said Dr. Bo, "but I would guess that was a Prire decision that they were aware of when they married right after national service."

"How much education would a fellow like that get in Prire?" I asked.

"He probably left school at twelve, I would guess, and went to work in the pottery factory or one of the other factories around here," Dr. Bo replied. "Mr. Ononi told me he's a very good worker and very careful with the plates, so they value him quite highly. Did you notice the variety of the berries that they had in the back there?"

"Yes, I did, I was so pleased that she wanted to give me some of the jam to try."

"Well, Mr. Tors, according to what Mr. Ononi told me, has as his community service job the raising of the berries and is the man who is the consultant for the berries grown here."

"I would have thought you would have chosen a man from one of your agricultural colleges, a botanist or some expert on berries, not a chap like Mr. Tors," I remarked.

"Well, we go by what works," Dr. Bo answered. "I would assume that Mr. Tors had raised more berries, and better ones, than anybody else in Shin Village, agricultural training or not. Since he produces the best, he gets to be the consultant."

"What does Madame Tors do as her community service job?" I asked.

"You had a sample of it," Dr. Bo replied with a smile. "I knew that before we went there, so that's why I was very quick to accept the offer of tea and bread. She makes the bread for the schools."

"It was certainly good," I said. "She doesn't make it there in that house, does she?"

"No, she uses a bakery in one of the schools, and she trains other people in baking bread. It was an excellent bread, I thought, didn't you?"

We had no more chance to talk because we had to get back to the train by 11:30. Dr. Bo parked the transit, we picked up our baggage from the stationmaster and made the train for the hour trip back to Capital City.

When we started the train ride back to Capital City, I used the chance to ask Dr. Bo several questions about the pottery factory we had visited, and how factories in general were operated in Prire.

"What do you do about unions?" I asked.

"Unions?"

"Yes," I persisted, "unions. You know we have unions in our society which are organizations that represent workers. They bargain with the management of a factory to get them better working conditions and wages. They make contracts and go on strike sometimes."

"Oh yes," Dr. Bo replied, "unions. I have read about them. No, we don't have unions as you describe them."

"How do you protect your workers, then?" I asked. "How do you keep them from being worked too hard or paid too little or fired by their employers?"

"They are protected as long as they are productive," Dr. Bo answered. "We have many different answers to the question you ask. As far as wages are concerned, all the jobs in Prire are assigned a basic rate. These basic rates are established by the Trustees for Human Resources. Working conditions are also governed by a number of different groups, including health conditions, pollution, exposure to dangerous materials and so on. What else do your unions do?"

"Mainly," I answered, "they protect the worker by representing him and his needs against that of management."

"Well, maybe that is where the difference lies then, since the management of a factory is really the people of the same community. In that pottery factory, for example, Mr. Onomi who is the manager has no particular interest in trying to—what do you say? 'exploit', is that right?—the people who work for him because they are his neighbors, for one thing; and secondly, Mr. Onomi is not going to get any more money if he does so. A third reason is that Mr. Ononi works with all of those people in different roles in his community service job. He is dependent on them half the week for other kinds of productivity in the community."

"But why wouldn't your Mr. Ononi just lay down on the job then, if he's not going to get any more money for running that factory?" I exclaimed.

"Theoretically he could," Dr. Bo agreed, "and occasionally it certainly happens. But Mr. Ononi's pay is dependent upon the job he does as a factory manager. We keep records on that as well."

"You mean he wouldn't get paid if he didn't turn out any pottery?"

"Yes, that's correct, unless there was some very good reason for it. His pay is within a particular range that has been set for that job, but what he gets within that range depends entirely upon his performance."

"I don't see how that would motivate anybody to do a really first rate job," I said. "You can't convince me that people are going to work hard for a small difference in pay."

"People will work very hard for small differences

if those are the only differences available," Dr. Bo answered. "Of course, you must remember we do have points and the possibility of working for certain experiences, so that there is a range of rewards other than just the money involved."

"I find that very hard to believe," I answered.

Dr. Bo was silent for a few minutes, apparently thinking about something. Then he asked, "Tell me about your unions. I'm curious about how they work. It seems to me that they must suffer from the problems of short-term rewards, don't they?"

"What do you mean, 'suffer from the problems of short-term rewards'?" I asked.

"If I understand how they operate, and perhaps I do not, would it not be true that the leaders of your unions would do whatever would be needed to be elected the next time?"

"Yes, I think that's largely true. What's wrong with that?"

"That's what I mean," Dr. Bo said, "by short-term rewards. Won't their behavior be governed by the immediate payoff of anything they do for the people they represent?"

"Yes," I answered. "So?"

"Well, then," Dr. Bo said, "I would make some predictions about their behavior, if you would indulge me."

"Predict ahead," I answered, "I'd like to hear what you'll say."

"I would make the prediction," Dr. Bo replied, "that such union leadership would put the most effort into getting immediate benefits for its membership, such as increased pay and better working conditions and whatever benefits you have in your society—they would go for an increase in all of these at each opportunity. Is that prediction correct?"

"That is essentially correct," I answered.

"Then my second prediction," Dr. Bo went on, "is that in the long run such behavior will be detrimental to the factories and industries, or whatever organizations those union people are working in, because those short-term behaviors are going to be against the long-run economic health of those enterprises. The conflict is inevitable, it would seem to me, is it not?"

"What do you mean, 'an inevitable conflict'?" I asked.

"The conflict between the short-term rewards and what the long-term rewards would be. The union behavior that I have predicted would be endless. The union leadership would always want more and more and more in order to get reelected on the basis of having done something for the people it represent. The more and more and more is going to have to be paid for somehow. I would assume the costs of the products in your society would go up, or else a lot of businesses would fail, one of the two."

"That is partially true, I guess," I answered. "I'm no expert on economics, as you know."

"Have there not been businesses in certain areas that have had to stop because the cost of their employees had mounted so, due to the unions?" Dr. Bo asked.

"I suppose so, I really don't know," I answered.

"I have read somewhere that some of your larger cities have had some problems along these lines," Dr. Bo said.

"Yes, you are probably right about that," I

said. "I think that the construction industry also has had such problems from what I have read."

"Here in Prire we would probably see that as a basic conflict, one that would be resolved in favor of short-term rewards, which of course will only lead to long-term disasters," Dr. Bo remarked. "We have a term for it here in Prire—we call such cases Short-Term Blindness. It is very easy to get into short-term traps. It is particularly easy when people want to be reelected every few years. Then their behavior is really dominated by Short Term Blindness, don't you think?"

"I wouldn't go so far as to say that," I replied. "I think you've made a point, but I don't think that democracy is at fault here."

"Oh, you misunderstand me, my friend," Dr. Bo replied quickly. "I was not criticizing your democracy. I was pointing out what I thought were some problems where people must be reelected every so often. It seems to us, from our Prire point of view, that Short-Term Blindness would become an ever-present problem. I just don't see how you ever get any long-term behaviors out of such people."

"I must admit that is a bit of a problem for us," I replied. "How do you prevent that?"

"By some of the things that you have seen this week," Dr. Bo answered. "You know we keep records on the long-term behaviors of our officials. Someone has to reward the long-term behaviors, of course, or we are not going to get any of them, are we? The immediate is so appealing, and the remote so far away. But it is those long-term behaviors that make the difference in the quality of life and we have found it is the short-term behaviors that destroys it."

"Speaking of the quality of life," I said, "could you tell me a little more about the census that you talked about? What kinds of questions do you ask on that quality of life census you spoke about?"

"There are many questions on the census. I'm not sure I can recall any of them exactly for you," Dr. Bo responded. "But we do ask questions about whether the people in Prire feel in control of their lives; whether they feel the same level of independence they did at the time of the earlier census; the degree of loyalty they feel toward the various institutions in Prire; do they feel that they matter in the eyes of their local community organizations; whether they feel treated as human beings in their daily contacts and whether they are afraid of strangers; if they are afraid to go anywhere in Prire; if the quality of foods has been maintained or gone down —all sorts of things like that—I really can't remember them well enough for you, I'm sorry. That is only one of the national censuses that we take. You do understand that, don't you?"

"No," I answered in surprise, "I was not clear about that. How many censuses do you actually take?"

"I've never counted them up, but among the other ones that we do is one that the Trustees for Human Resources put out on the use of skills in Prire. Each person lists—every three years, I think it is —the skills they have or have acquired in the interim, so that we have a national inventory of available skills. This gives us some picture of what we are missing and helps us to encourage young people to take up such skills. We also look at it in terms of whether the skills are available to the community in a broad enough range. It also prevents us from letting skills disappear, something we are very concerned about."

"You mean like horse-shoeing, for example, which has been a disappearing skill in my own society?" I asked.

"Yes, that's one example. Another might be the making of barrels by hand, which we do in some places here in Prire, or some forms of masonry like building a dry wall. These are all important skills and we do not want to see any of them lost, so we maintain a national inventory of all these skills to make sure they're being handed down from one generation to the other."

"What do you do if you see a skill disappearing? Do you order the young people in school to take it up, or what?"

"No, we don't order them to take it up. We would put out a notice that such and such a skill seemed to be disappearing and ask if there are young people or adults that are interested in learning it. We would be very likely to accept a sabbatical application, for example, from a person or a couple who wanted to learn a particular skill if it were needed in their community. They might have a sabbatical granted to them much sooner than the seventh year in order to learn that skill."

"You mean that a person or couple could apply for a sabbatical out of turn if they wanted to learn, let us say, making dry walls if that skill was needed in their community?" I asked.

"Yes, that's a very common pattern," Dr. Bo replied. "We feel it is a good investment for Prire and for the community if they have the talent and interest in learning that skill. We maintain a list of needs for all of our regions. We use short-term volunteers to fill these needs, whether skills or services, that are not being fulfilled. You see, we try to make each community as self-reliant as we possibly can, but at the same time we think that communities should be complementary to each other in the same region. Not every community has to have every skill, or every piece of equipment, or every service. We try to keep a reasonable balance between self-sufficiency and complementary communities. —I see we're getting in to Capital City on time," Dr. Bo ended, looking at his watch.

The train pulled into the station which I was now familiar with and I was not surprised to see that it was exactly on time. Dr. Bo suggested we leave our luggage in one of the vaults at the station, which we did. He guided me over to the park a few blocks from the station to have lunch out of doors. It was another lovely day in June and I appreciated his suggestion. This park, like all parks in Prire, was full of flowers and vegetable gardens. There was a booth over to the left of the entrance where Dr. Bo picked up sandwiches for us and some milk and fruit. These were sold in very attractive baskets which looked hand-woven. We each took our basket and strolled through the park to where I heard some music. We sat down on a bench underneath a beautiful sugar maple, watching from a distance a group of young people who were rehearsing a musical play of some kind on an open air stage. Dr. Bo said that he did not know this group but he assumed it was one of the theater groups in Capital City. I asked him about how drama was handled in Prire. He said there were those whose occupations were in the drama field and who were employed in it. They had theaters throughout the cities, and touring theaters that came to each of the communities. Another method was for people who wished to do community service to do it through their local theater group. He explained that people paid to go to the theaters as they did to concerts. This income enabled them to maintain a production. (The price of theaters that he quoted would be extremely cheap by comparison to our theater. An equivalent price would be 50¢ to $1.50.)

While I was eating my sandwich, which was made with some kind of nut butter and sprouts, really quite good for a prepared sandwich, I looked around the park and noticed that there was no litter anywhere. The flower beds remained intact and were a pleasure to look at. I asked Dr. Bo how they maintained their parks. Dr. Bo explained that this was partly the result of continual education, but he thought that a lot of the credit had to go to the Prire civilian police.

"What civilian police?" I asked. "Who are they? How are they different from your regular police?"

"Look over there," said Dr. Bo pointing, "there is one of our regular policemen standing over there watching that rehearsal."

I looked over and saw a man in a gray uniform eating his lunch and watching the players.

"But where is your civilian police?" I asked.

"Well, you're sitting next to one," Dr. Bo answered laughingly. "I am one myself and you've passed any number of them on our walk to the park."

"You are a member of the civilian police?" I asked incredulously. "Now when would you have time for that, when you are an Overseer of the Future and have so many other responsibilities?"

"I think that you misunderstand what we do as civilian police," Dr. Bo answered. "A person who is a member of the civilian police does not do anything in particular but simply acts as eyes and ears for the regular police as they go about their daily duties."

"What do you mean, 'act as eyes and ears'?" I asked.

"I mean that as I go about my regular duties during the week, which of course brings me into streets and in many parts of Capital City, I act as a trained and reliable observer. If I see something that is amiss or that looks suspicious, I notify the regular police immediately."

"Tell me how you do that," I asked. "I'd be really interested in hearing about it."

"Suppose for example," Dr. Bo replied, "that we are sitting here having our lunch and I see a person tramping in the flower beds, or bothering somebody's lunch basket that's been left on the next bench, or anything of that nature. I would simply notify the regular police immediately and they would have someone here in no time at all, if not the policemen we see right across there at the rehearsal."

"How would you do that?" I asked.

"We carry a small broadcasting unit with us," Dr. Bo answered pointing to his watch. "This watch that I wear," he said, "contains a sending and receiving unit that's very tiny but quite adequate for the job because there is always a police receiver within a mile of any place in Capital City."

"But suppose you saw someone being robbed or hurt or murdered?" I asked. "Would you call the police then, or would you be afraid that you'd be hurt yourself?"

"I don't think we've had a murder in Prire for

several years," Dr. Bo answered, "but we do have fights occasionally. No, I would not hesitate to call the police if I saw a fight. I can do so without drawing attention to myself. I just give my identification number and the police would be right there."

"Then your police don't patrol the way ours do, do they?"

"What do you mean 'patrol'?" asked Dr. Bo.

"I mean they don't ride around in cars—oh, excuse me—I mean in transits or on bicycles or walk around Capital City in the streets, do they?" I asked.

"No, they don't, unless there's some sort of special occasion. We rely on our civilian police to be the eyes and ears and they do a remarkably good job of it. The job of the regular police is to be available for calls immediately. We can get them to almost any place in our cities within a minute or less."

"Within a minute?" I asked incredulously.

"Yes, within a minute," Dr. Bo said. "You must remember our police are assigned each to their own community, so they are not so far away."

"You mean that there would be police assigned to this community?" I asked.

"Yes," replied Dr. Bo. "We're sitting in one of our many city communities right now, and this is their park. This community is called the Fishboat Community and I know you're going to ask me why it's called Fishboat. In the olden days, the fishing boats used to come up the South River to this part of Capital City. There used to be a fish market not far from here, but of course, that's been moved. The police of Fishboat Community would be located right there and it's not that far for them to come."

"Can anyone in Prire become a civilian police officer? Doesn't that mean that you could have some

criminal elements becoming part of your police system?"

"No, not everyone in Prire can become a member of the civilian police," Dr. Bo answered. "Anyone may apply. But again, we go by the record of that person's behavior on which, as you know by now, we keep so many records! If they have been responsible and law-abiding citizens of Prire, they are very likely to become members. It is considered quite an honor, you know. We encourage all of our government officials, both at the community level and at the regional and national levels to be members of the civilian police themselves, so that as they go about their business every day they too will be alert to the behavior in their communities. Some prefer to be consumer officers but I would say most of them have become members of the civilian police."

"What are consumer officers?" I asked.

"Oh, I'm sorry," replied Dr. Bo. "I thought you knew about them. We have very much the same set-up for observation and protection of our consumers as we have with our civilian police. We have people who volunteer to become civilian consumer officers. In their daily activities they watch to see that the people in the stores are fair in what they sell, that they give true weight, do not overcharge, that products are labeled correctly, all those things that mean that the people in Prire who are buying products and services are getting a fair exchange."

"How does that work?" I asked.

"Let me see if I can give you an example," responded Dr. Bo. "Oh yes, now that I think of it, I remember Coco reported someone last week. You'll be meeting her—that is my daughter. She is a consumer officer and if I may be allowed a little fatherly pride, I think she's very good at it. She told me that she was in a shop the other day, a fish shop, I think it was—yes, it was a fish shop—and she noticed that the weight on the scale did not look right and she thought that the man was using two sheets of paper to help increase the weight. She said she stepped back and watched several of the weighings until she was sure that this was so. She then called in to the regular consumer inspectors and had one there in a matter of a few minutes. He checked the scale and found it wrong. He also found the man was using more than one sheet of paper."

"What happened to the shopkeeper?" I asked.

"He was not allowed to sell any more fish until the scale was corrected, for one thing, and then he was in court after work that evening."

"What would be likely to happen to such a person?" I asked. "Would he stand trial or be fined or what?"

"No. If the charge were proven correct, and there was some estimate of how much he had been overweighing, he might have to increase his weights by that same percentage for a specified period of time, for example."

"You mean he'd have to give his customers extra weight for a while in order to make up for the cheating?" I asked.

"Yes, that's one likely outcome. We try very hard to make the punishment act as a corrective for what had gone before."

"How many of your people in Prire belong to the civilian police or the consumer officers?" I asked.

"My goodness," said Dr. Bo, "I don't know, I don't remember those figures. But I would say at least 20 percent of our population belongs to one or the other."

"I guess it makes your shopkeepers think twice about cheating anybody if they don't know which of their customers is a consumer officer," I asked, "or do they know?"

"No, they might not know at all, because they would never know which person had called the consumer inspectors. And yes, we do think people will be more honest if they know that they will be observed. It certainly helps, let me put it that way," answered Dr. Bo with a twinkle.

"Do people in one community shop in that same community or are they permitted to shop anywhere in Capital City?" I asked.

"Oh, they can shop anywhere," answered Dr. Bo. "We don't force people to stay in the community as some kind of compound, if that was your impression. We just use a community as a way of organizing our cities. Each city is nothing but a cluster of communities, because we find that the quality of life goes up when people deal with each other on a personal basis, rather than an anonymous one. It ties down responsibility."

"It is an appealing idea," I answered. "It might solve some of our problems perhaps. But I still think it must make for an awful lot of red tape and bureaucracy to get things done."

"Not at all," replied Dr. Bo. "As a matter of fact, you could make a good argument that local communities can be more efficient than larger ones. A small community can get more things done that need to be done, and faster, because the people there live in the community and know each other."

We finished our lunch and returned our baskets to the man at the gate. I noticed that everyone returned their baskets so I assumed that the civilian police officers must be thick as flies in that park.

Dr. Bo had promised me a visit to a hospital. We walked two blocks from the park and went up a few steps to a stone front building. Dr Bo told me that this was the local Fishboat Hospital. He said he had not made any arrangements for us to visit there but he thought that we would be welcome. He suggested that I wait a minute while he went to talk to the manager of the hospital to make sure it would be convenient. He came back within a few minutes and said that we were more than welcome to walk around as long as we stayed out of the areas marked "Against Entrance."

The hospital was quite a surprise to me. There was nothing about it that reminded me of our own hospitals. As I came in the front door I passed immediately into a large living room with comfortable chairs in it. There was a lady at a desk that I passed to get into the room. She seemed very pleasant. I noticed her talking to people who came in who I assume were visitors. I saw no signs around about visiting hours. The building itself was small, I would guess that there were not more than 50 beds in that particular hospital. To the left of the living room was the emergency room. I saw some people bring in a youngster who had cut his head and was looking quite scared. Dr. Bo had returned by this time and, of course, I was full of questions. He explained that visiting hours were not limited but that visitors would have to wait if there were something being done with the patient. The typical community hospital, he said, would not have more than 40 beds. The Fishboat Hospital was specialized in eyes, he

236

said, and might have as patients people from other parts of Capital City who needed help with their eyes. Dr. Bo said that he had been here once when he had gotten something in one of his eyes and had liked the hospital very much.

"Do each of the hospitals in the communities specialize in something?" I asked.

"No," said Dr. Bo, "not necessarily, but for each need that we have in Capital City, there will be one hospital designated as the specialist in that particular need. The others are regular community hospitals."

"Why don't you have centralized and specialized hospitals as we do?" I asked.

"I suppose the same reason that we keep everything in Prire on a small and local scale," answered Dr. Bo. "We find that people are better cared for in smaller hospitals located in their own communities. You see, everybody in this hospital will know everybody else. If you lived in Fishboat Community, Dr. Aldworth, and had to be hospitalized, you'd be taken care of by your neighbors, who would be the doctors and the nurses and the physical fitness specialists and so on."

"I'm beginning to think that in Prire everybody knows everyone," I answered laughingly. "Can't you ever lose your identity in this country?"

"Not very easily I'm afraid," Dr. Bo said. "That is one criticism that's been made of our type of society. People have told us that this is not the country where people can go off and sow their wild oats anonymously. Maybe that is a fault, I don't know, but I warn you if you're going to sow wild oats in Prire, everybody's going to know about it!"

We walked upstairs and I looked into a few of

the rooms. Dr. Bo encouraged me to go in wherever I wanted to, but I didn't feel that I should intrude upon people who were ill. The rooms were small, most of them singles, but were cheerful and with good light. Each room was furnished differently. I noticed that there was a monitoring screen in each of the rooms such as I'd seen at the center at Blue Lake Village. I assumed that each patient could be in direct contact with whoever was in charge. Dr. Bo assured me that that was true. The nurses were of all ages, from sixteen to the seventies, and there were quite a few men who were nurses also. Dr. Bo said that that was true throughout Prire just as there were women who were in various medical specialties. Some of the people would be doing their community service work here, whereas for others the hospital was their occupational jobs.

"Is medical care expensive?" I asked.

"I don't know how to answer that question," Dr. Bo said. "Expensive is always in comparison to something. Our hospitals are not very expensive to run if I compare them to what I've read about in your society, for example. But again, of course, you see many of our people who work here are on their community service jobs, plus the fact we believe in the small units."

"Do people in Prire pay to go to the hospital, or is that furnished them free of charge?"

"There is nothing given anyone free of charge in Prire that I can think of," said Dr. Bo. "We really do believe that people should work for what they get. No, there is a charge based upon how long you stay in the hospital, what kind of service you need, but it is a modest charge that people can afford."

"What about the physicians' and surgeons' fees? Are they expensive also?"

"No, they are not expensive. I think you were told at one point, were you not, that our medical teams are paid on the basis of the health of the people they care for? We would not find it a good plan to pay them handsomely when people were sick."

"If they're not paid when a patient is sick, what makes them come to see them at the hospital or even take care of them?" I asked.

"That is part of their responsibility and again we keep records on that," Dr. Bo answered. "If they failed to give service, that would show up on their annual evaluation."

I was struck by the atmosphere of this hospital. It did have a cozy feeling. It reminded me of one I had visited many years ago which was run by a Catholic order of sisters. People called each other by their first name, including the patients, and it was more like a large boarding house than anything else I could think of. I had no way of knowing whether the health care was adequate at all. I saw nothing that I could make any judgment of, except that the hospital was clean, the patients looked comfortable enough, and the staff impressed me as being concerned about their duties. I did not see staff members standing in the corridors, drinking coffee and talking to each other. I noticed that their contacts were with patients a good part of the time.

After we had finished touring the hospital, Dr. Bo suggested that I might like to go to another part of Capital City, but he would not tell me what our trip was for. I could not imagine what he had in mind. We got on one of the trams and rode up a hill, past another park, and down the hill perhaps thirty or forty blocks. Dr. Bo told me we would get off at the next stop and we did. He took me by the arm and started me down the sidewalk past a number of stores.

"I noticed that you were quite taken with the pottery at Shin Village this morning and I thought you might like to see some of the pottery in these stores. This is a special part of Capital City where china and pottery from all over Prire is brought," he explained.

We went by one store window after another with varieties of pottery, china, and ceramic ware. I was overwhelmed at the sight. I have never seen so many different styles of pottery, so many different motifs, so many different shapes in my life. I picked out two very different cups for Marjorie and Jack. Marjorie's cup had some flowers painted on it that I had seen at the Inn of the Eight Bridges, and Jack's had a duck on it that I thought was a wonderful-looking duck. Knowing Jack, I knew he would like that.

Dr. Bo escorted me another few blocks to a very large hall which was the arts and crafts exhibition hall, according to the sign over the entrance. He explained that here were brought the arts and crafts from all the communities across Prire and that this was a new exhibit that had just been mounted that week. He'd had it in mind to bring me here in any event, but he was delighted we could go by the pottery stores first. I was overwhelmed inside the hall. There was booth after booth of all kinds of arts and handiwork, from old-fashioned crafts to modern ones. Over in one corner an elderly gentleman was giving a demonstration of how to use an old-time ax to cut out a watering trough and a pipe. I was amazed at his dexterity. It seemed to me he used that ax in the way one would an electrical saw. The sign said he was a woodsman from above Ponyo City.

There were all kinds of farm crafts such as spinning and weaving, needlework, quilting, dyeing of yarn; and then there was bootmaking—I hadn't seen anyone make a pair of boots by hand before —and all kinds of leatherwork; silvermaking was a big exhibit in another corner; glass blowing, forging —they even had a real forge set up in the middle of the floor with a big hood over it—every kind of woodworking tool that I could imagine was ex- hibited in operation including shingle-making, which fascinated me. I can't think of a farm skill that was not represented except milking cows or caring for the animals. There were no animals in the exhi- bit. I was impressed with the level of skill that I saw, and particularly when so many exhibitors were youngsters perhaps fourteen or fifteen and old peo- ple in their seventies and eighties. It gave me plea- sure to see these skills being demonstrated at such a high level of competence. Of course, I've always been interested in farm tools and what people could make for themselves. Dr. Bo must have realized how much enjoyment these things gave me because he presented me with a catalogue with pictures of all the different tools and techniques. (That catalogue is one of the treasures I have from my visit to Prire.)

I could not resist purchasing a few gifts to take back with me. Everything was so reasonably priced that I would have liked to have taken two of every- thing, but I did not want to appear to be a glutton, and I had the problem of getting things back to Dr. Bo's house. I finally bought a finely tooled leather diary for Marjorie. For Jack I got a belt with fancy leather tooling on it I know he would be wild about. I also picked up a knife for him which was made right there in the exhibit. It looked very good to me, as though it would hold a good edge.

For Marjorie I found a hand-woven wool hat that I thought would be attractive on her. I had no idea what size she wore but I found a girl there just about her height and we tried one on her. She said it was quite adjustable anyhow. (I suppose she won't like the colors or something. Marjorie is at that age where I'm not sure I can pick things out for her anymore.) For Susan I found a wool sweater that was intricately knitted in a design typical of the Lake Luko region. I also could not resist a set of teaspoons made by a young woman who said she came from near Long Valley, which we had passed through. They were exquisitely designed and executed and I knew that Susan would get a great deal of pleasure from them.

When Dr. Bo stayed behind to watch an exhibit I found an opportunity to talk to this young silversmith and I asked her for her help. I explained that I was staying with Dr. Bo and I noticed she knew who he was right away and seemed very impressed that I was staying with such a distinguished person. I explained to her that I wanted to get a present for him in return for his hospitality, but I knew so little about what would be appropriate. She agreed it had to be something that was just right. She suggested that she walk with me over to the glassblower's booth who was a friend of hers and said she thought that we would find something there that would be appropriate. What she suggested to me, and which I agreed was a fine selection, were a half dozen hand-blown goblets which were exquisite.

The silversmith explained to her friend, a young man in his thirties, that I was buying the present for Dr. Bo. He insisted on picking out the six glasses, which of course he had blown himself, because he wanted only the best to be in Dr. Bo's home. The price was very reasonable—I would have expected to pay two or three times as much for equivalent quality back home—and he packed them quickly for me, which I appreciated because I was afraid Dr. Bo would catch up with me too soon, and then I pushed off into the aisle.

Dr. Bo finally caught up with me at the needlework exhibit which was impressive, but I really don't understand much about needlework. He suggested we go back to the station to pick up our bags if we were to get back to his house by a reasonable hour. He thought I might want to have a little rest before dinner. We took the tram back to the station this time, picked up our baggage and then took the subway back to his neighborhood. It dropped us about two blocks from his house and we were able to manage the luggage without too much trouble. As a matter of fact, I thought Dr. Bo did better than I did. I never got over my surprise at that man's vitality, it was just amazing. He suggested that I rest for an hour and he would expect me downstairs at 6:00.

At 6:00 I went downstairs and found Dr. Bo in his book-lined living room with a woman in her fifties who had the same erect carriage as Dr. Bo, although a little more on the plumpish side, with light hair and those same eyes. Dr. Bo introduced her to me, but I had guessed already that she was his daughter because of the likeness. He introduced her as Coco, which is the family name, and asked me to call her that which I agreed to do only if she would call me Charles. I then presented my gift to Dr. Bo, saying how much I had appreciated his great hospitality to me and that this was a very small way of showing my gratitude. Dr. Bo and Coco both said I should not have done a thing. When they opened the package I thought they were quite pleased with the glasses.

"I hope you bought these at an NVC store," said Coco to me with a joking expression.

"I don't think he knows about our NVC," said Dr. Bo. "Perhaps you'd better explain what you mean, Coco."

"I was teasing you, Charles," replied Coco. "NVC means No Verified Complaint and we try to do our shopping only in the stores that have the NVC sign up for the current year."

"You will have to excuse her, Charles," Dr. Bo interrupted. "My daughter is a little bit crazy on the subject of her Board of Product Standards. She is in nutrition as you know, and she has been largely responsible for extending the work of her board. I'm afraid she'll give you a lecture on it if you're not careful."

"Now Father, I was not going to lecture Charles at all, but I think he should know this part of Prire. It's important for him to take these things back with him," protested Coco.

"I would be interested in having you explain the NVC to me," I protested.

"I will give you two minutes, Coco, and then we

must be going," said Dr. Bo with an indulgent glance at his daughter.

"The NVC system is a way of making our services and stores responsive to customers," explained Coco. "Any customer who finds that a service or a store has provided inadequate products or inferior service, or has been misleading in some way, makes a report to the local Board of Product Standards. Our civilian officers, of course, are always on the alert in checking out services and products. Any complaint that is verified by a consumer inspector is registered against the shop or the service and even one such verified complaint means that they cannot have their sign up for that year. Stores or services that have no verified complaint during the year may put a sign up for the past year. When we go shopping we always look to see if the sign is in the front of the store."

"It is taken very seriously here," added Dr. Bo. "People hate to lose their NVC sign because it means that they will lose business. As Coco said, we try to give our business to those stores and services that show the sign because we feel that we should reward them for their good relations with customers."

"Well, that certainly does explain a mystery to me," I replied. "I had seen that sign in some of those stores in the pottery area where we were this afternoon and I'd wondered what it stood for."

Dr. Bo picked up the glasses and put them on the mantle where he thought they would be safe, and then he turned to me and said, "We have a surprise for you tonight. It is really Coco's surprise so I'm going to let her tell you about it. She was sorry not to have seen you when you flew in the first day, but she has done some research and has come up with an evening that is designed to give you pleasure."

"I hope I am right, Charles, in thinking that you love music, and especially opera. Am I correct?" asked Coco.

"Yes indeed, you are, Coco, but I don't know how you knew about it," I replied.

"That was part of my research!" she laughed. "I had some of my friends at the university do a little checking on your background. We found out about this, so we have planned an evening that I hope you are going to like. I think Father has shown you enough serious things in Prire. We thought on your last night here we should do something that would be particularly enjoyable for you. Here is our plan. First, we'll go to a restaurant because I don't think Father's taken you to a single one, has he?"

"He took me to the Inn of the Eight Bridges, Coco, which I thought was the most wonderful inn I have ever been to."

"Yes, that is lovely," Coco answered, "but here you are in Capital City, and it's your last evening, and so we are going to take you out to our favorite restaurant. We want you to meet some people. You'll be meeting Mr. Senius who is one of the Overseers of the Arts and Madame Geara who is our best-known singer in Prire—"

"Oh, I have heard of her!" I exclaimed. "It will be wonderful to meet her."

"I'm glad that you are so pleased," Coco said. "And there will be Mr. Lan, a very able painter and Madame Threet, who is a very well-known composer. And then after dinner we are going to hear one of Madame Threet's operas. It will be a very important time also for Madame Geara. I'm sure she's going to tell you about that when you see her," said Coco. "Madame Geara is not likely to keep it a secret, is she, Father?"

"No, she's not, Coco, I'm sure she'll tell Dr. Aldworth all about what is going on this evening before we get to our first mouthful."

They both laughed at the thought of Madame Geara and her talkativeness.

"There's only one thing," Coco said looking at me anxiously I thought. "We do hope that you like fish. Do you?"

"I happen to love fish," I said quite honestly.

"Good, everything is settled then. Now, we have a transit for the evening and we'll meet them there. We're going to take you to what Father and I think is the best restaurant in Capital City. Sometimes I think it is the best restaurant in all of Prire."

We went out the front door and into the transit, which Coco drove. We passed around a large park which Dr. Bo explained was the park around the Capitol itself. It was a huge park, it seemed to me —because we took a long time to get around it. I wondered why we didn't drive through it. Dr. Bo explained that no cars were allowed in the park at all, that in fact there were no roadways except for the maintenance trucks. We drove then to what would be the east side of Capital City, over the South River. Just on the other side of the river Coco parked the transit near a high wall. We got out and followed the wall up to a large wooden door over which hung a crude wooden sign that read "Old Wharf Inn."

As we went in Dr. Bo told me that there had been a wharf here at one time many years ago and that the inn took its name from that. Coco spoke to the manager, who knew her, and we were led to a table in the corner overlooking the garden. As we sat down, Coco explained that she had chosen a table inside rather than in the garden because we would be able to hear each other much better here.

We had not been seated more than a minute before our guests arrived, almost in a group. I picked out Madame Geara before she was introduced because she had to be either Madame Geara or Madame Threet and I decided that Madame Geara looked much more like an opera singer. She was a very handsome woman, quite tall, with a proportionately large frame. Her height and her excellent carriage made her seem to be just the right proportions. She wore her black hair high on her head so that she really was well over six feet. Many people in the room turned to look at her as she came toward our table. She threw her arms around Coco and kissed her and then Dr. Bo. Clearly they were great friends. She shook my hand warmly, hoped I was having a good visit in Prire and said they all had a special treat in store for me that night.

"You can't imagine what a wonderful thing we're going to see tonight," she said.

Dr. Bo winked at Coco so I knew that they had won their bet.

"We are going to hear Belle's opera which is absolutely wonderful, but even more—perhaps Coco has told you? No? We're also going to hear the debut of my own Lee who is going to be absolutely sensational, I guarantee it."

"That sounds wonderful," I murmured not really following what she was talking about but it sounded like a grand evening.

"Charles does not know Lee, Gigi," Coco said to Madame Geara. "Lee Solonay has been a very good friend of Gigi's for years, in fact, her protégée, and you cannot imagine how much Gigi has done for her. Tonight Lee is having her first real part in Belle's opera. She has the lead and it's her opening night so it's a very special occasion for all of us. We're very fond of Lee and think she's very talented."

"Talented!" snorted Gigi. "She's not talented, she has genius. There's a big difference between the two, Coco."

"I'll stick to my statement," said Coco. "Right now she has talent and in time she will be a genius, I think. You have genius, Gigi, not talent."

"Oh, fiddle! What you mean is I was born with the right lungs and larynx and that's just a piece of good luck," retorted Gigi.

"Not to mention the hard work, the self-discipline, the training, the studying, the acting lessons and the voice lessons and the language lessons —I suppose none of those make any difference, do they?" Coco teased her.

"Oh, of course they make a difference," replied Madame Geara, "but if you want something badly enough you just work at it, that's all."

Mr. Senius had come across the room. The room itself was not too impressive. It looked like most fish restaurants, with fish nets on the wall and aquatic decorations. The tables were covered with what looked like a shiny white canvas which seemed to be waterproof. There were shells here and there. It was very clean, however, and there was very pleasant chamber music coming from somewhere on my right. Mr. Senius was in his sixties and an Overseer of the Arts. He was extremely thin, about six feet tall with a white goatee and a very ascetic face. He welcomed me cordially and hoped that I was having a good visit in Prire which I assured him I was.

Mr. Lan appeared next, the painter, I remembered. He was an especially attractive person in his mid-forties with sandy hair and blue eyes, a boyish face and the most charming smile. He greeted me warmly as though we were great friends and made me feel comfortable immediately. Finally Madame Threet arrived looking a little dishevelled and harassed, not surprising in view of what she must have been going through. She was a short women in her fifties, with her hair up on her head, but it was flying down around her neck also. She had vivacious brown eyes and a warm smile, and simply bubbled over with enthusiasm.

"We have just finished rehearsing this very minute, my dear," she said to Coco, "and you must excuse me for being a bit late. I think we have things under control for tonight and it's going to come off splendidly. Your Lee is doing a simply marvelous job," she said to Madame Geara.

"I knew she would, I knew she would," said Madame Geara. "That girl is going to be really something."

"I think she is, Gigi," replied Madame Threet. "She's got the will and she's got the talent and she's got you. I don't know what else she needs."

"What she needs is a bit of luck," answered Madame Geara quickly. "Don't ever forget that. You

250

can have everything else, but without a bit of luck, you're not going to make it. I know."

"You would have made your own luck, Gigi," said Mr. Lan quietly.

"She would have called up the office in charge of good luck," added Madame Threet, "asked them where her portion was, and told them she wanted it delivered tomorrow!"

There was a lot of joshing of Gigi after that while we were ordering our dinner, but I could see they were all very fond of her and well aware of her determination. She took it all very good naturedly. I was surprised at how modest she was about her own abilities. I knew of her reputation, which was enormous, but I had never dreamed that I would have the opportunity to meet her. Only two of her records were available in our country. I had them both, and had played them so often that they were in poor shape. I thought she had as fine a voice as any soprano at the present time.

I let Dr. Bo and Coco steer me through the menu. The first course was a huge bowl of salad, in which everything was so fresh it seemed to have been just picked from the garden. Coco, who was sitting on my left, noticed how much I was enjoying it.

"Father always teases me about the salad here at the Old Wharf Inn. He says I make him come here because the salad is my favorite nutritional meal."

"I don't know much about nutrition," I said, "but it's a wonderful way to start a meal."

She went on to explain the nutritional elements of the salad, about which she seemed very knowledgeable. I learned that she was the head of the nutrition department at Capital University. I was surprised when she told me that her community service job was to teach painting. She was helping to supervise a mural being installed the next week in one of the buildings on the edge of Capital City. I discovered she was divorced, with two grown children, a son, who was in biology, and a daughter who was a writer and lived in the City of the Plain. I learned from her that the son was the advisor to the national service camp I had visited near Ponyo City. I now realized that Dr. Bo's business of that day had been to see his grandson. I asked about her daughter, who was trying to establish herself as a writer and was going through the usual difficulties faced by young writers. Coco thought she was going at it the right way and was very determined. I asked about her daughter's community service job, because I had become accustomed now to realizing that one had always to ask two questions about what people did. Coco said her daughter was a beekeeper and was in charge of producing and retailing honey in her community near City of the Plains.

Everyone ordered a different first course, so that when the waiter brought the dishes it looked as though we had a piece of everything that grew in all the lakes in Prire, and in the ocean as well. For me they had selected a dish made with their local oysters. It had been so long since I had eaten oysters that I was hesitant to try them for fear of pollution. They assured me that they were absolutely safe. These oysters had been steamed and then put back on the shell and seasoned with a sauce of fennel and crumbled cheese. They were absolutely delicious. I had twelve of them and I think I could have eaten a dozen more, but I did not give myself the opportunity. With our dinner came an excellent white wine, from the Ponyo region and for dessert we had ice cream, made in the restaurant, from real cream and eggs.

I was asked several times during the meal if the food measured up to the kind of meals we had in our country. They asked me what a restaurant similar to this would be like. I said it was far better because much of our food came long distances, and therefore was not so fresh when we got it. They did not understand why we did not grow our food around our cities and in the local areas. I do not think my explanation was very satisfying to them.

I shifted the conversation around to the arts because I felt it was a wonderful opportunity for me to learn about the arts in Prire from this group. Dr. Bo explained to them that I was always full of questions and that they should be able to eat and answer questions at the same time. I will summarize what I learned about the arts in Prire.

The arts are taken very seriously, as seriously I think as any occupation or industry. Children may elect to go into the arts at age twelve as they would begin any other occupation. They can wait and enter their chosen field after college training, or advanced training, but the opportunity is open for an apprenticeship very early. I asked a number of questions about how artists supported themselves. There were a variety of ways, Mr. Lan said. He described his own experiences as a young man in his twenties trying to find his own style. He had found it very helpful to live off only his community service job, which took up about 2½ days a week. He said this was by no means fancy living, but one could exist on it, as he had done, in a community not far from

Mountgate. He said this gave him the time he needed to paint and to find his own way, but without starving. He said it had also been helpful to be in a community of artists because he learned a lot from seeing other people work and from talking with them. I gather that this opportunity was open to anyone who wanted to pursue an art on a full-time basis. The community service job would always give them enough to eat and get by on. His community service job, by the way, was as a house painter. I thought that was rather funny.

There were regular occupational jobs open to artists of all kinds, as musicians, painters, sculptors, choreographers, dancers—in the community or cities where there are a number of companies available for the performing arts. Artists such as painters and sculptors—and other nonperforming artists—can earn a living at their art in a number of ways. One way is to submit works to their regional art shows which occur twice a year. Any art work that is accepted for the show carries a payment with it so that one is paid just for the acceptance. In this way one can earn a small living from having works accepted in the regional shows. And there are many other opportunities. All the community-owned buildings commissioned paintings and sculptures for their rooms and their gardens. These were competitive. Anyone could enter a proposal.

In addition, there were teaching jobs in the universities. Mr. Lan said that he made quite a comfortable living because he was fortunate to be asked to do a number of commissions for the community-owned buildings in Prire. I was curious about this system because it seemed to me there would be an oversupply of paintings and sculptures that were on the theme of community-owned buildings. He told me that this was not so, that the community-owned buildings commissioned the paintings, but the paintings could be on any subject. They felt it was important to have paintings hung on the walls of state-owned buildings and to have sculpture in and around those same buildings. The money came out of community funds. It has been a long tradition in Prire, he told me, that the community budget include items for the arts and for aesthetic development. I asked whether these appropriations would not get cut when a community was strapped for funds. He said that they were very rarely cut, because in Prire a lot of value was placed on the arts. It would be much more likely, he said, for some other service to be cut which people would then supply out of volunteer labor. As an example, he told me that in Capital City, which of course is the largest city in Prire, there were twelve ballet companies of which the one we were seeing tonight is considered the foremost, innumerable neighborhood acting companies, and he had no way of estimating the amount of music. He doubted anyone could count the number of chamber music groups there were.

I had a chance to speak with Madame Threet a little later during the meal. I was surprised, although I did not tell her, to see a woman composer because that is so unusual in our country. I was interested in her training, which she described. She had started out as a pianist but in her teens had decided that she wanted to be a composer rather than a performer. She had studied with two or three of the better known composers in Prire, whose names I did not recognize, then at the advanced school of music in Capital City which was part of Capital University. While she was at the advanced school, she had many opportunities to write music and have it performed, which she thought was the best kind of training for a composer. She told me that even now she often goes to the performances of the advanced school to hear the work of younger composers. She said she finds it very invigorating to hear what young people were doing these days.

I asked Mr. Senius about the role of the Overseer of the Arts and although I did not have very much time to talk with him, I surmised that this group's influence was very strong throughout Prire. He told me that in Prire it was felt that the arts added very much to the quality of life and were therefore one of the things on which they put a high priority. I thought this was quite admirable, although I never did understand the financing of it. Of course, my bias toward music was evident and I was glad to hear that so much music was available to everyone. I asked Madame Threet what we would be hearing this evening and she said that I would have to wait and hear for myself. She said it was a very simple opera, based on Prire history, but "quite popular" and that I should not expect a great deal from it. I thought she was being overly modest. She was not going to conduct the opera, as she thought the conductor at the house was doing a fine job. She would just sit in the audience and try to relax. I thought how hard it must be for her to sit there and watch people bring her own work to life.

Madame Geara was getting nervous, looking frequently at her watch, as was Coco, and soon they had us all gathered up and off we went in the transit with Coco driving a little casually for my taste. We went up one side of the park toward the Capitol itself, already floodlighted in the June evening. We turned left off Capitol Plaza into a second smaller plaza where the opera house stood. We were able to park the car within two blocks and walked across the plaza to the opera house.

This was the most elegant building I had seen so far in Prire. It was made of white stone and looked the way an opera house ought to look—impressive, as though it contained great sound. Madame Geara had arranged for us to have a box in a wonderful location. I had to pinch myself to make sure it was all real. Here I was, just another music fan, sitting in a box with Madame Geara at an opera by Madame Threet and hearing the debut of what promised to be a fine new voice.

The opera turned out to be quite a surprise to me. Madame Threet had suggested that it was just a light musical comedy. Instead, as I learned from the program notes, it was based on an episode of Prire's early history. A long time ago, there had been a very bad winter, with much starvation and suffering. A young man became a leader of a group proposing land reform. The opera was about his fight with the existing political powers, and, of course, the inevitable romance. It reminded me more of a Verdi plot than anything else. The music was extremely powerful, the chorus in the scenes of political agitation was well rehearsed, the tenor was good and believable as a young hothead—but it was Solonay's night, without a doubt. She was a bit shrill and tense in the first act, nervous I am sure over her debut. But she had acting talent, she looked the part of a young girl who matures through the three acts into a major political figure. Her aria in the third act was a great triumph. She walked on, against a night scene in the city, alone, with a spot on her, very stark, a symbol of determination and strength while the others have deserted. Her aria, "with hope I am not alone," brought the house down, calling her back for nine curtain calls.

Madame Geara was ecstatic. She told us and everyone in the next box, and the box beyond, what a wonderful future Lee had, and how they must be sure to come and hear her sing again. All the others shared the view that the performance had been splendid. We congratulated Madame Threet on her opera. She was called to the stage, joining Madame Solonay and the rest of the cast in the final curtain bow.

We left our box to go backstage to congratulate Madame Solonay. The feeling in the opera house was high, everyone seemed to be drunk on it. Madame Solonay's debut was clearly a success. There was champagne and wine and congratulations, people smiling and weeping and throwing their arms around each other. It was a very moving scene. I felt fortunate to be a part of it, thanks to my Prire friends. I shall never forget that night.

Finally Dr. Bo and Coco thought we should leave, as it was getting quite late, and we drove home by ourselves. Coco asked me several times if I had really enjoyed the opera. I assured her over and over again that it had been a tremendously exciting evening, one that I would never forget and that I had enjoyed the opera very much, as well as Madame Solonay's debut. I found to my disappointment that she had not made a record,

258

but they promised they would try to get one for me later and send it to me.

I could not imagine a more wonderful evening for them to arrange for me. I had only had a brief word with Madame Solonay in her dressing room—it was a madhouse in there and, of course, she did not know me from a hole in the wall—but I was as impressed by her in person as I had been by her on stage. She had more than talent. She had that determined look about her that made me certain she was going to be a great voice. I thanked Dr. Bo and Coco over and over for the wonderful evening, the dinner, and meeting such nice people. In fact, I said, I had met only nice people since I had come to Prire. I was beginning to wonder where they kept all their unpleasant people. Dr. Bo said they had their share of them, but he saw no reason why I had to put up with that in this brief exploratory visit. He promised jokingly that on my next visit they would see to it that I met only unpleasant people.

I was so excited by the opera that I had trouble getting to sleep. I wrote in my journal, but I kept seeing scenes from the opera—the scene where Madame Solonay sang alone on stage in the third act. I could hear the aria in my head as I went to sleep and that beautiful round tone of her voice, "With hope I am not alone. . . ."

# 7

## Saturday, June 23rd

I must have been more tired than I realized. It was late when I woke up. I dressed hurriedly and went downstairs to find Dr. Bo and Coco out in the back yard looking at their flowers. I apologized for my lateness. They said they understood perfectly and were glad that I could get a little extra sleep. They came in with me to the dining room where Coco had put out some fruit and cereal, which I ate quickly, knowing that time would be short today. Dr. Bo, however did not seem to be in a hurry to leave. I had just finished my breakfast when there was a knock on the door. In came a woman with a young girl and boy. Dr. Bo must have been expecting them. He brought them into the dining room and introduced me to them.

I was completely taken by surprise! It turned out that this was all part of a plan set up by Dr. Bo and Coco at least two months before. The woman, Madame Tashmin, was from the Overseers of the Future, picked by Dr. Bo because he knew that she was about the same age as my wife. The girl was the daughter of a member of the Overseer's Department and the boy, the son of another member. They were picked because they were the same ages as Marjorie and Jack. Madame Tashmin made a very nice speech in which she welcomed me as a guest to Prire. She and Naomi and Josh, the girl and boy with her, wanted to send a remembrance back from Prire to my wife and my daughter and son. She then presented me with a shawl which had been hand-embroidered with these words: "For Mrs. Susan Aldworth, from her friends in Prire who hope to see her on the next visit." I know almost nothing about embroidery or handwork of any kind, but I recognized the care and pains that had been taken to make such delicate designs. I thanked her profusely, told her I was sure that Susan would be overwhelmed by the amount of work that had gone into a present for someone whom Madame Tashmin had never even seen. She told me she had not worked on it alone, several people at the Overseer's Department had worked on it who were skillful at needlework.

The girl, Naomi, then presented me with a small box of hand-carved miniature replicas of the geese that are famous on Lake Luko. I asked her if she had carved them herself. She had, and wanted Marjorie to have them as a present from the girls of Prire. There were four tiny white Chinese geese, two ganders and two hens, cut from hard wood and exquisitely carved. I asked her how she became interested in carving. She said she had been doing it for a long time and hoped to become a naturalist when she grew up. That, of course, struck a warm chord in me because Marjorie had said she would like to grow up to be someone like Jane Goodall and study animals in their natural habitat.

The boy, Josh, then gave me his present, which turned out to be a heavy bracelet of silver with the symbol of Prire on it. I knew Jack would be very proud to own such a bracelet. (I hoped he wouldn't lose it.) Josh told me he had cast the metal himself and had cut out the Prire symbol. It was surprisingly good work, I thought for someone so young. He said his instructor at school had encouraged him to consider silversmithing as an occupation when he grew up. I agreed that he definitely should think of it.

While the present giving was going on, Dr. Bo and Coco stood at one end of the dining room, watching what went on and smiling with approval. After Madame Tashmin, Naomi and Josh had left, with as many thanks as I could possibly express, Coco asked me if I thought that the presents would be appropriate for my family.

"I can't imagine anything nicer," I said. "How in the world did you ever think this up?"

"It was Coco's idea, really," replied Dr. Bo. "We wanted you to have something as a remembrance to take back to your family. Coco thought if we found people the same age as your wife and your children we'd be likely to hit upon the right gifts to please them."

"You really must be psychic, Coco, because you could not have picked anything that would please Susan or Marjorie or Jack more than these. I just don't know how to thank you enough for what you have done."

"We have a saying in Prire," said Coco. " 'To give to another warms the heart.' It has warmed all of our hearts to be able to do this, knowing that your family will have something from Prire to remember us by."

"I think you'd better get your things together, Dr. Aldworth," Dr. Bo remarked. "We'll use the transit today so I can take you out to the airport, but I think we should be leaving."

I went upstairs to finish packing my bags, including the three new presents which I put in very carefully. I got my dictating machine and journals together, brought everything down and put it in the transit which Coco had left out front last night. I said good-bye to Coco, thanking her for all she had done to make my visit so pleasant. I urged her strongly to visit me and my family if she decided to make a visit to our country.

Dr. Bo drove us to the edge of that same park we had passed the night before. He parked the transit just outside the entrance. The park was surrounded by a wall which I had not seen very clearly the night before. We walked inside. The wall apparently ran around the inside of the park, which was very large. On my left I saw young people in groups walking along the inside of the wall, sometimes stopping and pointing to it. There was some writing on it which I could not read from the distance. Dr. Bo was standing over to the right, apparently waiting for me. He went up to the stall near the gate and purchased something. I did not know what to do, whether to wait there for him or what. I finally decided to go over to the stall. Between the stall and the wall was a walkway of tan bark perhaps ten feet wide. The wall itself was about five feet tall, made with stones in a dry wall manner —I couldn't see any cement. There was a marker opposite me. It read "The land was being colonized during this period."

"What does that mean, on the wall?" I asked Dr. Bo. "That wall must have some special significance, I suppose?"

"Yes," replied Dr. Bo, "I thought you'd be curious to see this. Have you read about our 'Life of Earth Circle'?"

"Oh yes," I answered, "Yes indeed. I've come across it in several places."

"This is the 'Life of Earth Circle'," said Dr. Bo. "These young people you see are walking the circle. It is a tradition in Prire for young people to walk it at least once a year."

"You mean they walk around the entire wall? That must be quite a walk."

"It's not so bad," he answered. "It's about 7½ miles around, more or less. Of course, the younger children can't do this. That's why we have the life of Earth Circle in each of our school yards."

"So *that's* what those circles were that I saw!" I exclaimed. "I wondered what they were. Does every school have one?"

"Oh, yes," said Dr. Bo. "Every school has one and children are required to memorize the months and days in the circle."

"Do we have time to walk the circle today?" I asked.

"No, I'm afraid not," replied Dr. Bo, "our schedule is too tight. But I did find a replica of one here for you which I thought you'd like to have."

. Dr. Bo pulled out of his pocket what he had purchased at the stall. It was a bracelet made of several small imitation stones, inscribed in minute writing. Dr. Bo identified the stones for me.

"These first nine are the beginnings of life on earth. Each of these stones represents a month. All twelve represent the lifetime of earth, as though it were a year. This one here is November and that is when the colonizing of the land began. You can always tell the December stone because it is broken into tiny fragments. This one shows the dinosaurs. That would be about the middle of December. This one is the mammals, that would be close to your Christmas. This one is the beginning of primates, on the last day of the year. This tiny one here, the very last one, represents recorded history. That takes up about thirty seconds, just before midnight on the last day of the year.

"That is a very interesting way to portray the lifetime of earth," I commented. "Do you think that your young people are impressed by the 'Life of Earth Circle'? Do you think it makes any impression on them?"

"We think it does, very definitely. In Prire we try to remind ourselves constantly of how recently man came upon earth. It tends to keep us all a little humble. We have a saying here that we're very fond of—'We are but one day of earth's year'. You'll hear people say that to each other sometimes, meaning that man's hubris is not very appropriate."

As far as I could see there were walkers following the path along the wall, many of them with knapsacks and lunches, some with walking sticks.

"You will have to get a magnifying glass to read what's on there," Dr. Bo said pointing to the bracelet I had just put on my wrist, "but it will be something for you to remember. Next time you come, we'll have to walk the circle. It has a very salutary effect, I can assure you! Now we have just time for a quick look inside the main hall before we go to lunch. Would you like that?"

"Yes, I would. That would be very nice," I said.

We turned to our right and took a diagonal path across the park to the main hall, which was not far from the opera house where we had been the night before. The park itself, as we walked through it, reminded me of a combination of the park in Mexico City and Central Park in New York City. There were children playing soccer and flying kites, people of all ages walking or sitting on benches, some eating their lunch, some feeding the birds. My first thought, of course, was whether the park was safe.

"Do you have any problem of safety in the park, Dr. Bo?"

"No, these things are extremely rare in Prire. I think that's due to the way we handle anti-social behavior, as I mentioned to you the other day. The park is one of our great joys," Dr. Bo said, "but then, of course, we have parks throughout Prire as you noticed. We think they do something for a man's soul. It keeps him reminded that he's just part of nature."

"I love parks myself," I replied. "It's too bad they have become unsafe in so much of the world.

"Would you feel free to walk through here at night, for example?"

"Oh, it's absolutely safe," Dr. Bo said. "We just don't have that kind of problem here."

"Do you mean you don't have any robberies at all at night? No bicycles being stolen or things like that?"

"We think we have the answer to that," said Dr. Bo. "You have to make sure that such behavior has no payoff if you want it to stop. I'm sure there are quite a few people in Prire, much as I hate to say so, who would take up a life of crime here in this park if it had an immediate payoff for them."

"I'm surprised to hear you say that," I retorted. "The people I've seen in Prire don't look at all like criminals to me."

"They are not criminals. But I'm saying that the nice people in Prire are quite capable of behaving in an antisocial way if there were enough payoffs in it for them. Human nature is human nature, Dr. Aldworth."

"I am still surprised to hear you say that," I answered.

Just then we went up the steps to the main hall. The main hall was as grand a building as the opera house, perhaps grander because it was on a much larger scale. It was made of pink and white stones with large columns and steps leading up to it. It stood at the head of the park. At the foot of the steps we turned around and looked back over a gorgeous vista right down through the park. It gave me a feeling of serenity. Certainly one would not imagine oneself in the middle of a large city. Inside the main hall we crossed a large reception area and passed through a pair of huge doors. We were now looking into the main meeting room where, as Dr. Bo explained, the regional representatives met to form national policy for Prire. The room was not very much different from those that I had seen in other capitols. It was large, with chairs and benches and working desks, and a raised dais at the end for whoever was in charge. I noticed what appeared to be television cameras in the four corners of the room. There were ample galleries around all four sides of the room so I assumed that the sessions were open to the public. The only thing I noticed that was different was that all the walls of the room, including the front and the balconies, were covered with photographs—huge, overlapping photographs of people.

I turned to Dr. Bo. "These photographs, do they have some special meaning?"

"They are meant to," Dr. Bo said with a smile. "These are photographs of the people of Prire."

"What is the point of having them in there, in your meeting place, in your assembly room?" I asked.

"We thought it was a good idea for our regional representatives to look at pictures of the people they represent when they debate policy. A kind reminder, perhaps."

"Do you think it has any effect?" I asked.

"That would be hard to say," Dr. Bo replied. "It's difficult to differentiate between the effect of the pictures and of the galleries themselves, but we think it helps to keep the representatives aware of the constituents they serve."

He closed the vast doors and we turned to our right to go through the reception area toward one of the wings. I noticed the busts of several people at eye level and asked Dr. Bo who they were. He said there were busts of the first Overseers of the Future who were associated with the Great Reform. He pointed out several whose names I had read about. What interested me most was that below each person's bust was a bronze table that gave their dual occupations. I was interested to see the variety among those that made up the first Overseers of the Future. The first one I came to was a man who had been a farmer and a photographer; then a woman who was recorded as a behavioral scientist and a carpenter; then a man whose tablet read lawyer and beekeeper; then a housewife and wildflower collector; then a teacher of music and cook; a mechanic and composer; a printer and mason; a mailman and swineherd; a shopkeeper and fruit-tree grower. I was beginning to enjoy the Prire custom of seeing people in two occupations.

Dr. Bo led me toward the right wing saying I might want a quick look inside one of their museum rooms. We entered a large room with a photographic exhibit, very nicely mounted, some of the photographs quite large. I began on my left. The first group of pictures showed crowds of people taken from several angles. The next was a series of pictures showing the banks of the rivers full of trash. That made me stop and I asked Dr. Bo, "What in the world is this exhibit? I haven't seen anything like this in Prire."

Dr. Bo chuckled. He said, "I thought you might react to this. Look at the title of the exhibit."

I looked up to the title, which I had missed as I came in.

"These are pictures of the way things used to be before the Great Reform," he said. "It's hard to believe, isn't it?"

I toured the exhibit quickly, seeing photographs of traffic jams, cars, pollution—it was more than I could stand. It was simply overwhelming. As I came around the corner on my way out, the far wall was

270

hung with one huge photographic mural of Capital City, taken from the air on a clear day. It showed a blanket of brown smog overhanging the Capitol. I had a very funny reaction to that exhibit. I felt sick to my stomach, left the room as quickly as possible. Dr. Bo must have noticed that I was upset because he followed me out quickly.

"I'm sorry," he said, "I didn't think you would react that strongly. I should have known better."

"Oh, it's nothing," I replied. "It just came as a bit of a shock after what I've been seeing. I can't believe that things looked like that here—ever. It just seems impossible."

"I know," Dr. Bo said. "It does seem impossible. That's one reason we have the exhibit."

He led me back through the reception area to the other wing.

This is something I don't think you'd want to miss," he said, pushing me into the room.

It was a huge room containing only one exhibit, an enormous bronze tablet that must have extended twenty feet in the air, and ten feet across. From the vaulted dome high above us, sunlight filtered down in a pattern of light and shadow on the tablet.

"I am sure you read about this." Dr. Bo said.

"Yes," I said. "I know what it is. The tablet of the Rights of Earth."

Dr. Bo nodded. "I thought you would want to see it."

I walked to the side of the room where I could face the tablet. There were a number of people standing there, all very quiet, reading the tablet to their children. I made a copy of the inscription.

'The Rights of Earth'

1. All that is living upon this earth, below it or

above it, has the right to its own survival and to flourish.

2. No species has the right to endanger another species.
3. The waters of this earth shall remain clear.
4. The air around this earth shall remain pure.
5. The sounds of this earth shall remain natural.
6. The continuation of a balanced and diversified life upon this earth takes precedence over all other rights.
7. Man must act as guardian of the rights of other species.
8. Man is the protector of the rights of earth.

I finished my notes and followed Dr. Bo out of the room.

"Do many people come to see the tablet?" I asked.

"Oh, yes, many," said Dr. Bo. "One of the high points of coming to the Capitol is to see that, and visit the assembly room, and of course, to walk the Circle. We have a similar tablet in each of the schools, as you probably noticed."

"I did not at the time, but now that I think back, I guess I do remember seeing them," I said. "But do you think any of this really helps, Dr. Bo?"

"Yes, we do," he answered slowly. "We think all of us need to be reminded over and over again about what the important values are."

"Isn't that a kind of propaganda though, if you really look at it?" I asked.

"I don't think so," answered Dr. Bo. "I think of propaganda as a distortion of the truth for some end. We see these just as reminders of what we hold to be the more important values. It is all part of our belief, you see, that the long run is the important one. That is so easy to forget for the short run."

"But I wonder about so much repetition and reminders," I asked.

"My dear Aldworth," Dr. Bo replied, "the advantages of the short run are repeated constantly in all of our lives. One has to make sure that the long run gets a chance."

"What do you mean, the short run is around us all the time?" I asked.

"The short run is with both of us right now. We are thinking of having lunch. You are thinking of having to be at the airport, of how we are going to spend the rest of our time together. We are thinking of today, and only today. What in this day will remind us that we should spend today for the long run?"

"Not very much," I admitted. "It is even worse in my own society."

"So I have read," remarked Dr. Bo. "But we all need reminders. That is why we see to it that they are available and become part of our thinking, whenever we are faced with decisions. Now we may not succeed. I do not want you to go back thinking we always make the good long-term decisions. But there is a conscious effort to try to do so."

We walked out of the main hall and down the steps, taking another long look at the park. It was such a lovely sight. We turned to our left and walked past a smaller white building. Dr. Bo turned to his right down a small path and we came upon an outdoor restaurant in the middle of the park. It was set among trees with partial shade and was quite informal. Dr. Bo said two friends should be waiting for us there. Although it was not a very fancy place to eat, he knew that time was important to us today, so he thought this would be convenient.

Dr. Bo waved to two people seated at a table at the end. He went over and he introduced me to Madame Adamac and Mr. Luwee who were, like Dr. Bo, Overseers of the Future. Madame Adamac was of medium height, with brown eyes, reddish brown hair and quite fair. Mr. Luwee was tall, perhaps 6′2″ with jet black hair, dark skin and brown eyes. Though I guessed both to be in their fifties, neither had any gray in their hair. We picked up our lunch from a buffet at one side and took our trays back to the table. Dr. Bo explained to Madame Adamac and Mr. Luwee that we had a very tight schedule today because of my departure, so he would like to use this time at lunch to present some things that had been overlooked in my visit so far.

"One thing that troubles me," said Dr. Bo to Madame Adamac and Mr. Luwee, "is that Dr. Aldworth has really seen the better side of Prire. He keeps asking me if we don't have problems in Prire, and I keep saying, indeed we have. But I don't think I've really shown him many of them. One reason, of course, is that he came here to see how we solved some problems. But I don't think he has any feel for the current problems we're working on, do you, Dr. Aldworth?"

"I don't really," I said. "Everywhere I look I see problems that have been solved. But I assume there must be problems you're working on now, or aren't there any?"

Madame Adamac and Mr. Luwee both broke out laughing.

"Problems!" exclaimed Mr. Luwee, "You think we don't have problems! You should sit with us in

274

some of our meetings and you would know what kinds of problems we have."

"My goodness," added Madame Adamac, "it seems to me we have nothing but problems!"

"That's what I want Dr. Aldworth to hear," said Dr. Bo. "Why don't you share with him some of the problems that come up in our meetings?"

"I don't know where to begin," replied Madame Adamac. "We have been debating for three months now about whether our budget should be a two-year budget or a three-year one."

"And we've been arguing all spring," interjected Mr. Luwee, "about the appropriate role for intensive hydrophonic culture."

"Some of our citizens," said Madame Adamac, "want children to have the option to leave school at ten or eleven, at least before twelve. There are others who think it should be extended to fourteen. This is an annual argument that goes on all the time and so far we've stayed with twelve, but the pressure is on again this year to change it."

"Don't forget our concern about improving educational opportunities for older citizens," added Dr. Bo. "One of the things we are concerned about, Dr. Aldworth, is that we think people over sixty need some new skills. We have not provided adequately for their learning these skills. We are coming up with an after-sixties school plan next year, I think."

"The biggest debate this year though, don't you agree," asked Mr. Luwee, "is the one over the news?"

"Yes," replied Madame Adamac, "I think that is the most important debate we've had. Why don't you tell Dr. Aldworth about it?"

The debate is between two different points of

view. One is that the news should be reported freely
and openly and objectively and in its entirety. The
other point of view is that the way in which news is
reported influences behavior. This debate has been
going on a long time. We have been running studies under the sponsorship of the Overseers of the
Future about the effects of various kinds of news
selection and presentation, both on our television
and in our press. As Dr. Bo has probably told you,
we keep very extensive records on almost all forms
of public activity. In one of our better experiments,
we encouraged several communities to feature re-
ports of antisocial acts both on television and in the
papers. In other communities we encouraged the reporting of the consequences of antisocial acts, rather
than the act itself."

"I don't think I follow you," I said. "Can you
explain that to me?"

"Let us say," answered Mr. Luwee, "that in all
communities in region 'A' they report antisocial acts
such as robbing. They show acts of robbery on television news, and report them in the papers with
pictures of people being robbed and hurt. In other
communities, what we'll call the 'B' communities, the
antisocial behavior is never shown, only the consequences of the act. For example, if someone is
robbed, this is reported in the back of the paper
under a register of antisocial acts so that it is actually reported. In one column you would read the
antisocial act and in the second column you would
see the punishment given to the person involved,
and the person is named. No pictures are shown of
the actual act itself. The only pictures allowed on
television and in the newspapers are pictures of the
punishment, such as a person going to prison, or

276

being executed—something of that sort. That's a quick rundown on our experiment."

"And what happened?" I asked. "Did you find any differences?"

"Yes, we did," replied Mr. Luwee, "quite a marked difference. We found in the 'A' communities the amount of antisocial behavior went way up —and in just those ways that were shown in the television and newspapers' pictures."

"If I may interrupt, Mr. Luwee," said Dr. Bo, "that is why we have the policy which I don't think Dr. Aldworth is aware of. At the present time our policy is the 'B' policy. This means we have guidelines for all of our regional television stations and our newspapers, which state very specifically what behaviors are to be modeled. They also permit the reporting of all information and of all news events in one form or another."

"That's a form of censorship, isn't it?" I asked.

"That is one way of looking at it," replied Dr. Bo. "We think a more accurate description is that it is careful modeling."

"But who sets these standards?" I asked. "Who decides that stations can only show this or that? Isn't that a limitation on freedom of speech?"

"We don't think that that limits freedom of speech, because we do permit all news to be reported, and reported freely. Our concern is with the form of it, because we know the form can influence behavior."

"I don't see how letting the news be reported freely is influencing anything," I said.

"But it does, very effectively," replied Dr. Bo. "When you show pictures of people stealing or harming others, we have very good evidence that such pictures act as model behavior for some of the people who watch. We don't want to model that kind of behavior in Prire."

"I still think that's censorship, I don't care what you call it," I replied.

"We still think it's a question of controlling the modeling. I read somewhere that in your society, for example, the news is reported in any way that the television people feel will appeal to the largest audience, is that not correct?"

"It varies a lot," I answered, "but it is essentially true that the news is presented from the point of view of what will interest people the most."

"That is the problem," said Dr. Bo. "What interests people is not necessarily how you want to model their behavior. If you want to interest people, you can always show acts of violence and antisocial acts because they are innately interesting—for the moment, at any rate—but we do not want to teach people those behaviors. Then newspapers and television teach people a great deal. We think they are tremendously powerful forms of education and that's why we think it important to regulate them."

"Who owns the newspapers and the television? Is it a state monopoly, a sort of propaganda arm of the government in Prire?" I asked.

"No, it's not that. The television stations are owned by their regions and are monitored by citizens of the region, often in the larger city of the region. The newspapers may be published either on a regional basis or on a local community basis and they are monitored by a community group as well. We have issued standards for reporting the news. It is the responsibility of the editors and of the citizens' committee to see that the standards are maintained."

"You mean you don't have any commercial television?" I asked.

"No, we don't," replied Madame Adamac. "We changed that many years ago, long before I came to work at the Overseers, because of the effects we knew it was having on our children. We found it was silly to try to educate parents of our Prire children and then turn them loose to be influenced by all sorts of commercial television."

"Who pays for television, then?" I asked.

"It comes out of our tax money just as any other service does."

"What sort of programs do you run on it?" I inquired.

"We run all kinds of programs, from educational programs to entertainment. I don't think you'd find them that different from yours," said Mr. Luwee. "But the content has to fit the standards, and as Dr. Bo explained, these standards are very strict about the kinds of behaviors that may be modeled."

"It sounds awfully goody-goody to me. Isn't it boring?" I asked, I must say, rather rudely.

"We don't find it so," replied Madame Adamac slowly as though she hadn't heard the rudeness in my question. "But what makes it different from your country, I suppose, is that our newspapers only come out twice a week and our television is on a limited schedule. We do run special longer programs for people who are confined at home or in the hospital."

"Your newspapers are published only twice a week?" I asked.

"That's right," she answered. "We have experimented with that."

"It seems to me you are always running experiments, aren't you?" I said.

"Yes, that is true, Dr. Aldworth, that is absolutely true," she answered. "We are always running experiments to see what policy works best. We all plead guilty to that one!" She laughed, and Mr. Luwee and Dr. Bo joined in with her.

"You might even say," added Dr. Bo, "that we're the Overseers of the Experiments and you would not be too far off!"

They all laughed at that.

"But why only twice a week? What experiment is that?" I asked.

"We ran experiments on this too, which you won't be surprised to hear. We found that we got better reporting and more perspective on the news if it was not so immediate. We found that people reacted with less sense of crisis if the news was two to three days old, and it gave the papers time to put events in some sort of perspective."

"Is that true of television also?"

"No, we have television news every night but it is short and very selective and only hits the highlights."

"I don't think you are giving Dr. Aldworth a very fair picture of our television," Madame Adamac stated. "I don't think you've given enough credit to our sports coverage at all. I have to tell you about this, Dr. Aldworth, because my two children are absolutely crazy about sports. They are glued when the sports are on our television."

"That's true," added Mr. Luwee. "You have to understand that we do have lots of sports coverage on our television, of all of our sports, including our higher schools, the colleges, as well as our local teams and so on. We also cover endurance races, all

280

forms of fitness competition for people from ten to a hundred. We run what is called the Master skills series in which the master craftsmen in each of our occupational areas teaches his particular skill. We have excellent television series of these kinds."

"Yes, I know," added Madame Adamac," I watched the one in silversmithing and found it invaluable. My daughter watched the one on building a log cabin. We thought we were going to have one right in our own backyard if we weren't careful."

The rest of the lunch was filled with their questions of me about my visit to Prire, what I liked and what I had not liked, and how it compared with things in my country. Again I met this complete wall or disbelief as I tried to describe certain things to them, such as our television, our supermarkets, our lack of good mass transportation. They could not understand how things could be that way, or why our citizens did not insist on their being changed. They were appalled at what they called age discrimination in education and employment. They thought it was terrible that communities lost all the skills of people when they got to be sixty-five. I tried to describe to them a retirement community in Florida, but I could see that they were horrified, and I changed the subject.

"I think we'd best be getting on," interrupted Dr. Bo. "I hate to stop this good talk, but we have to get to the airport and make sure that your baggage is in order."

Time was getting short. I thanked Madame Adamac and Mr. Luwee for their time. I realized they had taken time out of their busy day to have lunch with someone who was, in their eyes, abysmally ignorant of Prire. I told them I had enjoyed everything in Prire, especially the food, and I certainly was going to miss it. They laughed and seemed to like the compliment because they acknowledged that the standards of food in Prire were considered important. They wished me well on my return trip. I invited them to let me be their host, if they came for a visit. I thought they had little enthusiasm for such a visit, but they said they would let me know if they did come. Dr. Bo and I walked back along the wall to where we had parked the transit and he drove me out to the airport.

I found it very difficult to express the appreciation I felt for what he had done for me. We had spent seven days, almost all of it together, and I knew what this had done to his work schedule. Were it not for the importance of this first preliminary visit and for the official visit that might follow, I could not justify his spending that sort of time with a person of my position. He turned aside all my expressions of appreciation very lightly, suggesting that he had all the time in the world, that it had been a great vacation for him to visit different parts of Prire and to see his grandson. I asked if he would allow me to host him if he visited our country and he said, should he decide to come, he would accept that invitation. He indicated that there were other people in Prire, particularly some of the regional representatives, that he thought might benefit more from such a visit. He said this as a kind of joke. I thought that he meant that there were some people in the government who were critical of what Prire was doing, who would benefit from seeing what we did in our country.

When we arrived at the airport I found everything in order—my baggage and my presents and the tape recorder and my journals. The pilot and co-pilot were waiting for me, looking very tanned and fit. They said that their hosts had taken them fishing up into the Stone Mountains and that they'd had a perfectly wonderful time. I asked them if they had stopped at the Inn of the Eight Bridges. They had stayed there two nights ago and we exchanged our impressions of the Inn.

Everything had been checked out that morning. The airport was as quiet as when I had come in. I saw two ambulance planes out in front of one hangar but no planes taking off or landing. Our two pilots obviously enjoyed having the airport to themselves.

I was very touched when I said good-bye to Dr. Bo. I had come to admire this man so much during these seven days, his kindness and his generosity to me, his patience with all my questions. I sensed how idiotic some of them must have sounded to him, particularly during my first few days.

I started to say good-bye to him when Dr. Bo interrupted: "We don't say good-bye in Prire, my dear Aldworth. We always say, 'I'm only looking forward to your return.'"

"I'm only looking forward to your return," I said to Dr. Bo, "if I can ever persuade you to come visit us."

"Perhaps we should say that we will meet again when you return here on your next visit."

As I went up the stairs to the plane, I must confess my eyes were wet. The door was closed and we started the run to the end of the field. I waved out the window to Dr. Bo who stood there smiling, tall as ever and so vital. The plane turned and we took off. I looked out the window as we shot past the airport building and the hangars, then I could see Capital City as we banked. I could see the Capitol, the Main Hall and how large the park really was. I could even see glimpses of the wall at one end as we turned. I saw the river and thought I could identify the area where we had had dinner the night before.

As we climbed higher I could see Capital City in more perspective. The air was clear, another perfect June day. I had been very lucky with the weather. There were a few puffy clouds to the west that suggested rain was on its way, but the Capitol was still under a bright blue sky. I kept looking at Capital City wanting to make sure that I could keep the picture of Prire in my mind as long as I lived.

Prire . . . I leaned my head against the plane window, watching Capital City become smaller and smaller. Will anyone believe what I tell them? Or will they think it is some fantasy of mine? I said to myself. "All I can do is report what I saw and heard, as honestly as I can." I doubt if anyone will believe me, but some day there will be a second visit to Prire, and then they will know I tried to report it as exactly as I could.

I pulled out my typewriter on the table, arranged my journals and tried to compose myself. I must be objective, I reminded myself. Point out your biases so the committee will be aware of them. Don't be afraid to indicate your areas of ignorance. Write it down in order, from the very first moment you landed, and report everything, just as it happened.

I put paper in the typewriter, and started to type:

June 17th. "My first view of Prire was a surprise. As we came in over the Prire countryside it looked so familiar yet so different. I saw hedgerows, green rolling fields. . ."

# GREAT SCIENCE FICTION FROM WARNER...

**MEANWHILE**
by Max Handley                    (87-643, $5.95)

From the depths of the ocean a man emerges onto a world devoid of males for centuries. A stunning, illustrated Science Fiction novel that signals the emergence of a major new talent.

**ALIEN**
by Alan Dean Foster                (82-977, $2.25)

Astronauts encounter an awesome galactic horror on a distant planet. But it is only when they take off again that the real horror begins. For the alien is now within the ship, within the crew itself. And a classic deathtrap suspense begins.

**STRANGE WINE**
by Harlan Ellison                  (89-489, $1.95)

Fifteen new stories from the nightside of the world by one of the most original and entertaining short story writers in America today. Discover among these previously uncollected tales: the spirits of executed Nazi war criminals, gremlins, a murderess escaped from hell, and other chilling, thought provoking tales.

**THE PHILOSOPHER'S STONE**
by Colin Wilson                    (89-442, $1.95)

A prophetic novel whose premise is "that man must come into active, conscious control of his own brain, or the species will become extinct."

**MALEVIL**
by Robert Merle                    (81-658, $2.50)

In an isolated wine cellar, a group of friends escape the nuclear explosion which incinerates the earth. They are survivors, condemned to go back to man's roots and reinvent the means of existence.

# GREAT SCIENCE FICTION FROM WARNER...

## A CITY IN THE NORTH
*by Marta Randall*                    (94-062, $1.75)

They are set out to discover the secrets of the dead among the ruins — and found, instead, the secret of their survival.

## THE BEST OF JUDITH MERRIL
*by Judith Merril*                    (86-058, $1.25)

A collection of the best works of science fiction by the pioneering, feminist, activist author whose stories reflect penetrating studies into the psyche of the women of the future.

## THOSE GENTLE VOICES
*by George Alec Effinger*                    (94-017, $1.75)

What will happen when men from Earth encounter other intelligent forms of life — a race so primitive it hadn't even discovered the spear, or fire . . . .